You're holding in your hands one of the first in a new line of books of dark fiction called Abyss. Abyss is horror unlike anything you've ever read before. It's not about haunted houses or evil children or ancient Indian burial grounds. We've all read those books, and we all know their plots by heart.

Abyss is for the seeker of truth, no matter how disturbing or twisted it may be. It's about people, and the darkness we all carry within us. Abyss is the new horror from the dark frontier. And in that place, where we come face-to-face with terror, what we find is ourselves. The darkness illuminates us, revealing our flaws, our secret fears, our desires and ambitions longing to break free. And we never see ourselves or our world in the same way again.

"Melanie Tem may well be the literary successor to Shirley Jackson and be destined to become the new queen of high-quality, psychologically disturbing horror fiction. Melanie Tem's writing is a cry from the very heart of the heart of darkness.

"*Prodigal* is Melanie Tem's first novel, but all of us who value quality in horror fiction offer the heartfelt wish that it will not be her last. *Prodigal* is a descent through the corridors of a very human hell never dreamt of by Dante; Melanie Tem makes a very able guide through these deepest regions of fear."
     —Dan Simmons,
          author of *Carrion Comfort* and *Summer of Night*

"*Prodigal* drew me in from the very first and didn't let go till the final page. Melanie Tem has written a compelling and eerie tale that is all the more insidious for its subtle blend of innocence and horror. It attacks us where we live—at home, and takes us to the dark, inside places where true monsters dwell."
     —Lisa Cantrell,
          author of *The Manse*

"Melanie Tem has a knack for getting beneath the skin to the ambiguities of fear and desire, and she never flinches from depicting emotions in all their disturbing complexity. *Prodigal* isn't just about a young girl's coming of age as she discovers her own sexuality in particularly dangerous circumstances—to read it is to feel the shifting currents of love and anger, security and forbidden longings within a very real family. It's an unusual, unsettling novel."
     —Lisa Tuttle,
          author of *Gabriel*

Prodigal

MELANIE TEM

A DELL BOOK

Published by
Dell Publishing
a division of
Bantam Doubleday Dell Publishing Group, Inc.
666 Fifth Avenue
New York, New York 10103

ISBN: 0-440-20815-7

Printed in the United States of America

Published simultaneously in Canada

June 1991

10 9 8 7 6 5 4 3 2 1

OPM

*For my daughter Veronica,
who taught me how to tell this story,
and who goes on teaching.*

And, of course, for Steve.

1

Ethan came into Lucy's room without warning, without knocking. He always did whatever he felt like. She didn't even see or hear the door open; she had her eyes closed and her earphones on. Before she knew he was there, Ethan was beside her bed, leaning close over her and breathing bad breath into her face as if he was trying to say something, and he had his hands around her neck.

Ethan had been missing for a long time. Everybody knew he was dead.

Lucy slapped his hands away and pulled back from him against the wall. "Ethan!"

This wasn't a dream. She had lots of weird dreams about her dead brother Ethan; in some of them, he tried to kill her because what had happened to him was somehow her fault. In the dreams, and for a while before and after, Lucy believed it was her fault, even though she couldn't understand how, even though Ethan was the one who'd kept getting in trouble, who'd gotten into drugs, who'd run away and not come back. The times when she believed it was her fault weren't as scary as the times when she knew she couldn't have done anything to keep her brother safe, and neither could Mom or Dad.

This wasn't a dream. She wasn't asleep. It was the middle of a drizzly Saturday afternoon in May, and she was taking a break from chores and lying on her bed listening to the Top Forty Countdown, hoping she'd get through to number one before Mom or Dad found her and made her finish dusting. Maxx Well the deejay had been just about to announce number three when Ethan showed up in her room.

She took the earphones off and laid them in the sheets. Now the music sounded funny, voices without mouths. Ethan was still leaning over her, still had his mouth open, still had his hands raised and cupped to choke her. He could still reach her if he just straightened out his arms, and she couldn't move any farther back. She drew up her knees, crossed her arms over her chest. "What are you doing here? What's going on? Are you in trouble again?" That was a dumb question. Ethan was always in trouble.

He didn't say anything. She turned off the radio. Now she never would know what this week's number one was. Ethan's mouth hung open. She could see his tongue, coated white, and his dirty teeth. His breath made her sick to her stomach.

"God, Ethan, don't you ever brush your teeth?"

He still didn't say anything. He was trying to; his mouth twisted and awful choking sounds came out. But she couldn't understand him. He leaned and shook till she thought for sure he'd fall on top of her.

She longed to hug him again, like when they were little. She'd dreamed about hugging him, about punching him for all the stupid things he'd done, about holding on to him so he couldn't run away again. But she knew Ethan was dead.

"I'm going to get Mom or Dad." She scrambled to her hands and knees on the bed and started to crawl toward the foot, thinking she could circle around him. He put both hands on her shoulders and pushed her down.

Lucy screamed. "Mom! Dad!" She covered her head with a pillow, pulled the bedspread over her. When Mom came running into her room and Lucy opened her eyes again, Ethan was gone.

2

Mom sobbed and rocked back and forth on Lucy's bed. She was bent over and hugging herself with the arm that wasn't holding Lucy, as if her heart and stomach would explode if she didn't hold them in. Lucy hadn't seen her cry like that for a long time; she'd thought she was over it.

Lucy sobbed, too, and they clung to each other. That helped some. But Mom's body felt as if it had holes in it that Lucy's hands could go right through, and she thought probably her body felt the same way to Mom. The other noises of the household sounded thin and not quite real, as if they were coming from earphones that had been knocked off her ears: the dishwasher rumbling in the kitchen under her room; Priscilla running the vacuum cleaner on the stairs and singing; the little kids squabbling; Dad's saw in the basement. She wondered irritably what the number-two song was, whether it had moved up or down the charts from last week. She bet it was "You'll Never Be Free of Me."

The harder Mom cried and held her, the surer Lucy was that they were both going to slide off the edge of the earth, and that Mom knew it, too. Ethan had. He'd been missing for almost two years, and nobody had seen or heard from him, nobody had any idea what had happened to him. The cops couldn't find him. That social worker Jerry Johnston couldn't find him. She didn't think they'd looked very hard. Mom and Dad couldn't find him, and they'd looked everywhere.

"I'm . . . sorry . . . Mom," she gasped. Her chest hurt and her throat was closing around the words. She didn't feel scared like this much anymore, except when she made Mom cry. "I'm . . . so sorry!"

Mom took a few deep, shuddering breaths and smoothed Lucy's hair. Lucy liked it when her mother touched her hair, and she tipped her head back into the unsteady stroking. "No, baby, no," Mom whispered. Her voice shook, but she'd stopped crying. "You have nothing to be sorry for."

"I scared you."

"Lots of things scare me since Ethan disappeared. That's not your fault, and you can't fix it. I have to fix it, or I have to learn to live with it."

"Why did he run away?" She'd asked that lots of times; she didn't know why she was asking it again now. "Why did he do all that bad stuff? Stealing cars and doing drugs and stuff?"

Mom shook her head. "We don't know, Lucy. We may never know."

"Do you think he's dead?" She'd never come right out and asked that before.

"No," Mom said flatly, and when she didn't say any more, Lucy thought she was mad.

That made her burst into tears again. She'd always hated it when Mom or Dad was mad at her, and since Ethan had disappeared she could hardly stand it. Rae didn't care; half the time she went out of her way to get them mad at her, and the other half she didn't seem to notice. But then Rae was almost fourteen. "Oh, Mom, I'm *sorry*!" Lucy wailed.

Mom hugged her, stroked her hair, and said, so quietly that Lucy had to hold her breath to hear, "*I'm* his mother. *I'm* the one who was supposed to keep him safe."

Lucy buried her face in her mother's shoulder and curled her knees up, for the moment not caring that fifth graders shouldn't act like babies. Her mother's guilt was too much for her, but she had to say something. She mumbled, "You didn't know. You and Dad didn't know."

"We did our best, just like we do with all you kids. But our best wasn't good enough for Ethan. It still isn't good enough."

Chills raced through Lucy's body, and she cried again, "I'm sorry!"

Mom was rocking her, as if she were Cory's age. "Lucy, Lucy, none of this is your fault."

"I'm sorry I called you in here and scared you. It was just . . . a dream."

Mom held her by the shoulders a little away from her. "Lucy." Lucy fought against the separation, but finally looked into her mother's face. Her eyes were red and swollen, frantic with a love that made Lucy, every time she saw it, swear she'd never have kids. "I don't think they are dreams. He comes to me, too."

Lucy's heart suddenly pounded against her rib cage, and her head swam. For a minute she thought she was going to throw up. "He does?"

"Maybe ten times over the past year."

"What does he want?"

"I don't know. He won't talk."

"Where does he come from?"

"I don't know. I've tried to follow him, but I always lose him."

"He . . . tried to strangle me." Lucy put her hands to her throat.

Mom's eyes widened. She tipped Lucy's head back, pushed Lucy's fingers aside, and put her own there, probing, rubbing. "Are you hurt? I don't see any marks. Did he hurt you?"

"No. He wasn't trying very hard. I got away from him." Lucy laughed a little. She and Ethan always used to fight like that. Once she'd shut the car door on his hand; she'd insisted it wasn't on purpose, and her parents and even Ethan had believed her, but it was.

Mom bent her head and kissed Lucy's throat, then pulled her close again. "He's done things like that to me, too. But I think it's just that he needs something. He's in trouble and he needs something from me, and I can't help him now any more than I could when he was at home or at New Beginnings because I don't know what to do."

"Does Dad see him, too?"

Mom smiled sadly and shook her head. The white streak in the front of her hair showed a lot in the rainy light, and a lock fell over her forehead, a white lock out of her dark brown hair. Lucy's hair was dark brown, too; she was afraid she'd have a white streak like Mom's when she got that old. She wished Mom would just dye it. Mom said it was her badge of courage, from having seven kids. Lucy resented that. And, anyway, she hadn't noticed it getting any bigger since all the trouble with Ethan—but then, it was hard to remember a time in the family when there hadn't been trouble with Ethan, when they hadn't all been thinking mostly about him. "Dad and Ethan haven't gotten along very well the last few years," Mom said. "They haven't been very close."

Lucy didn't see what that had to do with anything, and it seemed to her that somehow Mom was putting Dad down. "Ethan wasn't close to anybody in the family," she said angrily, and sat up on the bed away from her mother's arms.

"I don't know about that." There was a dreamy look on her mother's face that made Lucy even madder. "There was always something special between Ethan and me. I guess there still is."

"Does Dad know you see Ethan?"

"I used to tell him. I don't anymore. He thinks it's all in my head, because I *want* so much to see him. He says it's just grief. He believes Ethan is dead."

"He *is* dead."

"I don't think so."

Now Lucy was furious. She knew she wasn't as special as Ethan because she didn't get in all kinds of trouble and she hadn't disappeared and she wasn't dead. She turned the radio up loud again and slammed the earphones onto her head. Then she took them off long enough to demand, almost yelling, "So does Rae know?" She doubted it. Rae spent most of her time away from the house these days and didn't know anything that was going on. Didn't know about the cute new guy in Lucy's math class. Didn't know that Cory was finally potty-trained, mostly. Didn't know that Ethan kept showing up without knocking, except that couldn't be true because everybody but Mom knew he was dead.

Mom cupped Lucy's chin. Lucy closed her eyes tight so she wouldn't have to look at her and put the earphones back on, but she could still hear Mom say, "I won't be telling anybody but you," and then Lucy felt very special, indeed, and very much afraid.

3

 "Jerry Johnston doesn't work at Nubie anymore," Mom said to Dad.

"He doesn't? What happened?"

"I don't know the circumstances, whether he was fired or quit or what. I guess the turnover at places like that must be pretty high."

They were sitting back in their chairs at the two ends of the dining-room table, drinking coffee and talking to each other. They almost always did that after dinner, when the kids had left the table. They hugged in the kitchen, too; you'd carry your plate in to put it on the sink and there they'd be, arms around each other, maybe even kissing, sometimes dancing to some silly old song they sang together.

For a long time after Ethan had disappeared, Mom and Dad had hugged each other all the time, as if they didn't dare let go. It had scared Lucy. They'd touched the kids all the time, too. It was embarrassing; you'd be standing in line at the grocery store and Dad would put his hand on your head, or you'd be crossing the street and Mom would grab your hand as if you were Cory's age.

Lucy kept wanting to yell at them, "Leave me alone! Nothing's going to happen to me! Nothing can happen to me!"

Then there'd been a long time when she hadn't seen her parents touch each other at all. They'd hardly even looked at each other. Dad had kept touching the kids; sometimes you could find enough room to sit beside him in the big chair even if you were almost twelve years old. But Mom didn't touch anybody unless she had to. She'd braid Priscilla's hair, she'd put her hand on Molly's forehead to check for fever, she'd put her arms around Dominic from behind to get his jacket zipper started. But she didn't hug, she didn't spank, she didn't kiss the top of Dad's head when she passed behind his chair.

That had gone on for months. Lucy was relieved they were kissing and dancing in the kitchen again, even though she didn't know how they could do it when Ethan was still missing and everybody knew he was dead. Everybody but Mom.

Their chairs had arms. None of the others

did. Someday Lucy would sit in a captain's chair with arms and a high back at the head of a long table. There'd be flowers on the table. There'd be a lot of kids, and Lucy would take care of them all.

She poured herself another glass of milk and dished up more chili into her bowl. She pretty much knew how to make chili now, even though she still did need Mom to tell her how long to brown the hamburger and how much chili powder to put in. Rae couldn't, or wouldn't, cook anything. She didn't know that Ethan kept coming back.

Rae would eat all her meals in her room if they'd let her. She took tiny servings and gobbled her food, all hunched over her plate and not looking at anybody. She said she wasn't hungry. She said she had to lose weight. But Lucy knew there were Reese's cups and M&M's stashed in her top dresser drawer under her bras and panty hose.

The little kids chattered and ate a lot, but they couldn't sit still for very long. They didn't care, didn't even understand what the grown-ups talked about.

Lucy didn't care either, most of the time, but she kept thinking that she ought to, that there was coded information in their conversations that someday she'd need. Only recently had she realized that they talked about stuff when she wasn't around. That bothered her.

"He's in private practice now," Mom was saying.

Lucy didn't know what that was, or why it mattered what Jerry Johnston was doing. She had other things to worry about. She was afraid she'd flunked the math test today. A couple of sixth-grade boys had called her and Stacey a dirty name; Lucy wasn't even sure what it meant. Stacey had promised to show her how to use eyeliner today, but the teacher had caught them whispering about it in class and had confiscated Stacey's entire makeup bag. Stacey said her dad would sue. Stacey always said that, but her dad never did. Her dad lived in California with his new wife and a baby brother Stacey had never seen.

"How do you know?" Dad asked Mom.

"I called him at Nubie and they told me. They gave me his number, but all I got was a snotty answering service."

When Lucy grew up, she was going to have a beach house on Malibu with Emilio Estevez or Charlie Sheen, whichever one of them waited for her. She'd have a pink stretch limo and she'd drive it herself, even though most rich people had chauffeurs. Lucy couldn't wait to drive. Dad said he'd teach her when she was fifteen. In the back of the limo there'd be a pink-and-white marble hot tub. She'd drive around with all her friends in the hot tub, cruising.

Dad's scolding voice brought her attention back to what he and Mom were talking about. "I thought we decided to quit doing that."

"*I* never decided that. *You* decided that. You and Jerry."

"I thought you agreed that calling him or the cops every other day is just making it harder on you."

"Not knowing is harder. Not doing anything is harder. I can't just let them drop it."

"Carole, it's been two years."

"It's been one year and nine and a half months."

"The chances of turning up anything get slimmer and slimmer. You know that."

"You're so sure he's dead. I think you'd rather believe that than admit nobody knows."

Dad rested his forehead on his hand. "You think I don't fantasize that someday Ethan will just stroll in here like none of this ever happened and he'll be fine? You think I don't look at every brown-haired teenage boy on the street to make sure it's not him?"

Mom shook her head sadly. "I'm sorry, Tony. You don't talk about it—"

"You think you're the only one who dreams about him?"

Mom didn't say anything for a minute. Lucy was listening carefully now, blowing bubbles in her milk that made a ring around the rim of the glass like a necklace or a noose. Finally Mom said quietly, "They're not dreams."

Dad slammed his hand down on the table and Lucy's milk spilled. "Carole, for God's sake, after all we've been through!"

Mom had started gathering up the dirty dishes, the crockpot with the scum of chili in the bottom, the salad bowl littered with lettuce and celery leaves. She wasn't looking at Dad. She wasn't looking at Lucy either. *I saw him, too,* Lucy knew she ought to say, but she didn't, and Mom didn't give her away. Mom just said, "They're not dreams. That's all," and left the room.

Dad sat still with his head on his hand. Lucy mopped up the spilled milk with her napkin, chugged the rest of it, and stood up. She stacked the bowl on her salad plate and the glass in her bowl, remembering only then that Mom didn't like them to do that because it got food all over the outside of the glass. There were so many rules, so many ways you could do things wrong.

She started to go around the back of Dad's chair. He pulled her to him and kissed the top of her head. Her glass tipped over, dribbling little white specks of milk onto the floor. She kissed him back. His cheek was scratchy, and he smelled nice, the way Dad always smelled, the way dads were supposed to smell.

When Lucy went upstairs, Rae was lying on

her bed. They'd put the shelves in between their beds for privacy, so Lucy couldn't see what her sister was doing over there, could only hear her breathing. Rae didn't say anything when Lucy came in, so Lucy didn't say anything either.

The first thing she did, as always, was to check for her diary. She moved it often, and she hadn't written in it for a long time because there wasn't anything to say, so sometimes she forgot where it was and thought somebody had stolen it. But there it was now, under the dirty clothes in her laundry basket. She'd have to remember to take it out before it got washed, but she couldn't move it now because Rae was in the room. She patted its cover, imagined what the blank page with today's date would look like, put the dirty clothes back on top of it.

She sat down in front of the mirror and stared at herself, leaned so close to the glass that her breath made little clouds. Her skin looked funny up close, but at least she didn't have zits. Rae had zits.

All of a sudden Rae was in the mirror with her. It surprised Lucy, scared her a little. "Want me to do your hair?"

"Sure."

The brush caught in the tangles, and Rae didn't hold on to the roots like Mom did to keep it from hurting. But Lucy didn't jump or say anything.

Rae brushed and combed Lucy's hair, pinned it this way and that. Sideways over one ear. Slanted across her forehead like a scarf. Twisted into pompons on the sides of her head. She never once asked Lucy which way she liked it, and Lucy didn't know, anyway.

Finally Rae settled on what she said was a French twist, and she pinned a white plastic flower in the middle of it that Lucy could just barely see if she turned her head a certain way. "There," Rae said. "Now turn around this way and I'll do your face."

Lucy sat very still, although her heart pounded with excitement and the little brushes tickled her nose and cheeks and eyelids. She could see the tiny wet wrinkles in Rae's lips when the older girl leaned over her. She could smell the perfume and lotion on Rae's fingers.

"There," Rae said again, and stepped back. "You're done."

At first Lucy didn't know what she was supposed to do. Then she turned to the mirror. She looked the same as she had before, but she also looked very different. She looked like Rae, and Mom, and Dad, and Ethan, who didn't look like each other at all. She looked the way she would when she grew up.

"Like it?" Rae asked.

Lucy nodded. "I guess."

"Go show Mom and Dad," Rae ordered, and went back to her side of the room.

4

Later that night Lucy sat in the living room hugging Patches and watched her mother check the outside lights again. The fat old cat meowed and twisted, trying to scratch, but most of the time she could avoid his claws. Her mother glanced back sharply but didn't say anything, which pleased Lucy; if it had been one of the younger kids, her mother would already be scolding, "Don't be mean to the kitty! He'll scratch you, and he'll be right!" Lucy eased her grip. Patches shook his head furiously, glared at her, then settled solidly back onto her lap.

Her mother stooped to pick up a sock from the floor, and the white streak glistened. She should dye it. The rest of her hair was so dark it was almost black. Lucy wished her own hair was that color, or blond like her sister Rae's and like the little kids' before it started to turn. She suspected Rae of lightening her hair, and she suspected Mom of suspecting it, too, even though they'd said she couldn't until she was sixteen.

There were two round switches on the wall beside the door, one above the other like buttons on a card. One was for the hall light that hung like an umbrella from the high ceiling. The other one worked the porch light and the lamp at the top of the outside front steps.

Nobody in the family could remember which switch worked which light. You'd think people would guess right at least half the time, but almost every time they pushed the wrong one first, turning the outside lights off by mistake and then hastily turning them back on again. Her mother did it every night, more than once if anybody was away from home. In the two years since Ethan had been gone, Lucy bet her mother had turned those lights off and on, off and on, half a dozen times a night, looking for him, making sure he'd be able to find his way home.

Which was stupid, because Ethan was dead. And even if he wasn't, he wouldn't come here. And even if he did, they wouldn't let him in.

"What happened to your brother?" She must have answered the question a million times. Even if she told them it was none of their business, she was still answering it. If you timesed how many questions she'd had to answer or not answer about Ethan by the number of minutes each time took by the other six kids in her family, that was a huge amount of time Ethan had already taken up out of their lives. Which didn't even count the time Mom and Dad spent talking about him and thinking about him, which sometimes Lucy thought was all the time and sometimes she thought was never.

"He's in jail, kind of," was what she'd said at first.

"How can you be 'kind of' in jail? Either you're in jail or you're not."

"How old is he? He's only fifteen, right? They don't put kids in jail. Do they?"

"It's a place called Nubie. New Beginnings."

"What's *that*?"

She'd asked Mom what it was. "It's a children's home."

"You mean, like for kids who don't have parents?"

"Ethan has parents! He's got a whole family! We visit him every week and he comes home on pass on Sunday sometimes and we have family therapy and Mom and Dad—"

"So what'd they do, give him up?"

Once she'd understood what that even meant, she'd been astonished at the very thought. "No!"

"My dad says parents are supposed to raise their own kids. He'd never put *me* in a place like that."

Lucy had asked Dad what to say to that. Then she was sorry she had; his face and his voice had stiffened; he'd said it wasn't her he was mad at. She'd said what he'd told her to say, though it hadn't satisfied either her or her questioners. "Ethan was out of control. He just kept stealing and doing drugs and nothing Mom or Dad did could stop him, so finally the judge put him at Nubie to get him to stop. He'll only be there for a year. Then he'll come home."

But Ethan hadn't come home. He'd run away from Nubie. No one had known where he was for more than two years. He would be seventeen now. It was hard for Lucy to comprehend that she hadn't known him at all when he was sixteen, and never would. The cops were supposed to be looking for him, but Mom and Dad didn't think they were looking very hard anymore. They must think he was dead. It was easier to think that than not to know where he was or when he might show up again.

It had been so long that people didn't ask much anymore. But when they did—when they came to her house, for instance, and saw the pictures that Mom and Dad wouldn't take down—Lucy just said, "He doesn't live here anymore," which was what her parents had told her to say, or, "He died," which she knew they wouldn't like but was probably the truth.

Now Mom reached to turn off the dusty hall light. Lucy waited. Her mother hit the wrong switch as usual and turned off the outside lights. She swore under her breath and punched the switch to get them back on.

Lucy wasn't allowed to say words like that, but she practiced them a lot in her mind and out loud with some of her friends. Her parents had pretty much stopped yelling at Rae for swearing a year or so ago, and they'd given up on it altogether with Ethan when he hadn't been much older than Lucy was now, because they'd had so many other things to yell at him about.

That was one way to do it: be so bad all the time that grown-ups couldn't keep up. The other way was to be so good all the time that you never broke any rules, never got into any trouble. Either way was hard.

If any of the neighbors were watching, Lucy thought—as she thought every time somebody pushed the wrong light switch—the lights flashing at the big old house on the hill would look like a distress signal. Lucy put a considerable amount of time and energy into thinking up ways you could let somebody know you needed help when the phone lines had been cut and the murderer was standing in your living room with a gun in one hand trained on you and his arm around one of your little brothers or sisters. Or when your crazy teenage brother came back from the dead and your parents didn't know what to do, your father didn't even believe he was there, and your mother welcomed him home.

Sneakily flicking the outside lights was one of the ways she'd come up with and kept on a list in her head. But it had been ruined. By now, the neighbors had seen the lights go off and on so many times that they would ignore the signal. So Lucy would have to find some other way, a *lot* of other ways, to save herself and her family from the man with the gun, from the lady who put razor blades in the Halloween candy, from Ethan sneaking around the house at night or in broad daylight, from nuclear war.

Her mother opened the door to look out, then went out onto the porch. Soft summer air drifted in; Lucy smelled flowers, heard the hum of the city at night. Someday she was going to live in the country, maybe in the mountains. Her mother had grown up on a farm and had always dreamed of living in a place where there were sidewalks, where a date could walk her home. It was weird to think of Mom as a girl, with dates. Sometimes Lucy liked that a lot.

Patches had pricked up his ears when the

door opened but, not hearing the rattle of his food dish, settled back down into her lap. She rubbed a knuckle under his chin. He stretched out one spotted paw to claw at the arm of the couch, which was already worn from bright blue to gray blue by so many hands and feet, knees and bottoms.

Lucy whispered, "Stop that, you bad cat!" and pulled his paw back, liking the way his toes stretched and separated under her fingers. She was fascinated with the inner workings of things: bones and veins, pipes under streets, electric wires in the walls of the house, thoughts and dreams. You called that stuff *infrastructure;* Mom had said that word over and over one night while she was studying for a test, and Lucy had asked what it meant and how to spell it. Lucy liked big words that looked like what they meant; written out on the page, "infrastructure" *looked* like the inside of something, the frame you could hang something on. Patches let her play with his toes for a few minutes, two white and two black, then languidly put out his claws.

Her mother came back in carrying Molly's yellow dump truck, an empty white plastic grocery sack, and a pink tennis shoe that was either Lucy's or Priscilla's. Lucy frowned; she got blamed for everything.

Sometimes Lucy was mad at Mom and Dad because they still loved Ethan, after all this

time and all the awful things he'd done. Sometimes she was mad at them because they didn't
talk about him all the time; they went on with
their lives. Mom went back to school. Dad
changed jobs. They took care of their other
kids. They kissed in the kitchen. It seemed
they'd forgotten all about Ethan. Someday
they might forget about her.

Lucy sighed. "They're all right. Nothing happened to them."

"Of course they're all right."

The sharpness of her tone brought tears to
Lucy's eyes, and she buried her face in the
cat's fur. He gave a very low growl, so quiet
she knew it was a secret message meant for
only her to hear. But she didn't know what it
was supposed to mean.

"But they've been gone a long time," her
mother said. "It doesn't take an hour to go to
the corner store for the paper." She looked at
her watch. "Over an hour."

"They're with Dad. They're safe," Lucy said,
only half believing it.

"He could have called."

"Molly's probably giving him a hard time,"
Lucy said wisely. "You know three-year-olds."

"More likely it's Rae," her mother said,
laughing a little. "You know fourteen-year-
olds." And Lucy felt the fear and excitement,
like a cyclone threatening to blow her off her
feet and set her down somewhere else, that

she always felt when she thought about being a teenager.

It wouldn't be long now. She was almost twelve. She had to wear a bra with most of her shirts, and Rae had finally convinced her that if you were going to shave your legs, you had to put up with all those tiny cuts.

Her mother reached to pet the cat. Lucy admired the shape of her hand where it caught the lamplight, although the nails were too short and there were nests of wrinkles across the knuckles. Her mother's wedding ring glinted silver. Dad wore one just like it, and when she was little, Lucy used to set their hands side by side and slide her two index fingers around and around their rings. She liked the rings, because they had pretty designs in them, and because they made circles that went around and around and didn't stop, and because they meant that her parents were going to stay married forever.

When her mother's fingers expertly massaged his ears, Patches's purring got louder and his whiskers flared in pleasure. All the animals liked Mom best. If she was anywhere in sight, Dominic couldn't get the dogs to sit still while he put their leashes on. Patches slept on Mom and Dad's bed if he could, arranging himself like another of the black-and-white star patterns on their green quilt. Even Priscilla's canary, which Lucy didn't like to be around since she'd found out in science that birds have hollow bones, would let Mom catch him when he got out of the cage. Lucy could hardly stand to look at that fragile feathered creature wrapped in Mom's two hands, with just his head sticking out the top and just his feet like broken yellowish twigs out the bottom.

Mom said pointedly that the animals liked her best because she was the one who fed them, even though every time the Brill family acquired another pet one kid or another had promised to take responsibility. Lucy knew it was more than that. The animals liked Mom —kept an eye on her, followed her around— because they thought she would keep them safe.

Lucy used to believe that, too, and that Dad would keep everything bad away from her and her brothers and sisters until they were old enough to protect themselves. Sometimes, even now, she let herself believe that.

"I wish they'd get back soon," Mom said. "I'd like to get to bed. Rae has to catch the summer-school bus at seven in the morning. I don't know why they start these things so *early*." Chattering about normal, everyday things was her mother's way of reassuring her, Lucy knew—of reassuring both of them. It didn't work; instead, it reminded her that if something had happened to Dad and Rae and

Molly, not much would be normal tomorrow or for a long long time. Rae wouldn't go to summer school. Priscilla wouldn't have her birthday party. They wouldn't even have breakfast, probably. Just cereal.

"You can go to bed," she offered. "I'll wait up for them."

Mom smiled and patted her knee. The instant her hand left him, Patches stopped purring. The instant it came back, he started up again. Lucy thought it must be wonderful to have power like Mom's, to stop and start a cat's purring. Maybe when she grew up, she'd be powerful, too. "That's all right, honey. You need your sleep. Priscilla's party is tomorrow, and amusement parks are tiring enough on a good night's sleep."

"I'm not even tired," Lucy protested feebly.

"I wouldn't be able to sleep anyway until I heard them come home. It's all I can do to sleep with Ethan out there somewhere, not safe in his own bed."

"Ethan's dead," Lucy said automatically.

"No, he's not."

Though her mother didn't raise her voice, Lucy felt the tension, the slight pulling away, and was sorry she'd said anything. Ethan's name, just his *name*, came between her and her mother. He'd always tried to take things away from people. Hatred for her brother made Lucy say, "The cops think he's dead.

That social worker, that Jerry Johnston, thinks he's dead. Everybody but you thinks he's dead."

"I'm his *mother*. It's my job to believe he's alive. And anyway, nobody can say for sure that he's dead. Some kids are missing for a long time and they're still alive."

"Dad thinks he's dead too."

"Why do you think that?"

"I heard him say so. You guys were having a fight."

Her mother reached out to ruffle her hair. Patches stopped purring. Lucy felt like crying, but didn't. "It's also my job to worry about your father and your sisters until they get home. Even if it is silly." She got up and went back to the door, pressing her nose against the glass and cupping her hands around her eyes. Lucy didn't like it when her mother deliberately blocked out the reflections of what was safe and real inside the house—including the two of them—to see what might be outside.

Her mother's worry was like the earwig in the old *Twilight Zone* that Lucy had seen a couple of times: eating its way through the brain. Leaving eggs.

The phone rang. Lucy's heart beat so hard that her ears hurt, and she made no move to answer it. Her mother got to it on the first ring. "Hello?

"Tony, where are you? Is something wrong?

"Are the girls all right?

"I know, I know. It's the age."

A brief laugh, that tired, brave sound that always made Lucy feel guilty and indignant at the same time. Nobody'd *forced* them to have seven kids. There was nothing to say they wouldn't have more. Cory was the youngest, and he was already two, and they liked babies.

Her mother passed a hand over her eyes, ran fingers through that ugly white streak. Furiously Lucy wondered if she could sneak into her parents' room at night and dye it herself.

"Okay, Tony. Thanks for calling. I know it's silly, but it helps.

"I love you, too."

When Ethan had disappeared, there had been a phone call in the middle of the night, just like in the movies. Lucy had heard the ringing, had heard Cory start to wail at the monster sound of it, had dragged the pillow over her head. Finally Rae had got up, swearing, and stomped down the hall to the little boys' room. When Cory's howling had subsided and it had seemed safe to come out, Lucy had rolled over onto her back to stare at the gray ceiling and listen to the things that were happening in her house.

She could hear her father's voice, so low she was almost feeling it, like music through the walls. He wasn't saying much. Then she heard him put down the phone and say to her mother, "That was Jerry Johnston. Ethan's missing."

At first Lucy hadn't been able to place Jerry Johnston. Then she remembered: the social worker from the place where the judge had sent Ethan the last time he stole a car. New Beginnings Children's Home; the kids who lived there called it Nubie. Jerry was huge, actually not as tall as Dad but so big around that he seemed like a fairy-tale tree. With homes inside the trunk and branches for tiny scared creatures with made-up names. He was very pale, and his voice didn't change no matter what he was saying, and he'd keep asking and asking a question until he got an answer, whether or not it was the truth. Ethan liked him, as much as he liked anybody.

"He had Ethan over at his apartment this evening," her father was telling her mother, "to get him away from the institution for a while. He left him in the living room watching TV while he went to put the pizza in the oven, and Ethan just walked out the door."

Lucy couldn't hear what her mother said. Dominic hollered something about being hungry, wanting pizza. Rae said, "Shut up," gently, and he did.

"He thought he'd come back. He thought he could find him. That's why he didn't report it until now. He says not to worry, that when kids go AWOL they're almost always picked up in a matter of hours for jaywalking or disturbing the peace or some other minor offense. They'll find him. If he shows up here, we're supposed to call."

But in two years they hadn't found Ethan or any sign of him. Lucy wanted to believe he was dead; she also wanted to believe he'd come home someday and everything would be all right again.

Sometimes he'd be standing in the hall when she got up to go to the bathroom at night; his eyes were like punched-out circles of paper, white and flat. Sometimes he'd be hiding in the lilac bush outside her parents' bedroom window, and his flesh looked like the undersides of leaves when it was going to rain. She saw him often.

And now she knew that Mom saw him, too. She didn't want to know that. She was afraid of secrets.

"I'm going to check on the other kids," her mother said now, and started up the stairs with an armload of stray belongings.

Suddenly terrified of being left alone, Lucy scrambled to her feet, dumping Patches onto the floor. "I'll come with you."

5

It was a nightly ritual. Like cakes on birthdays and the smell of coffee in the morning, her mother's rounds had always made Lucy feel safe in the net of her family and her home. It hadn't kept Ethan safe, but her mother still did it, and Lucy still waited for her mother's footsteps in the hall before she let herself fall asleep. Now she watched closely to see how it was done.

Cory was asleep in the big-boy bed. The much-used crib—tooth-marked, toy-dented, the same crib Ethan and then each of the other babies had slept in—stood nearby in case anybody needed it again. Cory slept like a baby, with his knees bent under him and his bottom in the air and his thumb in his mouth. Asleep, he was awfully cute.

Across the little room, Dominic's bed was so crowded with stuffed animals that she could hardly see him in it. A big pink dog, almost as big as he was, had a Star Wars quilt tucked under what would be its chin if it had one. Sometimes it was hard for Lucy to believe that he was five already; she clearly remembered when he'd been born.

Both Dom and Cory were light sleepers; you didn't dare touch either one of them. Mom stood so still in their doorway that Lucy wanted to sneak up behind her and poke her in the ribs. *It doesn't work,* she wanted to yell at her. Right now Cory had a cat scratch that just missed his eye, and Dom had skinned both knees yesterday when he fell on the basement steps trying to carry the pink dog down to the playroom. *It doesn't keep us safe. Even when we're little, you can't keep us safe, and the older we get the more dangers there are.*

As though she'd thought of that too, Mom sighed sadly and moved on. The door to the younger girls' room was shut tight; Lucy grinned to herself. Priscilla had had her way now, but when Molly got home, she'd want it open.

Mom knocked, waited, then put her head in. Lucy could just see past her. Priscilla was asleep on Molly's bottom bunk, flat on her back, snoring. Lucy giggled, put her hand over her mouth. She couldn't wait to tease Pris about that in the morning. Pris said she never snored: "Girls in the fourth grade don't do stuff like that! Farting and burping and snoring! Yuck!"

Her mother lifted Priscilla under the shoulders and knees. The snoring changed key. Priscilla's red-brown hair fell across her mother's arm. She wouldn't get it cut, and so every morning she screamed when Mom brushed the tangles out, and Dad was always reaching over to push it out of her face.

Something was wrong with the room. Lucy was afraid to see what it was. But fear for her little sister made her barge in.

There was the hint of a face at the window, she thought, lit by the streetlight. She almost cried out. She pointed and knocked a doll off the shelf. Priscilla stirred in their mother's arms, kicked a little. Mom made a shushing gesture with her mouth and eyes.

Then the face wasn't there, and Lucy saw that the only thing different about the room was its colors. The walls were silvery instead of their usual white. The curtains, which by day were a crisp apple green, now looked gray. It confused her a little, made her wonder about tricks of the light, made her wonder which colors were real and which were just in her mind, then confused her even more when she wondered whether colors ever existed anywhere but in your mind.

For as long as she could, Mom stood rocking the little girl in her arms. *Put her down,* Lucy thought furiously. *She's too heavy for you. You'll drop her.*

Suddenly she was remembering: Ethan bigger than their mother, sitting on the floor at their mother's feet with his arms folded on her lap and his head on his arms, asking to be read to. It was the last weekend he'd had a home pass from Nubie. Mom had read him poetry from Grandpa's frayed old book. Lucy had seen him smiling, her mother with tears in her eyes. It had bothered Lucy at the time and it bothered her now; he'd been way too old for a bedtime story.

Finally, sadly, Mom lifted Pris up onto her own bunk, tugged off the dirty lavender tennis shoes, pulled the rumpled Strawberry Short-cake sheet up over her, stretched on tiptoe to kiss her cheek. Lucy's jealousy was like hot tar inside her, like when they've just done the street and your shoes stick in it and if it gets on your skin it burns and you can't get away from the awful smell.

"Why'd you guys have so many kids?" she whispered. Mom frowned and put her finger to her lips, but Lucy repeated more loudly, "Why'd you have seven kids?"

"We like being parents," Mom whispered, but she was looking at Priscilla and Lucy wanted her to look at her.

"You should have stopped after three," she said, almost out loud.

"We like children," Mom whispered. "We like babies."

The hot-tar feeling got hotter and stickier, and Lucy said, "How come Ethan and Rae and me weren't enough for you?"

"Lucy. Are you saying you wish we didn't have the others? Are you saying you wish Priscilla and Dom and Molly and Cory had never been born?"

Not exactly, Lucy thought fiercely. *But sort of. I wish Ethan and Rae had never been born, too. I wish it was just me.*

Priscilla stirred, snored, brushed at her cheek as though shooing away a fly, settled into her pillow, snored again. In the corner, under the cage cover, the canary chirped sleepily; Mom cooed at him, almost soundlessly, and he quieted.

Downstairs the front door opened. Lucy heard Dad's voice and Molly's, and a third set of footsteps—jerky, like Cory's when he pounded his heels on the floor in a tantrum—that were her sister Rae's. Relief made Lucy sick to her stomach. She saw it mirrored on her mother's face and said quickly so that she wouldn't have to hear her mother say it, "They're home!"

Mom turned Lucy by the shoulders and pushed her out of the little girls' room. She was too rough; Lucy would have gone by herself. It wasn't worth saying anything about now; Lucy just added the small hot resentment to the pile of little bad things kept in the back of her mind about her mother, her father, her family, her life. Every day, the pile got bigger. Every day, she looked at every hard stone in it, knowing that someday she'd find a use for them all.

"You go straight to your room!" she heard her father say. His voice was raised, just a little but dangerously, the closest he ever came to yelling at any of them except Ethan. When Ethan had been at home, she'd sometimes been afraid of both of them. Now she was only afraid of Ethan.

"You already said that," Rae snapped back.

"Hey!"

Lucy heard scuffling and rushed to the landing to see.

Dad half turned Rae before she could shake him off, and she was shrieking, "Get your hands off me!" while he said in a voice like low thunder, "Don't you get smart with me, young lady!"

Paying no attention, Molly ran to her mother at the foot of the stairs. "Mommy, look at my telecoat! It makes stars!"

Lucy saw with disgust that it was just the tube from a roll of paper towels. It was soaked; when Mom took it, it drooped in her hand. "It doesn't *make* stars, honey. The stars are already in the sky. A telescope helps you *see* them."

"Daddy said it *makes* stars," Molly said stubbornly, and grabbed her tube back.

Rae had slammed the front door so hard that the umbrella lamp was still swaying. She stormed up the stairs, bumping into Lucy on purpose and muttering, "Son of a bitch" just barely under her breath. Dad had sat down hard in the blue chair in the living room and Mom sat beside him; they didn't seem to know Lucy was there.

"Mommy, I'm hungry!" Molly was wailing.

"You may have a banana, and then it's bedtime."

"I don't want a nana! I want ice cream!"

"I just bought her an ice cream cone," Dad said in a tired voice.

"I want ice cream!"

"Molly, it's a banana or nothing."

Molly ran down the hall to the kitchen. She'd stopped whining, but Lucy could tell by the way she moved that she was mad, and she could imagine her pouty little face. Suddenly infuriated by her own terror of what would happen if they weren't all very good, she thought: *You better make her behave while you still can.*

Dad said, "Shoplifting."

"Oh, Tony, no."

"Two movie magazines under her shirt. The manager came out after us. I never even suspected."

Her mother's voice was a flat rock that Lucy could slip on. "What happened?"

"The manager said pressing charges was more trouble than it was worth. I told him he ought to. We don't do her any favors by protecting her from the consequences of the things she does," he said, sounding like a social worker, like that Jerry Johnston.

It bothered Lucy to be thinking about Jerry Johnston again. She was sure he was a very nice person; she was sure he had a mother and father and brothers and sisters and maybe a girlfriend and maybe a cat. But he'd only been part of their lives because of her screwed-up brother. She hated remembering those endless family meetings, everybody in the family in tears but Ethan. Jerry had sat calm and sweet as a marshmallow Easter chicken, massive legs crossed, taking notes.

"This is how Ethan started, you know," her mother was saying. "Shoplifting from that same store."

"Candy bars," Dad agreed. "But let's not jump to conclusions. A lot of kids shoplift and never go on to bigger things."

"Come on, Tony, you know that isn't all. The cheating at school. The lying. I'm not sure she even knows what's true a lot of the time."

"There was a five-dollar bill missing from my wallet when I went to pay for gas this morning," Dad said, as if he didn't want to. "I've been trying to tell myself I lost it or miscounted, but it's the second time in two weeks."

"I suppose we better get her into therapy," Mom said. "Not that it did Ethan much good."

Dad rubbed his eyes. "Our job is to give her every chance we can think of, every resource. It's up to her what use she makes of anything. Just like it was up to Ethan."

"It still is," Mom said, and then hastily went on before Dad could say anything, although he'd looked up at her sharply. "I'll call Jerry Johnston in the morning. He already knows our family. Maybe that's an advantage."

"Who knows."

"Six more to raise." Mom sighed, and the stone in Lucy's chest twisted. She was one of those six. She couldn't help it. "I don't know if I'm going to make it till they're all grown."

"You'll make it. So will I. What choice do we have? Shit."

Lucy always wanted to laugh when one of her parents said a dirty word. She put her hand over her mouth, then hurriedly left the landing and went down the hall to her room. Below her in the living room, she knew her parents were hugging and kissing. That embarrassed her and made her feel good at the same time.

She almost smashed her nose against the door of the room she shared with Rae when it didn't open to her shove. She took a step back and pushed on it again. "Rae. Let me in." No answer. "Rae, come on. It's my room, too." She thought she heard the sounds of someone in there, but the door stayed shut. Lucy pounded hard on the door. "You pig! *I* didn't do anything to you!"

The door couldn't be locked; they weren't allowed to have locks on their doors, in case there was a fire. Rae had just pushed something in front of it. Lucy took a few more steps backward and then charged, hitting the door with her shoulder. It hurt, and it made a much louder bang than she'd hoped, but the door jerked open and she stumbled over the toy chest Rae had used as a barricade. It was Lucy's toy chest; Rae had no business touching it.

The room was dark, and unfamiliar because the furniture had been rearranged. Lucy had her hand on the light switch when she turned to look at the bed.

Her sister was lying flat on her back. The streetlight turned her skin blue and silver; her profile shimmered, as if somebody had drawn it with Dominic's Glo-in-the-Dark Etch-a-Sketch. Her breasts stuck up; Lucy couldn't help being shocked and envious at how big they were. Her eyes shone dully, like pennies.

"Are you all right?" Lucy stood in the doorway and left the lights off. Her knees were braced against the toy chest, out of which spilled toys she hadn't played with in years; she saw the glittery eyes of her blue panda bear, the green ribbons on the braids of her dancing doll, whose long stuffed legs seemed to be curled around her own neck. "Rae? Should I call Mom and Dad?"

"No!"

The word sounded dangerous, but Lucy kept on. "Are you sick?"

"I feel *awful*!"

"I don't know what to do. I better call them—"

"*I hate them!*" Rae's voice was like a growl. Lucy stopped with her back to the door and stared at her.

Her sister's face was twisting and twitching as if there were snakes under the skin. Her body jerked, knees brought up to her chest and then kicked straight again. She pounded her fists backward onto the mattress. A dark pool stained the sheets under her hips. "Rae," breathed Lucy. "Your period—" But then her sister was on her feet and coming toward her, and Lucy saw that it was just a shadow and not blood and that Rae was going to hurt her.

She fumbled behind her for the doorknob. "Stop it! I'll tell! I'll tell Dad!"

Rae burst into little-girl tears and collapsed onto the floor. "Dad hates me!" she wailed. "Oh, he hates me!" and then, "Go away! Get out of here!"

It was her room, too, but she didn't stop to say so. She opened the door, backed through it, shut it behind her. Something soft bounced off it on the other side. Probably one of her stuffed animals.

Her parents weren't in the front part of the house. Lucy reached way back into the hall closet and pulled coats and sweaters off hangers and hooks, until they covered the floor of the closet knee-high. She sat down on the mound, curled her legs up under her, lay down. Mom's torn gray jacket hung toward the back; it had belonged to Lucy's great-grandfather who had died when her mother was fifteen. Lucy pulled it down; the hanger pinged against the closet wall. Gently she folded the jacket; it held her mother's smells and her great-grandfather's, and it made a perfect pillow.

"Lucy?" Her mother's head poked around the closet door. "What are you doing?"

"Can I sleep in the closet tonight?"

Mom crouched, but she was still taller than Lucy was. "In the *closet*? What for?"

Lucy snuggled deeper into the nest of family clothes. "It's cozy here," she said.

Her mother hesitated, then smiled and bent forward on her hands and knees to kiss Lucy's cheek. "Why not," she said. "Pleasant dreams, honey."

Mom left the door ajar when she left, so that a pale streak of not-quite darkness cut the darkness of the closet. Lucy fell asleep to the quiet sounds of her parents readying themselves and the house for sleep.

6

From the middle of the amusement park, between the funhouse and the little train, there was a weird glow. Lucy thought it was just moonlight on the lake, but she wasn't sure. The sky was dark blue, like the eighth-grade graduation robe Rae had worn last month, and the lights of the Ferris wheel and roller coaster and Tilt-a-Whirl were like buttons and tassels, coming loose.

Lucy was ready to go home. She was tired. She had a headache from too much sun and noise and sugar. Her shoulders were sunburned. Her mouth and fingers were sticky from cotton candy and sno-cones, and so much dirt had stuck to her that she felt furry.

But Pris was still going strong, racing between rides and concession stands, trying to laugh louder than the mechanical lady in front of the funhouse, singing at the top of her lungs, "Happy birthday to me! Happy birthday to me!"

Nobody else in the family seemed tired. Even Mom and Dad were having a good time. Mom had ridden the roller coaster six times already and was in line again now with Priscilla. Dad, who'd always claimed that rides made him sick, was on the big Ferris wheel with Molly and Dom.

It wasn't fair. The kids who had summer birthdays got to have neat parties—here, or swimming, or slumber parties in the backyard tent. When your birthday was in January, like Lucy's and Ethan's, you never got to do anything fun.

Scowling, Lucy stood and watched the merry-go-round animals go up and down and around. Cory was on an elephant with turquoise tusks. He screamed every time it went up in the air, and Lucy wasn't sure he was having fun, but it was too late to get him off now.

The striped pole stuck right through the elephant's fat stomach and back made Lucy cringe. When the elephant went up, the scalloped shadow of the roofline seemed to cut off both its head and her little brother's. Cory was yelling and the elephant's painted wooden eye swelled out at her. She imagined how that huge, smooth, red eyeball would feel in her palm.

"Hey, Lucy! Look at me!" Cory's baby voice was muffled and he was carried out of her sight again under the red and white fringe.

The merry-go-round slowed down. It took a long time to stop completely, and even then she had the feeling that it could start up again for no reason, at any time, whether anybody wanted it to or not, that it could work itself back up to full speed before she knew it and send Cory and the others spinning out into space, way beyond her reach.

But the tinny, tinkly music kept on, never missed a beat. She used to imagine that the music and the motion were connected somehow, that the circling ran a hidden motor that created the music, or that the music actually made the platform turn. It bothered her that she didn't know which caused which, or whether there was some third mechanical force that caused them both. The animals looked different when they weren't moving. Scarier.

Little kids scuttled from between the animals' legs and from under their tails and necks. The cute teenage operator leaned his bare arms on the railing to talk to another boy. They didn't seem to care much about the merry-go-round or about Cory on it. They hadn't even noticed her.

Somebody stopped to talk to them. A huge man, not as tall as Dad but big around, legs like tree trunks in white shorts, a red striped shirt stretched over a hard-looking belly and shoulders like mountains, short thick arms, a short thick neck.

She knew him. Jerry Johnston, the social worker from Nubie where Ethan had been. She'd sat with her brothers and sisters and parents in Jerry Johnston's office every month for family meetings; she'd never said much unless they made her, but she'd watched the gold and silver fish in Jerry's aquarium and the gold and silver rings on Jerry's fingers that sparkled when he moved his fat hands.

Now she saw him put his hand on the arm of the ride operator's not-so-cute friend, saw the boy shrug and glance at his friend and then follow Jerry into the crowd. Lucy was relieved that she wouldn't have to say hello.

Cory must be on the other side. She started that way, making a tight, cautious circle. There were more kids on the ride than she'd thought. Uneasily she wondered where they all could have come from, who was taking care of them. She didn't see anybody taking care of them. She didn't see Cory.

Ethan walked by.

Reddish-brown hair cut very close to his skull, like a punker's. Everybody in her family had either reddish-brown or dark brown hair, except Rae, whose hair these days looked like lemon cotton candy. Brown eyes like hers and her brothers' and sisters', his going in every direction at once. Thin face, thin shoulders and arms sticking out of a gray sleeveless sweatshirt, thin ankles above tennis shoes that were so new they glared.

She'd never seen Ethan so thin. She'd always thought of him as big and strong, sometimes a bully and sometimes a protector, her big brother.

Suddenly it crossed her mind that maybe the only reason he'd seemed big was because she'd been so small. Maybe that was true about Dad, too. Maybe the older and bigger she got, the smaller and thinner and weaker everybody else would get, until she'd have to take care of them all. Ethan looked right at her, even turned his head as he walked past, but she didn't think he saw her.

She yelled, "Cory!" and pushed through the crowd, racing to the other side of the merry-go-round. But the thing had moved. It wasn't moving, but it had moved. The stiff, polished animals on this side were the same as the ones she'd been watching on the other side. The spotted giraffe. The cream-colored horse with the purple mane. The pink and gold flamingo with the beak that looked sharp but wasn't when she put her hand to it. Cory wasn't there. He wasn't anywhere. She'd lost him.

Lucy burst into tears.

Somebody sneered. "What's the matter with you?"

Lucy jumped and turned away from the merry-go-round, which was filling with little strangers for the next ride. She forced herself to peer into the crowd again. Just a few minutes ago she hadn't been able to find anybody she knew—though she always had the feeling that if she stood still long enough in any one place, everybody she knew, dead or alive or imagined, would come by like a parade. Now Rae was coming toward her. She had hold of Cory's wrist and was walking too fast for him. He was crying and stumbling.

"Nothing," Lucy said, and wiped her nose with a sticky hand.

Rae glared. "Then what are you crying for? You're always crying. God, you're such a baby."

Lucy kicked at the hard-packed dirt of the midway. Some of it came loose and puffed up against Rae's smooth leg. She hoped it got into the high-heeled sandal, stuck to the red toenail polish. "I couldn't find Cory," Lucy said sullenly, and took him away from Rae, picked him up though he was getting awfully heavy for her, pressed his head into her shoulder. Someday she'd have a baby of her own, just like Cory when he was a baby. She'd be a good mother. She'd never let anything bad happen to her baby, like Mom had let happen to Ethan.

Rae wiped her hands on her jeans. Lucy had watched her practice that gesture in front of the mirror; it called attention to her hips. "Jesus, sometimes I wish he *would* get lost. I wish they'd all get lost."

"That's a mean thing to say," Lucy said. "I'm telling."

Rae reached out both hands with the long red nails and pushed Lucy so hard that she almost fell, carrying Cory. "You, too," she sneered. Thick lipstick made her teeth look very white when she pulled her lips back. "I wish you'd get lost, too. Permanently. Like Ethan."

Nearly blind with fury, Lucy balanced her little brother higher on her hip and crouched. She swept her free hand across the ground in search of a weapon, found only an empty potato chip bag, threw it as hard as she could at Rae, who was laughing and walking away. A tall boy was with her. Lucy hadn't noticed him before. The glittery bag sailed back to the ground. "I hate you!" she shouted after her sister, though already she'd lost her among the colors and shapes of the crowd. "You bitch!"

"Bitch!" Cory echoed gleefully, tugging at her hair. His baby voice made the bad word sound even worse than it was, and she put her hand over his mouth. He turned his head and chortled: "You bitch!"

"Lucy, what's going on?"

Lucy was so glad to see her mother, and so embarrassed at being caught swearing in public, that she started crying again. Mom had her hair in pigtails, and bangs almost hid the ugly white streak. She looked too young to have seven kids.

Cory squirmed out of Lucy's arms and ran to his mother. She patted his head and smiled at him. But she didn't pick him up, even though Lucy could see that was what he wanted and knew that Mom could see it, too. When she had kids, she'd always give them what they wanted. "What's going on?" Mom asked her again, and Lucy could tell that she was already mad at her.

"Rae's being obnoxious. I hate her."

Her mother glanced around. The pigtails flopped. "Where is Rae? I haven't seen her since we got here."

"I don't know where she is. She saw some guy she knew and they took off." Lucy didn't know if her sister really had known the tall boy, if she'd even really gone off with him or just happened to be walking in the same direction for a while.

"Was she okay?"

Lucy scowled. Sure, she was okay. Why wouldn't she be okay? "I guess," she said.

Cory was wandering off, following a little girl with three pink balloons. Lucy started after him, but Mom reached him first and hoisted him onto her shoulders. Mom was really strong.

Dad came up with Molly and Dominic. He was holding his stomach and his face was pale, so that all the little hairs of his beard stood out like dirt on his cheeks and chin and down the front of his neck. "Three times in a row on the Ferris wheel," he groaned.

Mom patted his arm. "You'll earn a star on your daddy badge."

"The guy stopped us at the top. All three times. And then we *rocked*."

"And we could see *everything*!" Dom crowed. "We could even see you guys! It was *neat*! Huh, Dad?"

Dad groaned again and rolled his eyes. Lucy giggled. She went over and put her arms around him, but he pushed her away gently when she pressed her face too hard into his tummy.

"Lucy says she saw Rae," Mom told Dad. "She went off with some boy. I could hear Lucy calling her names from clear over at the hot-dog stand."

Lucy looked down guiltily, but all Dad said was, "Rae can be—difficult sometimes. It's her age."

"I'm not going to be like that when *I'm* a teenager," Lucy said heatedly.

"Oh, you probably will. But you'll get through it. And so will Rae."

"Ethan didn't get through it," Lucy said.

"He hasn't yet," Mom said sharply. "There's still plenty of time. He's still young."

"I bet he's dead."

"Stop it, Lucy," Dad said, and she did, her eyes glazed with tears, her mind pulsing with the image of Ethan in the short haircut and the white shoes, thin and silent and with eyes everywhere at once, maybe watching all of them from the crowd right now. She'd stop, if that's what they wanted. She wouldn't tell them. She wouldn't mention Ethan again.

Dominic and Molly were chasing each other around their father's legs. He wasn't really paying attention. Mom said, "We shouldn't have let Rae come, Tony. Not after last night."

Dad sighed. "You're the one who said how important birthdays are."

"I just think we should keep her feeling a part of the family for as long as we can."

"Hey, you guys! I wanna go on the roller coaster again!" Priscilla was yelling from all the way across the midway. She zigzagged over to them and didn't stop moving once she got there, dancing from one foot to the other, poking at Cory with the pointed cardboard tube from her cotton candy, tugging at her mother's arm. "Let's go again!"

"Oh, Pris." Mom reached to hug her and missed. "Do we have to?"

"It's my *birthday*!"

Pris was a year and four months younger than Lucy, but she was already taller. At the moment, she was also wearing Lucy's rainbow T-shirt under the long-sleeved blue shirt of her own, which she'd now rolled up and tied by the tails around her midriff. Lucy didn't care whose birthday it was. Infuriated, she grabbed for the T-shirt, but Priscilla twisted away and the shirt would have ripped if Lucy had held on.

"How about something else?" Mom pointed. "How about that?"

Everybody looked up. Molly cried, "Oooh! *Pretty*!"

A string of cars one after another, red and blue and red and blue, swung through the night air. Some of them were as high as the tops of the trees. They looked like big half shells—a giant's necklace, or the homes of giant slimy clams. They dipped and twisted, rose and fell, but they didn't make any noise. At first Lucy didn't see the cable holding them up or the people riding inside, and so it was easy to imagine that they were traveling empty, alone, and with no reason.

The cars were like bonnets, she thought, without any faces in them.

It would be easy to fall out, she thought. You probably wouldn't make much noise coming down. She heard little screams, like bugs.

"The Sky Ride!" Priscilla squealed. "All *right*!"

She started down the midway at full speed and bumped into a fat lady whose sundress showed lots of different sunburn lines on her neck and shoulders, layers and scoops of pink. The lady didn't say anything, and Priscilla kept going. Dom and Molly went after her.

Lucy was suddenly afraid. But all her family was leaving, so she went, too. Behind her she heard Mom calling to them to slow down, Cory howling to be let down, Rae laughing somewhere away from the family, and Ethan's quiet cold breathing as he watched.

7

Ethan was waiting for them when they got home. Lucy saw him right away when they turned onto King Street, standing under the apple tree out front. For a minute she thought the chain-link fence was wrapped right through him.

Lucy had lived on King Street all her life. So had Ethan, until he'd started getting in trouble, and now she didn't know where he lived. In a way you could still say he lived here; she didn't think he had any other home, and a person had to have a home *somewhere*. Someday she'd live in the Malibu Colony with Emilio Estevez, in a huge house with a giant pink marble bathtub shaped like a shell.

Mom was driving. Lucy saw her turn her head to look at their house, and was reassured. Mom always did that after they'd been away someplace, even for just a little while, even to the grocery store or to the dentist. She always turned her head to look at their house as they drove past on the way to the alley and the garage; it was one of the ways Lucy'd always been able to tell they were almost home, even back when she was so little she couldn't recognize the corner by herself.

Tonight Ethan was in their yard, by their house. Lucy braced herself. But Mom didn't say anything, so Lucy didn't either. Ethan was their secret.

He was camouflaged. Inside the fence with the roses climbing on it that separated the Brill place from the neighbors' on two sides and the street in front and the alley in back, he was hard to pick out. He was part of it. He belonged there.

Dad was talking to Mom about a project at his work. Rae had earphones on and was leaning against the door on the other side, as far away from everybody else as she could get. The little kids were playing old maid in the way-back. Beside her, Priscilla the birthday girl was staring dreamily out the window; the pale pink streetlight that must have just come on was right in Priscilla's face for a minute, and Lucy thought how much they all looked like Mom and Dad, even though Mom and Dad didn't look a thing like each other.

Suddenly Lucy was filled with such love for her family and her place in it that she felt like a hot-air balloon. It hurt her, there was so much love. She closed her eyes and held on to the edge of the seat. Mom slowed down for the turn into the alley. Two cars went by, and Lucy could tell they were carrying families or people who belonged to families, taking them home.

Mom took them slowly toward the garage, and everybody started making rustling sounds and little sighs as they got ready to get out of the car. Lucy twisted in her seat to peer out the back window, but she couldn't see Ethan anymore. Her knee bumped into Priscilla, and Pris complained loudly, "Lu-*cy!*" From the front seat Dad scolded without even turning his head, "Cut it out, girls!" Lucy sulked.

Dad got out of the car to open the garage door. As usual, Lucy wondered irritably why they didn't have an automatic garage door opener like Stacey's. She'd asked that so many times that Dad got mad at her if she even mentioned it, so she didn't. But she still wondered. Nobody could tell her what to think.

She watched Dad leave the safe shell of the family car. At first—mad at him because he'd yelled at her and because he wouldn't get a garage door opener—she was glad to see him go, hoped he'd disappear altogether into the smelly shadows around the garbage cans, hoped Ethan would get him.

Then she was sorry, and terrified, and had to clamp her mouth shut tight to keep from crying out, "Daddy!" Then she thought, with a rush of hot pride, that he looked like a hero, striding away from the car while they all watched and waited, lifting the heavy garage door with one hand, as if it weighed nothing, to let them all in.

When she got out of the car, Lucy went to her father and hugged him. They walked on into the house with their arms around each other, while the rest of the family chattered and yawned around them. "You're getting so tall," Dad said to her. "Look, you come all the way up to my second shirt button," and his big hand rested on the top of her head as he showed her how tall she was and held her for a minute against his chest.

Everybody just sort of drifted off to their beds. Even the little kids went without complaining. Lucy lay under her sheet and waited for Mom and Dad to come say good night to her. Rae still had the earphones on and was curled up on her bed across the room with a pillow over her head and her back to Lucy. Lucy stuck her tongue out.

Lucy kissed Dad and hugged him and said, "I love you." He said it back. He did love her, too. When it was Mom's turn, Lucy kept her arms around her neck and whispered, "Can I talk to you later?"

Mom tried to pull back a little in surprise, but Lucy held her close. "Can't it wait till tomorrow? It's late. You've had a big day. We all have."

"Can I come talk to you when everybody's asleep? I'll meet you in the living room in half an hour." Only when Lucy felt Mom's shoulders shrug and her head nod did she let her go.

She almost fell asleep. Or maybe she did fall asleep, because all of a sudden the house was awfully quiet. She could hear just the edges of music seeping out from around the earphones, and from Rae's breathing she could tell she was asleep. There was a cricket in their room, a big one from the sound of it; Lucy liked the sound crickets made but they looked gross, and she swung her feet gingerly over the side of the bed.

She didn't know how late it was. Maybe Mom had given up and gone to bed. Lucy hurried. She'd made it all the way down to the bottom of the stairs before she heard her mother whisper his name.

"Ethan!"

Lucy stifled her own cry of "Mama!" and tiptoed rapidly toward the sound of her mother's voice. The hall between the stairs and the living room was only a few steps long, and she'd probably traveled it every day of her life, but now she thought maybe she could get lost.

She was really *aware* of things, as if she had a fever: her own breathing, which filled her ears and hurt in her chest. The places under her bare feet where the nap of the carpet had been flattened by hundreds, maybe thousands, of footprints, including her own, including these she was making now. Patches's breathing that turned to purring when she passed him asleep in a chair, though he didn't open his eyes or flick his ears or give any other sign that he knew she was there. The way the house felt full, because of all the people and things in it that she loved.

The French doors at this end of the living room were ajar. Lucy could hardly bring herself to go any closer. She stood behind the lacy curtains and, afraid to look through, looked instead at each of the tiny holes that, if you looked from a little distance, made patterns of flowers and leaves.

She tasted coldness; her mouth puckered and her teeth hurt. She smelled Ethan, sour, as if he hadn't taken a shower in a long time, as if he were sick. She heard her mother say his name again. If Lucy hadn't already known what the word was and hadn't been expecting her to say it, it would have sounded like a sigh.

Lucy took a big sideways step, like in Mother May I? or Simon Says, and forced herself to peek through the crack between the doors. Her mother's back was to her, and she was close enough that Lucy could have reached through and touched her. Her brother Ethan crouched at the other end of the long room, facing them both.

He didn't speak. He didn't do any of the things he used to do: grin at them, or pout, or yell dirty words, or call out like in a bad dream. His mouth was hanging open, crooked, as if it hurt. It looked full of dirt or blood; Lucy felt sick. Furiously, she wondered what he'd been doing to hurt himself now. Maybe chewing snuff; she'd heard what snuff could do to your gums and lips and tongue.

Ethan started toward them. Lucy backed up, and her hand on the door opened it farther. Mom stayed where she was and said his name out loud. He was panting and his hands were in fists, as if he'd been running hard, but really he was hardly moving at all.

Mom raised her arms. Horrified, Lucy thought she was going to pull Ethan to her, the way she did the rest of them when they were hurt or sad, and then Mom would be filthy, too. But the distance between Mom and Ethan closed only a little bit at a time.

Ethan's face was blank. Lucy tried to tell herself that he looked tired, or sick, or mad, but really there wasn't any expression on his face at all. What he looked was *empty*.

But when he took another shaky step, she could see into his eyes. The same look was there that had been there for years, since before she'd been old enough to know that you could tell things about people from the look in their eyes. It was the same look she was seeing more and more in Rae's eyes, too. She didn't know what to call it. A wildness that good parents should be able to make go away. Lucy was suddenly furious with her father, asleep upstairs, and with her mother, who stood with her back to Lucy, close enough to touch, not doing anything.

"Ethan," Mom said again, and her voice broke. Lucy wondered savagely why she did that. In the seventeen years and six months since Ethan had been born, Mom had probably said his name a million times—maybe a million times just since he'd started getting in trouble, or just since he'd disappeared—and it never had done any good.

Help him! Lucy thought wildly, and the delicate threads in the lace curtain gave a little in her fist. *Do something. You're the mother. Help him, or make him go away.*

Ethan didn't answer to his name, of course. He didn't say anything. Seeing the way he strained, the way his throat worked and his wet mouth hung open, Lucy understood that he was trying to talk and couldn't.

Whatever had happened to him, whatever

big trouble he'd gotten himself into this time, he'd lost the power of speech. All of a sudden, Lucy hated it that he couldn't talk, even though, for a long time before he'd run away, all he'd said were ugly things to everybody, obscenities and accusations and lies.

Mom was begging. "Ethan, talk to me, honey. Tell me what's going on. Tell me what you need from me." He still didn't say anything, and Lucy knew why: Kids shouldn't have to tell their parents what they needed. Parents should just *know*. He took another long, labored step toward Mom's outstretched arms.

Suddenly Lucy realized that Ethan needed something he couldn't get from Mom and Dad, and that Rae did, too, and that maybe she herself would, too. Maybe she already did and didn't know it, like having some disease that you carried around inside you for years before there were any symptoms. Maybe all kids did. The realization both scared and excited her. *Help him!* she thought thunderously, but she could tell that at this very moment, Mom was failing him again.

Lucy's head swam. To keep herself from falling she held on to the curtains with both hands, and in several places her nails went through with tiny tearing sounds. The door creaked, but Mom and Ethan were paying too much attention to each other to notice that she was there.

"Ethan!"

Ethan lunged or stumbled and fell on top of Mom. Lucy dodged backward, pulling the door wide open although she didn't mean to. Her own cry was lost in Mom's. She saw them on the floor, Mom's white shirt and Ethan's pale skin against the dark brown carpet. She saw Mom close her arms around him, heard her actually start to hum as if she were singing a lullaby, then saw his hands go to Mom's throat.

"Ethan! Stop it!"

Mom's scream was a croak, but Lucy tried to help her by echoing it out loud. She fell to her knees beside them, afraid to touch them, not sure she should even be here, not knowing what to do.

She pulled at her brother's shoulders, his dirty shirt, his hair so short she couldn't get a hold on it. He wasn't very heavy, she could move parts of his body, but his grip was so tight that she couldn't even think how to break it; she clawed at his fingers, bit at them. His thumbs bored into the soft places in their mother's neck; the flesh was turning white around them, and Mom was coughing. Lucy wrapped her legs around her brother's thin waist and clamped her hands over his mouth and nose, trying not to think about the stuff she'd seen coming out of there.

There was a thin crash behind them. Ethan twisted underneath her, and she tumbled sideways onto the floor. She landed on top of Patches; he yowled and struggled free, but he didn't scratch.

"Lucy, Lucy, are you all right?"

"I guess." She was crying. Mom held her tight.

"What's going on?" Timidly Lucy opened her eyes. Dad was in the doorway, holding the fallen curtain rod. The curtains fluttered around him like torn skin.

"Lucy was having a nightmare," Mom told him, still panting, her voice strained as if she had a bad sore throat. She gathered Lucy up in her arms and carried her to the couch. Vaguely, Lucy was surprised that Mom could still carry her, that she could still fit into her mother's lap. She drew her knees up, put her thumb in her mouth, buried her face against Mom's soft shirt. "A nightmare about Ethan," Mom added.

"How did the curtains get torn down?"

"I think she was still half-asleep when she came downstairs. She lost her balance and grabbed them."

Dad came to sit beside them and put his arm around both of them. His cotton pajamas smelled like sunshine. Lucy snuggled against him. "Damn," he said softly. "It just goes on and on."

"And we can't protect them from their dreams," Mom said, leaning her head on his shoulder. "We can't keep any of them safe."

But Lucy, sitting in her mother's lap in her father's arms in her own living room on a quiet summer night, felt safe.

8

The doorbell rang before *Masters of the Universe* was over, so Lucy knew the social worker was early, it wasn't even nine yet. That made her mad. It was bad enough that he was coming to her house, upsetting everybody, making her dad come home from work; he could at least wait till the right time.

The police had come to her house very early this morning. They'd stood in the entranceway underneath the dusty umbrella-shaped lamp, a man and a woman. She'd only known it was a man and a woman because of their voices; otherwise they were the same, same height, same hair under the same hats. Ethan was dead, they'd said. It made her really mad. Everybody already knew that. They must have

said it a hundred times. She and Rae had listened at the upstairs railing, holding hands.

Mom and Dad had called everybody together before breakfast. "Ethan is dead,"
they'd said, a hundred times. "Your brother is
dead." Cory and Molly had started crying because Mom and Dad were crying. Everybody
else had just sat there, waiting to be released.
It wasn't like they didn't already know: Ethan
was dead.

So what was Jerry Johnston coming for
now? Probably to tell them that Ethan was
dead. Lucy scowled. Then she had the crazy
idea that maybe he was coming to tell them it
wasn't true, the cops were wrong, everybody
was wrong, Ethan wasn't dead.

When she heard Mom yell her name, she realized she hadn't cleaned up the kitchen like
she was supposed to. "I will, Mom!" she called,
and scrambled to her feet.

But at the door of the family room she
paused to look back at Cory, Molly, and Dominic. They sat in a row, cross-legged on the
crumb-specked brown carpet in front of the
TV, little shoulders rounded, little feet bare,
little toes like pebbles or like teeth.

It would be so easy for somebody to make
them sad. So easy for somebody to hurt them.
Right now, they seemed safe and happy. Molly
giggled at something on the screen. Cory unfolded his legs, leaned back on his elbows, and

stuck his feet straight up in the air. Dom yawned and made a sound like a car horn, in a miniature version of a game Dad played with all of them, one after another, until they got too old to play with him that way. Cheerios were scattered on the floor around them: lace on a wedding dress, or stepping-stones across a raging river, or tiny flying saucers carrying tiny aliens from a tiny distant planet to bring messages only Dominic could hear, or Molly, or Cory, just as they once had brought messages to Lucy.

Everybody had been like that once upon a time. All the grown-ups in the world had been kids, though some of them, she was learning, never had been safe. Mom and Dad had been children once. They hadn't known each other then. Lucy hadn't known them, either. She hadn't even *existed*. It was all connected, and hard for her to think about.

The doorbell rang again. Irritably Lucy wondered what Jerry Johnston was in such a hurry about, why Mom didn't answer the door. A cereal commercial came on, and Molly sang along; she knew all the words, even the whoop at the end.

Lucy pushed the door shut. It caught a breeze from the open kitchen window and slammed. She winced and waited, but nobody yelled at her.

The kitchen really was a mess. She didn't

see what was such a big deal. If the house was
clean enough for the family to live in, why
wasn't it clean enough for some stranger to
walk into? Even a stranger with power. Even a
stranger with terrible news about Ethan.

Her big brother was dead. She would never
see him again. Tears filled her eyes. The dishcloth was stiff and sour. Clean ones were in
the china cabinet in the dining room, next to
the living room where her mother would now
be taking Jerry Johnston to sit. Lucy didn't
want to go in there. Wrinkling her nose, she
held the dishcloth under hot running water.
An ant crawled across the counter. Lucy shuddered and watched it disappear under the
metal edge of the sink. Dad said everything
had a right to live, but Lucy didn't think that
ought to include bugs.

She wiped at the dribbles of milk across the
red tablecloth. Some of them were hardened
by now and she had to scrub. One of Ethan's
probation officers, a fat lady with soft white
hair like a grandmother from a little kids'
book, had put into a court report that the
Brills' house was "mediocre" and the house-
keeping was "passable." Lucy hadn't seen
what was so bad about that; she hadn't even
known for sure what *mediocre* meant until
she looked it up. But Mom had been furious.
"They read the damn things in open court!"
Mom had yelled at Dad, who was just trying to

calm her down. "It will be in our permanent record!"

"I don't think she meant it the way it sounds," Dad had insisted. "The whole report is sloppily written. I just think she picked the wrong words. I mean, look, Carole, if she'd said the house was 'modest' and the house-keeping was 'adequate,' it would mean the same thing literally but it would have an entirely different tone."

"But she *didn't* say that. She didn't *mean* that. Haven't you seen her, Tony? She noticed the spot where the paint is peeling on the outside of the front door. She brushed off the chair with her hand before she'd sit down. She examined her coffee cup before she'd drink out of it."

"Maybe she doesn't have kids or pets," Dad had suggested, chuckling. Then, seeing that Mom wasn't amused, he'd demanded, "Well, anyway, what do you care what she thinks?"

"I don't exactly care what she thinks. But it's such a gratuitous little cruelty to write things like that about a family that's already vulnerable, that's already going through hell."

Lucy hadn't understood much of that, except to see that she'd been wrong to think of the probation officer as a friendly, grandmotherly lady come to help them and to help Ethan. During the probation officer's second visit, Lucy'd had to leave the room, because all she could think about was the empty raisin box, crumpled and dusty, on the floor under the lady's chair, just behind her thick crossed ankles.

Now she ate bran flakes dry from her hand for her own breakfast while she scrubbed at a stubborn sticky place on the corner of the table. Good thing that probation officer lady never went in Ethan's room. The thought almost made Lucy giggle. There were posters all over the walls. Posters of naked ladies in all different poses. Sometimes Lucy and the other kids sneaked in there to look. Lucy would try to bend her arms and legs the way those ladies did, twist her face to arrange it like this one or that one, fluff her hair, push out her chest. Dom was always wanting to see "those naked ladies with the boobies and everything."

She stuck her hand inside the cereal boxes to check for prizes. Somebody had already taken them, of course. She folded down the plastic bags, closed the flaps, and stacked the boxes in the cupboard. She ran hot water into the sink, squeezing in enough of the green dish soap that it swelled up into a mound; Mom always said she used too much. One by one she slid the breakfast bowls and spoons and glasses in under the very edge of the soapy hill, disturbing its shape as little as possible. What was the point of having a dishwasher if you had to wash the stupid dishes first? When she grew up, she'd have a robot to do all the housework for her.

Adult voices came at her from both sides. Her mother was bringing Jerry Johnston in the front door, offering him a seat in the living room, asking if he wanted coffee. Her father had come in the back door, home in the middle of the day, and was talking to the little kids on his way through the family room.

The last time Jerry Johnston had been here, he'd taken away some of Ethan's stuff, and he'd never brought it back. Lucy had watched from the doorway, trying not to look at the naked ladies on the wall, while Mom and Dad and Jerry Johnston searched Ethan's room. The social worker had said maybe they'd find a clue to where he was, even though Dad had pointed out that Ethan had been on restriction for weeks before he'd run away and hadn't been home to leave any clues. Jerry had asked permission to take a few things away with him, and they'd let him. Lucy wouldn't have let him.

One dirty tube sock, stiff at the toe, white with green stripes. A blank book that had been in Ethan's stocking a couple of Christmases ago, before Mom and Dad gave up trying to get him to express himself some way other than stealing and doing drugs; still blank, but its spine was broken as if it had been opened and looked at a lot. A little metal thing kind of like a barrette with feathers that Rae had said was a roach clip and then later had to explain how you used it because Lucy couldn't figure out why Ethan would want to trap cockroaches. A *Playboy* centerfold of a red-haired lady with blue and purple scarves floating around her and her nipples filled in with red magic marker. A Garfield calendar from last year, with none of the pages torn off.

Jerry had put all that stuff into his briefcase, which had been empty when he came to their house. Lucy wondered if he had his briefcase now. The briefcase had a combination lock; Lucy had seen his fat fingers delicately turn the knobs around, then slide to the sides of the case to make sure it was locked.

Then Jerry Johnston and Mom and Dad had left Ethan's room. They'd walked single file right past Lucy and nobody had said anything to her, explained anything, even seemed to notice her. Offended, Lucy had decided they were trying to pretend that they hadn't been in Ethan's room without his permission, that they hadn't done anything wrong. But she'd seen them. She was a witness.

Now Jerry Johnston said yes, he'd have coffee, two sugars and a cream. A person that big probably never refused food or drink. Lucy heard Mom's footsteps and hurried to the cupboard to look for a clean cup, having to stand on tiptoe to see onto the second shelf and unable to see onto the top shelf at all. The only clean one was Molly's My Little Pony. That wouldn't be right for Jerry Johnston. Hastily, she fished a mug out of the dishwater and rinsed it out. There wasn't any dishtowel by the sink. The mug would be wet, but it would be clean. Unless she'd missed something. She peered into it again, ran her fingers around inside it to be sure. She still wasn't sure.

Mom and Dad came into the kitchen at the same time from different directions. Lucy stood at the sink hugging herself. "He's here," Mom said, and from the way she looked at Dad Lucy knew that she'd had the same crazy thought: Jerry Johnston was here to tell them that Ethan was alive.

Mom and Dad didn't say anything to her. Mom got a clean cup down from the back of the top shelf where Lucy couldn't have seen it. Her hands were shaking; she spilled coffee across the counter. Lucy wiped it up.

Dad asked, "Has he said anything?"

Mom shook her head.

"Does the kitchen look okay?" Lucy demanded. "I already got a clean cup out for him."

"It's fine," her mother said without even looking. "Thanks, honey."

"Can I come in and listen?"

"I guess so. Rae and Priscilla are already in there."

Lucy hadn't heard her sisters come downstairs. That bothered her, as if they were keeping secrets from her. She stalked down the hall to the living room, leaving Mom and Dad to close the kitchen door if they wanted it closed.

"Good morning," Jerry Johnston said to her. He didn't remember her name, she could tell. She wasn't about to make it any easier for him. She said hello only because her parents were there, and went to sit on the floor underneath the cuckoo clock, where she could play with the weights and chains.

Mom and Dad sat down. Neither of them said a word. That scared Lucy. She pulled up her knees. The clock struck nine and made her jump. She could feel the vibrations in the chains that rested against her back.

"I know you've heard the bad news about Ethan," Jerry began.

Mom was ready for him. "The police were here this morning. They told us Ethan is dead."

Jerry nodded. "I thought you'd want to hear how it happened." He stopped. Lucy kept her eyes on her mother's face, which looked like a mask. She couldn't look at Dad's. When nobody said anything, Jerry went on softly, like a bedtime story.

Ethan used to read her bedtime stories, when she was real little and he must have been about the age she was now. She'd forgotten all about that, and she didn't want to remember it now.

"He showed up at my place about five o'clock this morning. He said he'd split if I called you or anybody at New Beginnings before we'd had a chance to talk. That's against the rules, of course. But I knew he meant it, and I could see he was desperate for somebody he could trust, so I chose to take that personal risk."

He paused. He was smiling a little and his thin eyebrows were raised. After a minute he took a long drink of coffee. Over the rim of the cup his pale brown eyes floated like moths from one person to another to another around the room. Lucy cringed when they lighted on her and held her breath until they moved on, to rest for a long time on her sister Rae.

There was something special between Rae and Jerry Johnston. They saw each other every Wednesday in therapy. Lucy didn't like Jerry Johnston, and she didn't much like Rae either these days, but suddenly she wanted to be in therapy, too. Rae would never tell her what they talked about. Lucy hated secrets, unless they were her own.

Lucy had just finally realized that Jerry was waiting for somebody to tell him he'd done a good job when Dad said gruffly, "We appreciate all you've done."

Jerry nodded. He looked away from Rae, and his soft voice started up again. His voice was soothing; it seemed to say everything was all right. It was a lie. "He said he was hungry, and he looked as if he hadn't eaten in days. So I went to make sandwiches. I was only gone fifteen or twenty minutes, but when I came back he was dead."

Priscilla started to cry. Rae punched her and the crying got louder. Mom hadn't moved. Dad barked, "How?"

"I don't know," Jerry answered, and took another sip of coffee. "He was on his back on my living-room floor, and I thought he'd fallen asleep. He looked as if he hadn't slept in days, either. So I left him alone for a while. But then when I went to check on him, there was no pulse and he wasn't breathing."

"Drugs," Dad said, and slammed his fist onto the arm of the chair. Patches, who had been curled up there, meowed once and jumped down.

Jerry nodded. "Looks like it."

"Thank you," Mom said, in a child's voice, and Lucy was suddenly furious. She didn't like this big thick man, like a tree trunk where mean little creatures lived. He was the last one to see her brother alive. He was the first one to see him dead. And her mother was *thanking* him.

Not wanting to look at her parents, Lucy

looked instead at her sisters on the couch. Pris
was curled up like a baby, sobbing, her face
hidden against the pillow Lucy had embroi-
dered last year in school, her braids sticking
up. Rae's legs were crossed and her toes were
pointed in white high-heeled sandals, pink toenails glittering, the long pink nails of one
hand spread over one gleaming knee. Her eyes
were on Jerry Johnston.

"I'm sorry," he said.

9

They had to identify the body. They had to say out loud that it was Ethan, and some stranger had to write it down.

The place where they kept bodies was called a morgue. Lucy held the word in her mouth like a lump of old bread. When Mom and Dad wouldn't let any of the kids go with them to the morgue, Rae got really mad. "He was my brother! I have a right! You're always telling me what to do!"

Mom just kept saying, "No, no," as if she couldn't stop, and Dad tried to hug Rae, but she pushed him away. Lucy complained, too, that they wouldn't let her go, but secretly she was glad. She spent the night at Stacey's, and they stayed up till two o'clock in the morning eating popcorn and watching scary movies on

the VCR, and Lucy didn't have any nightmares.

"What did it look like?" she asked Mom
when she got home.

"Oh, honey, I don't know." They were folding laundry, and Mom bent her head over the
towels.

"I mean, could you see anything *wrong* with
him?"

Mom sort of stared off through the bay window where all the plants were. "He didn't have
any wounds, if that's what you mean, any cuts
or bruises. He was awfully thin and pale, as if
he'd been sick. The word I kept thinking was
ravaged." Her voice broke.

"What's that mean?"

"Used, sort of."

Lucy shook her head, bewildered. "What—"

"Patches!" Mom yelled, and the cat jumped
down from the window seat. A piece of spider
plant stuck to his fur. When he shook himself
and high-stepped away, the leaves like spread
fingers and the tiny white flower like an eye
dropped onto the floor behind him. Somebody
would step on it there, Lucy thought a little
frantically, or vacuum it up.

Stooping to rescue the broken plant, Mom
was crying. It was dumb to be upset over a
plant, Lucy thought, especially a spider plant;
there were always so many of them. On top of
the refrigerator were three or four cups of wa-

ter with spider-plant cuttings floating in them, waiting for roots, and there must be ten hanging or sitting in pots around the house. They always caught. Mom said it would be a shame just to let them die when they were so easy to save, even though she had all the spider plants she wanted and so did everybody else she knew, so she couldn't even give them away.

"It wasn't him, was it?" Rae was standing by the table, but she didn't fold anything. Lucy snapped a towel at her. Rae caught the end, yanked it out of her hand, and dropped it back onto the table.

Still crouched on the floor with the broken spider plant in both hands, still crying, Mom nodded. "Of course it was. It was Ethan."

"No, it wasn't."

"Stop it, Rae!"

Lucy fished a pair of tiny Mickey Mouse underwear out of the pile. Dominic's. They fit over her fist like Grandma's toaster cover. A red striped tube sock dangled off the edge of the table; there was no mate for it anywhere in the jumble of still-warm clothes.

Rae sighed, too, and Lucy looked up sharply, sure she was being mocked. But her sister's eyes were on their mother, who had stood up and was saying, "Rae, honey, I know how hard it is, but we all have to accept it. *Ethan is dead.* His funeral is today."

"You're glad! You hate him! You and Dad both!"

"You're wrong," Mom said dully, as if she'd run out of words. She poked at the plant in the palm of one hand with her other forefinger. "Have you talked about this in your therapy group? Maybe Jerry could help you—"

"You leave Jerry out of this!" Rae yelled, enraged.

Mom just stared at her. Lucy held her breath. A car went by on King Street with its radio blaring. Then Mom said, "I miss Ethan. I'll always miss Ethan."

"Gee, now he can't give you guys any more trouble, can he?"

Lucy added another folded washcloth to the teetering pile. *Hit her*, she thought grimly. *If you don't make her shut up, I will.* The washcloth had pretty blue designs on it; flowers, she thought, or birds. It was a new one, and it was folded, so you couldn't quite tell.

Mom said to Rae, "Oh, sweetheart, you don't understand. We loved him. We still love him. We'll always love him."

Mom and Rae were standing in the middle of the dining room, hugging each other. Lucy kept folding laundry. She found the missing sock balled up inside the corner of a fitted sheet. Rae was actually a little taller than their mother now, but Mom was stronger, steadier. Lucy supposed Mom used to hug Ethan too, although it was hard to remember a time when he'd let anybody in the family come that close.

"But he did all that—*stuff*!" Rae was saying into Mom's shoulder. "How can you love somebody like that? He did drugs. He dropped out of school. He wouldn't quit stealing. They finally locked him up in that place, that Nubie, and he still wouldn't straighten up."

"Yes. And there's a lot you don't know."

"Like what?"

"It doesn't matter. I shouldn't have said that."

"*Tell me!* He was my brother! I have a right to know!"

"No, you don't. What you have a right to know is that parents keep loving their kids no matter what the kids do. That's what parents are for."

"It is?" Rae's baby voice made Lucy sick, but she buried her face in Molly's cotton night-gown with the pink ribbons and held her breath and listened for Mom's answer.

"Yes. It is."

"Well, *I'm* never having kids."

"There were a lot of wonderful things about Ethan. There were a lot of good times. Joyous times. I wouldn't have missed having him." Mom's voice broke.

"Like what?"

"Remember the time you and Ethan were

butterflies for Halloween? You were barely two years old, so there were just the two of you."

"I don't remember that," Rae said suspiciously.

"We have pictures. You've seen the pictures."

"You and Dad think I'm turning out just like him."

"I don't think anybody 'turns out.' You're only fourteen. You'll keep growing and changing all your life."

"You're lying! You're just trying to get me mixed up! You think I'm just like him!"

"Well, Rae, in some ways you are. That's not such a terrible thing. He's not—he wasn't a monster. For instance, you look a lot like him."

"No! My hair is *blond*!"

Lucy said loudly, "Bleached."

"You both like to read. You both hate enchiladas. Or he used to, anyway, before he disappeared."

"I don't *want* to be like him! I hate him! You're his mother, so you have to still love him, but I don't and I *hate* him!"

"Rae, you're not *just like* anybody. You'll make your own choices and you'll do things your own way."

By now Rae was sobbing, her head down on the table, and Mom was standing behind her, rubbing her back. Mom seemed to have forgotten about the broken piece of spider plant, dropped it or broken it some more. Or maybe she'd put it in her pocket to keep it safe until she could stick it in water. "I love him," she heard her sister say. "He was the only big brother I ever had. I'll miss him."

"Me, too," Mom said, very softly. "Oh, me, too."

Me, too, Lucy thought deliberately, but she didn't know yet if it was really true. *I'll miss him, too,* she made herself think, but she wasn't even really sure that he was gone; he didn't *feel* gone.

The laundry basket was empty. Mom and Rae didn't seem to know she was there. She gathered up her pile of clothes and went up the stairs to her room. Ethan's funeral was today. She had to get ready.

She didn't know what to wear. She couldn't do anything with her hair. She stared into her closet for a while, into her mirror. Then she grabbed her diary and a pencil and shut herself into the bathroom with them. She turned the water in the tub on full force and straight hot; maybe she'd take a bath for Ethan's funeral and maybe she wouldn't, but she liked the noise and the steam.

She ought to write something about sadness. She ought to write something about death. Instead, she flipped through the diary's gold-edged pages, not looking for anything in particular except proof that there had been life and thoughts and words before this day.

There were lots of blank pages left, even though the year was more than half over. She didn't write in the diary very often. Most of the time, the things she thought about didn't stay still long enough to get written down, or didn't come to her in words.

She stopped to read a couple of entries about Jeremy Martinez, how cute he was, how one day he'd stolen her pencil and rolled it under the teacher's desk in math class, and they'd both had to stay after school. Dad had told her that boys Jeremy's age acted like that when they liked you.

Dad didn't know what he was talking about. She didn't know how you knew when a boy liked you, but that wasn't how. Rae would know. She'd ask Rae. She couldn't imagine how she'd ever thought Jeremy Martinez was cute. Jeremy Martinez was a dog. She had the fleeting, disturbing thought that she really hadn't written that, that somebody else was sneaking words into her diary.

Here was something about a spring day. Lucy remembered writing that one. "Now I know what the word *glorious* means." The word *glorious* stirred her, like listening to Tawanda Robinson play taps on her trumpet at the beginning and end of the sixth-grade assembly. She clearly remembered that particu-

lar day, that particular moment, the feel of the
pencil moving across the paper, filling in the
pale blue lines with shiny gray-black writing
that was now smudged a little. The day had
been filled with bird song and the smell of lilacs.

Lilacs were Lucy's favorite flower. Mom's,
too. Every year while there was still snow on
the ground, Mom worried that the lilacs
would bud too soon and get frozen, or there
wouldn't be enough rain at the right time and
they'd dry out, or there'd be a big wind right
after the buds had opened and they'd all blow
away. There wasn't anything she could do
about it, either. One year the ground had been
covered with petals like pale purple snow, and
Mom had stared out the window with tears in
her eyes, holding the baby Cory.

Here was an entry that at first didn't make
sense:

Ethan and Mom played hide-and-seek in the
basement today. They wouldn't let me play.

She had printed it, so the letters were neat.
Her cursive was still jiggly, like a little kid's;
she experimented all the time with different
sizes and slants and ways to make certain letters, and she didn't like any of them. She always got a *C* in penmanship. Once she got a *D*.

Mom called the police.

Quickly Lucy turned the page; gold flickered. Steam from the bathwater made the paper damp. Somebody was calling her. She turned the page back, smoothed it with the flat of her hand.

Sometimes Mom and Ethan are like the same person. Sometimes they're like total strangers.

Lucy tried hard to believe that she'd never written any of this, that somebody was sneaking into her room, into her dresser, into her diary and writing stuff that didn't have anything to do with her. Trying to get her in trouble. Trying to drive her crazy. She insisted to herself that she didn't remember this, but she did remember, and the memory curled around her like smoke, hurting her eyes.

It was a long time ago. Last Christmas vacation, after Christmas, just before they went back to school.

The furnace was huffing and puffing in its dusty, cobwebby corner of the basement. Lucy liked to think of the furnace as their pet monster, keeping them warm.

Snow was piled crookedly outside the little, high, dirty windows, like blankets somebody hadn't folded right to fit on the shelf. Lucy knew there were spiders everywhere, under everything, hanging from every beam, just waiting to spin sticky webs in her face, just waiting for their millions of eggs to hatch. The fact that she didn't actually see any only made her more sure that they were there.

She was in Ethan's room. She wasn't allowed in Ethan's room, none of them were, even though Ethan was long gone. Rae wanted this room, and Lucy wanted a room of her own, but Mom wouldn't let them do it. Once Priscilla had come downstairs wearing Ethan's green shirt, sleeves rolled like sausages above her elbows, tail long between her legs in front and in back. Mom had had a fit, even though Pris had insisted she'd found the shirt in her laundry.

Lucy was looking for the John Cougar Mellencamp tapes she was sure Ethan had stolen from her. Mom was in the upstairs bathroom giving Cory a bath; that would take a while. Dad was at the grocery store with a long list. Still, Lucy was being as quiet as she could, and listening hard to all the footsteps that crisscrossed the ceiling above her head. It was weird to think of a ceiling as being a floor, too, having another side, a top and a bottom.

She didn't leave his room as soon as she'd found the tapes under his bed because she was also hoping to find a clue. Maybe the grownups had missed something. Maybe Ethan had left a message in secret code that only she could decipher. Maybe in all the time his room had been empty it hadn't really been empty, Ethan's spirit or something had been hiding in there all the time, or something had grown or worked its way to the surface. If she could find it, she'd be a hero. Then Mom would quit crying, and Dad wouldn't be mad at her anymore.

Lucy left the closet door half-open and felt around. Shirtsleeves wriggled. A tennis shoe sat footless on a shelf. The closet smelled like the rest of the room, only more so; smelled like her brother Ethan. Until then she wouldn't have thought that certain smells went with certain people. Wondering suddenly if she herself had a special odor, she surreptitiously lifted her forearm to her nose. The ceiling light made huge shadows when she moved, even inside the closet.

She was on her hands and knees, gingerly poking through the clothes and papers and junk on Ethan's closet floor, trying not to think about spiders, when she heard a commotion, and then the door to Ethan's room banged open from the inside. Lucy froze. Something had been in the room with her all this time. Something was breaking out.

With her hands sunk to the wrists in her brother's things, she crouched and listened. If she turned her head, she could just see out through the opening in the closet door and then through the bedroom door, which she'd carefully shut behind her but which was now wide open, into the dusty, warm, inhabited basement that seemed to stretch on forever underneath the whole house.

Mom was standing out there in the basement, facing Lucy. The white streak in her hair made a dull glow, like the snow piling up outside all the windows.

Mom said, "Ethan!" and held out her arms.

From between Lucy and her mother, something jumped. There was a sudden, sickening, too-sweet stink, like a sick baby, or like when chicken gets left too long in the back of the refrigerator. It was Ethan. Lucy knew it was Ethan because Mom had called his name.

Mom cried out and dodged, covering her head. The creature that was Ethan hit the doorframe, which rattled, but only a little, as though he didn't weigh very much. He crumpled onto the floor like a balloon with the air let out of it, then got up and turned and started after Mom again.

Mom moaned, "Oh, Ethan, I'm so sorry," and then ran. Lucy struggled to her feet. Ethan's leavings on the closet floor tangled around her ankles, but she pulled free and stumbled to the door of the room, in time to see Mom halfway up the basement steps and

Ethan—thin, stiff as cardboard, unmistakably Ethan—right behind her.

He hadn't come back for her. She'd waited a long time, clutching a split plastic baseball bat because it was the only weapon she could find. As far as she knew, he hadn't caught Mom, either. She didn't know what had happened to him that day. Outside the basement windows, which were small as picture frames and not that high above her head, she'd seen feet in boots, big round knees in blue pants as somebody squatted in the snow, a hand with flashing rings wiping the glass, part of a face peering in.

When finally she'd gone upstairs, trailing the orange bat behind her, the cops were there. The family had been gathered around Mom like football players in a huddle.

The police hadn't found anything. No signs of forced entry, they'd said. No footprints in the snow, though it was snowing hard enough, Lucy thought, that footprints could have been covered up while they were standing there talking. Lucy had thought they looked at her mother funny. Lucy had hated them. She'd wanted them *out of her house*. She'd been afraid to tell anybody that she'd seen him, too, and that she'd also seen somebody else—a bigger man than Ethan, a man with blue pants and black boots and rings on his fingers.

But she'd written about it in her diary. Now,

sitting in the steamy bathroom on the day of her brother's funeral, she smoothed her fingertips over the page again, liking the way they looked against the pink paper.

Ethan and Mom played hide-and-seek in the basement today. They wouldn't let me play. Mom called the police. Sometimes it's like Mom and Ethan are like the same person.

If anybody ever broke into her diary and read that, they wouldn't know what it meant. They wouldn't have any idea what had really happened. But she knew. She turned the page.

Somebody else had written in her diary. Lucy stared. Thick black letters, sort of halfway between cursive and printing, catty-corner across the top of the page.

Mom's handwriting, like when she left a note on the refrigerator that she was at the store and would be home soon, and you were supposed to do the dishes before she got back. Lucy looked at Mom's writing compared to her own, and was suddenly, giddily, hopeful: someday when she grew up, she'd know what she was doing too.

Dear Lucy [the message from her diary said]. Don't be afraid. Ethan won't hurt you. Love, Mom.

Lucy read the words over and over, ran her fingertips across them to see if she could feel the words on the page. She lifted the diary to her nose, even touched her tongue to the paper. When had Mom written that? Now that Ethan was dead, would she still say those words to Lucy?

She heard the phone ringing. The water in the tub was almost overflowing, and not hot enough now for a bath. Lucy turned off the faucet, pulled the plug, and, carrying her diary under her arm, ran for the hall phone. She got to it just before Dominic. He made a face at her, mad, half playing. She poked him in the ribs. When he screeched, she couldn't hear what the person on the phone was saying, and she stuck her finger in her other ear to shut out Dom and the rest of the house noise.

Dom went running out onto the porch with his squirt gun. He wasn't ready for Ethan's funeral. Lucy told herself it was okay, the funeral wasn't for hours yet. They had to make it through the rest of the morning and lunch and the first part of the afternoon. Hot morning sunshine streamed in the front window, and you could see streaks in the glass and dust in the air that weren't there any other time.

Mites. She'd stared at the picture in her mother's book: huge mouths and pincers, lots of legs, no eyes. No eyes; that especially gave her the creeps. There were billions of mites in the world—in the air, on your food, in your sheets, up your nose. They lived off dead stuff: the hair in your brush, dead skin scales. Most people never knew they were there, but now Lucy did, and now she felt them and tasted them and saw them everywhere, and they made her sneeze. She felt her own skin dying.

"Hello?" she said again, impatiently, into the phone, and then suddenly, and for no good reason, the thought came whole into her mind: Ethan was dead.

His being dead kept sneaking up on her, the same way he himself had all that time he'd been missing, the same way he still did, though now she had the feeling he wasn't looking for her. Showing up in windows and mirrors and dreams. Following her too close down stairs, so that she almost fell. Making the floorboards creak and the curtains move when he played hide-and-seek in her house at night; it wasn't *his* house anymore, he'd lost it, he'd run away, he didn't live here anymore because he'd been so bad, he was dead. Singing. Saying to come with him and do what he was doing. Singing to Rae, really, but Lucy could hear the tune and most of the words.

He really was dead. Mom and Dad had seen the body. They'd identified it. They'd said, "Yes, that's our son, Ethan Michael Brill." Rae had asked Mom exactly what they'd had to say, and that's what she'd told her. The funeral was at three o'clock this afternoon. He really was dead.

The man's voice on the phone was asking again for Tony. It was almost eleven o'clock in the morning and Dad was still asleep. Lucy didn't say that right away, though, as if it were a shameful family secret not to be shared with a stranger. As politely as she could, she demanded, "Who's calling, please?"

"This is Jerry Johnston."

She still wasn't recognizing him right away; he could sneak up on her. He hadn't even said hello to her.

He had no right to be calling here anyway, invading her house, telling bad news, making her say stuff she didn't want to say. She imagined the phone lines like hypodermic needles in and out of her house, sucking stuff out, injecting other stuff in.

"Dad's still asleep," she said, finally.

"Oh."

"He's—he doesn't feel good."

"I'd like to speak to your mother then, if I may."

"Mom's taking a shower." Water in the pipes made the old house cough. It also made her think, unwillingly, about things that were hollowed out and then filled with other things: walls and pipes and molecules of water, dancing and sticking together.

"Well, then."

Jerry Johnston's voice on the phone was just a voice, without particular power. That was because he wasn't here in the room, with his bulk, his beige eyes, his baby-powder smell. At first, a long time ago, she'd liked his voice, but the longer she'd had to be in the same room with him, the more uncomfortable his voice had made her, even a little afraid.

"Well, then, is Rae there?" he asked.

"Rae?"

"Let me speak to Rae, please."

She didn't have to let him. She could have refused. She could have said that Rae was at a friend's house or taking the trash out or at the park with Molly. She could have said that Rae had run away, or Rae was dead. He'd never know. She had the power.

But Rae was sitting right there on the couch, and she'd looked up at the sound of her name. "Just a minute," Lucy said sullenly, and shoved the receiver into her sister's hand.

"Well, Jesus, you don't have to *throw* it at me!" Rae gave her the finger and then said into the phone, in the same mean voice, "What?" There was a brief pause, and then Rae said in a different tone altogether, "Oh, hi," and her face changed. Her whole body softened, delicately twisted, spread. She stretched out along the nubby blue couch and raised one knee. Her toes flexed like a cat's; the toenails were red. She was wearing baggy orange short-shorts, and Lucy could see way up to the lace on her yellow underwear. Her head was tilted, so that her bright blond hair draped across her cheek and across the hand that propped up her head, red-nailed against tanned skin and bent back at the wrist.

Cradling the receiver there, Rae smiled a little and nodded as she listened. She didn't say much, but what she did say had a tone to it that Lucy, no matter how much she practiced, couldn't quite get. Rae was *flirting.* Lucy felt a grudging admiration for her older sister, a strong desire to be like her.

"Oh," Rae said quietly. "Okay." Lucy wondered uneasily what she was agreeing to.

Jerry Johnston must have a penis and everything. The thought made Lucy blush, made her feel funny in the lower part of her stomach. Of course she'd seen her little brothers' penises lots of times, but they were like noodles, small and soft, and she really found it hard to believe that a penis ever got big and hard like the ones in Rae's magazine. If Jerry's went with the rest of him, it must be awesome. Lucy almost giggled.

Her brother Ethan must have had a penis, too. She'd never seen it. Ethan was dead. Pretty soon his body, all of his body, would start to decay. The funny feeling in Lucy's groin turned to nausea, and she pressed her palms there.

She forced her thoughts back to Jerry John-ston. He was kind of cute. He had pretty eyes and a nice smile. He was probably available, too; he didn't wear a wedding ring, though there was a giant square turquoise and silver ring on one of his pinkies, and she didn't think there were any pictures on his desk. Dad had a family portrait on his desk at work. Ethan was still in it.

"Sure," Rae said warmly. "I will."

It was disgusting to flirt with Jerry Johnston over the phone when Ethan was dead. Lucy turned resolutely away from her sister, but kept listening.

Finally, Rae said lingeringly, "Bye." Then she sat with the receiver still to her ear, wait-ing, Lucy supposed, for Jerry Johnston to hang up. Lucy stayed where she was, leaning against the wall; she expected Rae to yell at her for eavesdropping, and she got ready to yell back. Instead, the older girl lowered the receiver, sighed, and said almost dreamily, "That was Jerry."

"I know, dummy. I answered the phone."

"He called to tell us about Ethan."

"He already told us Ethan's dead. What else is there?"

"He called to tell us what he died of."

"Well, why'd he ask for you? He could have told me that."

"I guess because now I'm the oldest in the family next to Mom and Dad."

"You're only two years older than me."

Rae shrugged and tossed her hair. Dusty mite-filled sunshine puffed around her head. The voice of the recorded operator was leaking out of the receiver, trying to warn them that the phone was off the hook. Both of them heard. Neither of them did anything about it.

"Jerry says it was an OD."

"What's an OD?"

"Overdose."

"Oh. Well, big deal. We already figured that."

"Jerry says there were all kinds of drugs in his system. Downers, speed, crack, pot, acid." The names of the drugs sounded like dirty poetry coming out of her sister's mouth. "Some traces of stuff they couldn't even identify. Jerry says any one of them could have killed him. Jerry says drugs are really dangerous. *I'll* never take drugs, that's for sure."

"Just say no." Lucy sneered. "You better go tell Mom and Dad."

"Oh," Rae said dreamily, the same way she'd said it on the phone to Jerry Johnston. "Okay."

"Right now."

"Sure," Rae said. "I will."

Her legs gleamed as she swung them down. Her hair moved like sunny water; she brushed it back from her face with a practiced pretty gesture. Lucy tried it, but her own hair was tangled; her fingers got stuck in it. A red ant was crawling up Rae's leg. Apparently she didn't feel it, but Lucy saw it reach the little hollow at the back of her sister's knee before Rae's long slow strides carried it out of her sight. Now she'd never know what happened to it.

Lucy stood against the living-room wall. She heard her little brothers and sisters in various parts of the house and yard, like crickets. Patches was purring somewhere; he must be nearby, because the purring was loud, but she didn't see him.

She heard voices upstairs, where Rae was telling their parents the latest bad news about Ethan that Jerry Johnston had brought. Right now, it seemed important to know which voice was which. There was Rae's, singsong. There was Mom's, sharp, furious. There was Dad's, sleepy, asking a question, asking another question, crying.

Hearing Dad cry made Lucy slide down the wall until she was sitting on the floor with her knees drawn up and her face in her arms, as small a target as she could be. After a few minutes she realized it was hard to breathe, so she turned her head to one side, where she saw the blue triangle of the couch between her arm and her leg, the cat's black and white feet padding up to her, and Ethan.

Ethan was dead. Lucy raised her head.

Ethan was *dead*. His funeral was at three o'clock this afternoon. But there he was, just outside, between the living-room window and the lilac bush, hands cupped around his eyes, peering in.

Lucy tried to meet his gaze, but couldn't quite see his eyes in the hollows of his face and the shadows made by his hands. He didn't seem to see her. He seemed to be looking for something; he turned his head to scan the room. After a few minutes, he just stepped back away from the window, ducked under the branches, and was gone.

Upstairs, Dad was still crying.

10

A month passed, another week, another day. Things started to get back to normal. Sometimes Lucy had to remind herself that her brother Ethan was dead, she'd gone to his funeral, she'd seen and touched his body, and that he'd ever even been alive at all. And sometimes "Ethan is dead" was the only thing real.

She and Priscilla and Dominic took swimming lessons at the Y again. Lucy finally went off the high board headfirst. Water slapped her stomach and thighs and got up her nose, but it wasn't as scary as she'd thought it would be and she'd probably do it again before summer was over.

Rae went to therapy every Wednesday evening at Jerry Johnston's house. A few times

Lucy rode with Mom or Dad to pick her up, and watched the other kids come out. They looked like any other teenagers. That was disappointing. You couldn't tell by looking at them that they *had problems*, that they had to see a *therapist*. A couple of the guys were cute. Rae was always the last one out, and she was always very quiet on the way home.

Dad went to work every day, just as he'd always done, but now he didn't talk about his work at dinner anymore. The whole family used to laugh at his stories about how the computers ate up programs, or when they turned what he put into them into secrets and wouldn't let him have them back. Lucy didn't think her family would ever laugh again.

Mom went to her class every Tuesday night. She brought home a test paper with a big red *A* on it and showed it to everybody in the family. Dad said he was real proud of her, the same thing he said to the kids when any of them got good grades. Lucy didn't know exactly how to think about her mother as a student.

Rae went to a party at her friend Gina's, just four blocks away. Mom talked to Gina's parents about who was going to be there and what they were going to do, and she made Rae write down Gina's name and address and phone number. Rae threw such a fit about that that she almost didn't get to go to the party after all. And then she was over an hour late getting home and got herself grounded again. From the way she smirked, you'd have thought that was what she wanted. She was almost fourteen. Mom and Dad were starting to bug her about what she wanted for her birthday. She said she didn't want anything, but Lucy knew she liked the shiny black parachute pants they'd seen at the mall, if Lucy could just remember what store.

At the funeral, Lucy had actually touched Ethan's wrist. She hoped nobody had seen her do it. It was kind of weird, touching a dead body, even if it was your brother. The flesh had stayed white where she'd poked it down. His blood hadn't gone back to that spot. Hers did when she poked her own arm. He'd been really cold. She'd wished hard for his hand to move, but it didn't.

Pris fell off the parallel bars in gymnastics class. That same night, she rolled out of the top bunk; everybody in the house woke up from the thump and the yelling. Both times Dad took her to the emergency room and Mom stayed home with the other kids, turning the porch light off and on and waiting for the phone to ring. "It's weird there are only five kids at home now," Lucy had said, and then wished she hadn't because Mom got tears in her eyes and turned away. Priscilla had broken a little bone in each foot; she'd have casts and crutches until school. Already she was complaining that the casts made her feet itch. Lucy thought it would be neat to break something. She wrapped one foot in a towel and hobbled noisily around the house until Dad yelled at her to stop it.

Dad had cried through Ethan's whole funeral. Lucy had heard him cry before but she'd never seen him, and she was scared that he'd never stop. He didn't even try to hide it. In fact, she saw him turn his face up toward the sky, and sunshine glistened on his cheeks.

Mom was like a mannequin. Once, when Lucy was just little, there'd been a pretty pink blouse on a mannequin at Penney's and she'd reached up to rub the material between her fingers and then against her cheek, and then the mannequin had moved and smiled and said something to her. It was a real lady. It still embarrassed Lucy to think about that. At the funeral she'd been afraid to touch her mother, for fear the same thing would happen only in reverse: her mother would turn out to really be a mannequin, with no life in her.

Mom got a *B* in her class. Dominic's baseball team came in next to last in the league, but Dom learned to run the bases without tripping over his own feet. Molly's guppies had babies and the tank was full of little brown dots zipping around, leaving the tiniest ripples. Dad shaved off his beard and looked exactly like Benjamin Franklin; he had a dimple in his cheek that Lucy had never seen.

So, daily life swirled and puttered on, the same as always except that now Lucy kept thinking about what was not, what she had lost, what was going to die.

A bird with a song like a wind chime woke her up one morning; she'd never heard this bird before, and she lay there for a long time filled with it, feeling its notes slide inside her body over and over like sweet immortal flowers down a waterfall, trying to picture the bird that made it, thinking it might be a message from Ethan, or just about the world and her place in it. But then the song stopped, and all she could hear was the screeching of a jay, the neighbor revving his old car, dogs barking, a siren, and those things only made her nervous, didn't fill her with any sense of harmony at all. Rather than wait to hear that bird song again, Lucy decided it was gone forever, and that made her cry.

She went out to the front porch one afternoon and Mom was standing there holding Cory, and you could see their bodies through their clothes and their bones and blood and nerves inside their bodies. Ethan's bones and blood and clothes were in the ground now. She didn't know where he was. She didn't know where Mom and Cory were, or where they'd be a minute from now. She didn't know where she was; she was here, but not really.

They didn't have their own fireworks on the Fourth of July this year. Dad said they were too dangerous, and besides they were illegal. They'd always had their own fireworks, and it wasn't any more dangerous or any more against the law this year than any other year. It was because Ethan was dead. It wasn't fair. Lucy closed her curtains and turned her radio up loud and refused to pay any attention to the fireworks from the stadium, even though the view from her bedroom window was the best in the house. With a guilty feeling of relief, Lucy recognized this as something she could dare to be mad at her parents about for the rest of her life.

The world didn't come to an end, other people wouldn't die, just because Ethan Michael Brill was dead. It wouldn't come to an end if she died, either, Lucy Ann Brill. Sometimes she'd be thinking about starting sixth grade or something, and then she'd be ashamed of herself for worrying, for being excited, for thinking about anything but Ethan.

She watched Mom, paid close attention to what Mom said and what she didn't say. She listened for her to check on all the kids every night, waited for her own turn, and every night reminded herself that Mom would never again be able to check on Ethan, would never

again know where he was. She watched
how Mom made pancakes, rocked Cory,
kissed Dad, combed her hair so the white
streak showed. It didn't help. As far as she
could tell, Mom was just going through the
days, one after another. But then, Ethan came
to her again.

It was a sweltering Saturday morning in
early July. Sun in her window had awakened
Lucy early. She was restless. She didn't want
to watch cartoons; just the sound of them was
driving her crazy. She didn't feel like starting
her weekend chores. It was too hot to play outside. She thought about going back to bed, but
she wasn't tired. She was getting crankier and
crankier; when Dom asked her for the third
time where the Cheerios were, she threw the
box at him. He wailed, "I'll tell!" but then he
got so busy eating that she knew he wouldn't.

Rae had left a note that she was at the park
until noon. Lucy didn't believe it. Dad was out
mowing the lawn. Every once in a while she'd
hear the mower screech, and there'd be a loud
cracking sound, and she'd know he'd run over
some toy. He'd be furious and sweaty when he
came in.

Lucy hadn't seen Mom at all this morning.
She was probably still asleep. It used to be
Mom was up before any of them, even on
weekends; since Ethan had died, she slept in
as late as she could. Maybe she was sick.

Maybe she needed something and was too weak to call anybody, a glass of juice or aspirin or something.

Lucy went quietly up the stairs. Patches was coming down; she stopped to pet him and he rubbed against her hand. Sunlight was streaming in the stairway windows, and the carpet was warm in places under her bare feet.

Mom and Dad's bedroom door was open a little. That was so Patches could get in and out; otherwise, he'd yowl and scratch at the carpet and wake everybody up. The only time Mom and Dad closed their door tight was when they were doing something that had to do with being naked, like getting dressed or making love. Lucy still could hardly believe her parents did that. She wished they'd let her watch them so she could see how it was done.

She knocked on the doorframe, lightly so that if Mom was asleep it wouldn't wake her up. At first she thought the TV or the radio was on, but then she realized Mom was talking to somebody, a low stream of words like a lullaby, like the way you'd talk to a hurt dog that might attack you. Lucy pushed the door open just a little farther, wincing when it creaked, prepared to say, "Can I get you anything?" or "Are you sick?"

Ethan was in bed with Mom.

Horrified, Lucy took several steps backward, which brought her right to the top of the stairs. She didn't have to turn to look; she could feel the stairwell behind her, straight through the heart of the house. Dizzy, afraid she'd fall and nobody would come to pick her up because Dad was outside and Mom wouldn't notice, she clutched at the newel post with both hands. But the door to Mom and Dad's room had creaked far enough open by itself now that she could see right in, and she couldn't take her eyes off the scene in the bed.

Ethan was in bed with Mom. The weight of his body pushed down the rumpled sheets. She could see little shadows from him. She could hear him breathing, see the wet red hole that was his mouth, like a baby crying, only he wasn't making any noise. She could smell him, a cold smell, sweet and sour at the same time, like Cory when she used to give him his bottle.

Ethan was dead. She'd seen his body. His hand hadn't moved, and his skin had felt like cold blue rubber. She'd watched as they'd lowered his body into the grave. *Ethan was dead.* It had taken her a long time to believe that, to understand it, but at this moment she couldn't imagine why she'd ever thought it was a lie. She knew, in the same way that she knew she was alive and it was a hot summer morning and the stairs were waiting right behind her, that Ethan was dead.

But here he was, in bed with their mother,

and he was too old to do that, too big, he wasn't a baby anymore even though he seemed like one. He would hurt Mom. Mom would hurt him. There was something awful about this; Lucy wasn't clear, couldn't have put words to it, but her skin crawled.

There was also something so beautiful about it that the beauty seemed to get inside her, like mites, and it made her skin itch from underneath. Lucy ached to be where her brother was now, as close to their mother as he was, as he was becoming while she watched. She shouldn't be watching, but she clung to the post and didn't move.

Mom cried out, hurt, and then cooed as if to a hurt baby. Ethan was making sounds that came before words, gurgling, hiccuping, mewling. Mom wrapped her bare arms and legs around him. Ethan was naked, too, and Lucy couldn't tell one body from the other or how they fit together, except that she could see Ethan's mouth on Mom's breast, sucking, biting.

Ethan was getting smaller and smaller. Lucy didn't understand how that could be, but he was, and she tried not to blink at all because he might disappear while her eyes were closed and then she'd never know what had happened to him.

Ethan was tiny now, and curled, and colorless. He could be in anything, anywhere, and she wouldn't know it. Mom said his name one more time. "Ethan."

Then he was gone. Mom groaned and arched her back and spread her knees, fists flung back on the pillow, hair dark and tangled. Lucy thought clearly: *She looks like she's having a baby, only backward, because nothing's coming out. Ethan's going back in.*

Then, abruptly, Lucy couldn't watch anymore. She turned and ran unsteadily down the stairs. Nobody was around to yell at her for running; nobody was chasing her. She was careful not to trip, not to catch her heel, not to miss the bottom step. Her chore this weekend was to clean the living room. It took her a while to get the vacuum cleaner cord untangled from all the boots and backpacks on the closet floor. Then she was grateful for its loud noise and for the way it sucked up everything in its path.

11

"Lucy! Lunch!"

Dominic made each of the words two syllables, like a marching song. Lucy couldn't see him, but she could tell he was in the driveway, not really looking very hard for her, probably sitting on the ground playing with a bug or a rock with mica in it. He had a friend named Micah, and he never would believe that that shiny stuff like tin foil was called mica, even though she'd told him a hundred times.

Mom was inside the house. Ethan was inside Mom inside the house.

Lucy pulled up her knees and hid her face, trying to look like part of the tree. "Lucy! Dad says to come right now!"

She couldn't go in. She couldn't ever go in

that house again. She'd stay up in her tree for the rest of her life. Or she'd run away. She thought about running away to Jerry Johnston.

When she moved, the whole tree swayed. She hoped Dom wouldn't notice, or would think it was just the wind, even though probably none of the other trees in the yard was moving. Unless somebody was hiding in them, too. She shivered.

She didn't know if he could see her from the ground. This was her tree; nobody else in the family ever climbed it. So she'd never been the one on the ground looking up trying to see somebody.

Suddenly she was wondering if Ethan had ever been up here. She didn't remember if he had, but she knew he'd done lots of things that she didn't remember. It was weird to realize that she'd been alive and doing things and thinking things when she'd been one and two and three, and she didn't remember any of it, or just flashes: a red basin; snow on her face. It was weirder to realize that the little kids, Cory and Molly and maybe even Dom, wouldn't remember most of what was happening to them right now.

That meant that all kinds of stuff could have happened to her when she was real little, and it would be part of her now because everything that ever happened to you was part of you, and she wouldn't even know it. Ethan could have been up here in her tree lots of times before it was her tree, and she would never know.

"Lucy! Come *on*! I'm telling!"

Maybe Mom would do to her what she'd done to Ethan. Swallow her up. Keep her safe by swallowing her up. Lucy didn't know what to think about all this, how to think about it. She needed to talk to Mom, but Mom was asleep, Dad said Mom was sick and they all had to stay away from her.

She had already climbed as high as she dared. She was a lot higher than her usual reading place, which was a big forked branch that just fit her bottom, and curled up so she could lean her back comfortably against it, with knotholes and scars from sawed-off limbs that she could prop her heels into. Sometimes, when she'd been reading for a long time or writing in her diary or just looking at the leaves and the sky, a bird would come really close, or a squirrel, or a bug with a million legs would crawl up the tree trunk and even though she hated bugs, Lucy would think what a long trip that must be for him, like walking to the moon.

But the branch she was sitting on now was high and thin. It bent till she thought she could hear it crack, till she was almost resting on the stronger branches underneath, almost falling through the empty spaces between them. Maybe she would fall. Then Mom would come running and pick her up.

It used to be that when Mom kissed owies they really did feel better. Not anymore. Just ask Priscilla, with both her feet in casts. Just ask Cory, with the burn on his knee from the inside of the oven door. Just ask Ethan. Ethan was dead.

Lucy squinted up into the pale blue sky spotted with green leaves. She would climb higher if she could. She tested an even thinner branch right above her head, and it snapped off in her hand. She would climb all the way to the sky if she could. Disappear into it. Transform into blue air.

She didn't exactly understand what made the sky blue. Something about light bending and breaking. If light could break, anything could break. She clenched her fist, but no light was trapped inside and none oozed out between her fingers. She twisted her wrist sharply, but as far as she could tell, no light broke.

The branch between her legs was hurting a little. Lucy shifted her weight, and then a good feeling, kind of a bubbly feeling, gathered there, kind of squirmy and exciting, mixed up with the discomfort. She felt herself blushing, and she could hardly bring herself to think about what she was doing, but she moved the same way again, as if the branch were a rocking horse with a narrow back, and both the pleasure and the pain came again, strong. Reminding herself that nobody but the squirrels and the birds could see her up here, and the squirrels and the birds didn't care, Lucy did it again.

Then, abruptly, she'd had enough. She lowered herself precariously down to her reading place. Once she was settled into the fork she felt safe again, but exposed to anybody who might be watching from the ground. She looked down, felt dizzy, looked around. Dom had quit calling her, and she didn't see him. She wondered a little wistfully what they were having for lunch. She was hungry. She wondered if Mom was up. As she climbed quickly down from her tree, her foot slipped and for a second her heart raced painfully, but really she hadn't come close to falling. She went inside.

They were just sitting down to lunch. Grilled cheese sandwiches. Mom was at the table, still in her bathrobe, but holding Dominic on her lap and looking over his head at Lucy.

"Where were you?" Dad demanded as he ladled tomato soup into eight white bowls.

"Up in my tree."

"Didn't you hear Dom calling you? You almost missed lunch." Lucy just shrugged.

Dad always made great grilled cheese sandwiches. He wouldn't tell anybody what his secret was. Lucy didn't think he really had one. The tomato soup was a little lumpy, but Rae was the only one who cared. She sat all hunched over, staring into her bowl and squashing the lumps with the back of her spoon, but even she didn't say anything snotty.

Molly sang them a song she'd made up about bears, a *long* song. If she hadn't told you it was about bears, or that she was singing, you'd never have known. Dominic told a joke. He said the punch line first and gave it away, but he laughed and laughed until finally everybody else started laughing at him, so then he decided it must have been a really funny joke and told it again.

They talked about normal, everyday things. The snake Cory'd found in the gutter, so brown and flat that it looked like a piece torn off a grocery sack; he wanted to keep it as a pet and would not believe it was dead, so finally Dad just said no. Priscilla had a doctor's appointment this afternoon; she asked whether she'd be getting her casts off, and Dad said he doubted it, it had only been three weeks, and Priscilla said huh-*uh*, it was almost four, and there was a dumb little argument.

Rae said she was going to a movie tonight with friends. Dad said what movie. She said just a movie, we haven't decided yet. Dad said what friends. She said you know, just some of my friends, what's the big deal? Dad said she couldn't go unless he knew what movie and what friends and who was driving and what time they'd be home. Mom nodded. Rae slammed her spoon down so hard that tomato soup splattered out of the bowls. It didn't really look like blood; it was too thin and too orange. But Lucy didn't eat any more of it.

Lucy noticed that Mom didn't eat very much. She took one bite and put the sandwich back down on her plate. Her bite mark looked like somebody's secret smile.

Molly put her hands over Mom's eyes from behind. "That was a awful dream we had last night, huh, Mom?" She yawned noisily.

Mom tried to look around at her, but Molly wouldn't let go of her head. "I don't know what you mean, sweetheart."

"You do so. The bad dream where the monster chased me and I got scared and then you came and chopped off its head."

Mom chuckled. "Molly, honey, *I* didn't have that dream. That was *your* dream."

"But you were there. I *saw* you."

For a second Lucy thought maybe Molly had seen Ethan. That made her feel weird. Then she thought Mom must be lying to Molly, and to her, too. That thought didn't last long, but it made her feel guilty and nervous.

"Sometimes when you're little," Mom said to Molly, and Lucy knew Mom was talking to her, too, and she listened even though she pretended not to, "it seems as if your mom and dad are everywhere. Even in your thoughts and dreams. But we're not. Your dreams belong to you."

Molly lowered her hands until they were around Mom's neck. Mom put up her hands and loosened Molly's, then brought the little girl around to settle her on her lap, saying, as she almost always said about any of them, "Oh, you're getting so *big*!" Molly was frowning. Mom kissed her and smoothed her hair.

Right after lunch Mom went back to bed. Lucy and Dominic had to clear the table. Lucy took a long time on purpose, to give Mom time to write messages in her diary, if there was something she wanted to say to Lucy and to nobody else. Cheese from the sandwiches had hardened across the bottom of the skillet, and she had to scrub and scrub to get it off.

She wanted to take a bath. There weren't any clean towels. Lately there were never any clean towels. She went out to the back porch and found the dryer full. She fished through the tangled, faded pastels and found her favorite pink one, then defiantly shut the door and left the other towels for somebody else to put away. For Mom to put away. That was Mom's job.

She was hurrying toward the bathroom with her towel in her arms when she saw Dad on the living-room floor. She saw him out of the corner of her eye, and Rae leaning over him, and it took Lucy a minute to realize what she'd seen, and then she stopped and went back. If Rae was hurting Dad, she'd have to do something. She didn't know what to do.

Then she saw that Rae was giving Dad a back rub. His arms were folded under his head and Rae was straddling his hips. His back was bare. Lucy's face grew warm, and she lifted her towel to cover it, peering through the nubby folds. Dad loved back rubs, and he always said Rae was good at giving them, because her hands were small and strong. Sunlight through the window lit the room as if Dad and Rae were in a pretty box. Patches had folded himself onto the wide blue arm of the couch above them and was purring loudly. Lucy could hear her father and her sister breathing rhythmically together.

Rae looked up and saw her. Caught spying, Lucy took a guilty step back. But Rae just smiled. Her hands didn't stop in the circular motions along their father's shoulders, but she held her little sister's gaze for a long time, and she smiled. Lucy could hardly stand it, there was suddenly so much love. She stood there as long as she could, then ran up the stairs and slammed and locked the bathroom door.

12

Something woke her.

She sat up and opened her eyes very wide to see in the dimness of the sunrise and the fading streetlight. Rae was asleep in the other bed; Lucy could see the mounds of her shoulder and hip, the shiny blond tangle of her hair that looked silvery green.

She listened. There weren't any sounds that weren't always there when she woke up in the night: just the dripping of the bathroom faucet, Patches purring on the heap of Rae's clothes in the corner by the closet. In the tree outside her window, birds were starting to sing because the sun was coming up, and next door Dudley's daughter yelled good-bye to her father because he was hard of hearing and slammed the back door on her way to work.

She did that every morning. Usually Lucy put the pillow over her head and went back to sleep.

This morning she got up. She didn't think Dudley's daughter had awakened her, or the birds. Maybe it had been a dream, a good dream, because she wasn't sad or afraid. The shadows were just tree limbs, eaves, Dudley's chimney. Nothing lived in the shadows. They had no hands or eyes. Her house was a safe place and all her family was safe in it. Except her brother Ethan. Who was dead.

She was wide-awake and had to go to the bathroom. She swung her feet over the side of the bed. Patches trilled good morning and came to rub around her ankles.

Lucy went down the hall to the bathroom. Patches came with her, and noisily used the cat box while she used the toilet. That made Lucy smile. From across the hall she could hear Dad snoring, tiny little round sounds like seashells.

She was combing her hair in the full-length mirror on the back of the bathroom door, trying to decide whether it looked better behind her ears, and Patches was sitting at her feet watching, when she heard the noise that she knew had awakened her. A regular snipping sound. The sound, she realized, of garden clippers. And singing. Her mother's voice, singing a song.

Standing on tiptoe, she could just see out the
bathroom window. There was Mom, in the
pink flowered robe the kids had given her for
her birthday and short white gardening gloves
that made her hands look like a child's, on her
hands and knees in the peachy light of the sunrise, working in her flower garden and singing
a song that, as far as Lucy could tell, didn't
have any words.

This was a wonderful thing. An adventure. A
beautiful experience she would remember all
her life. Lucy propped her elbows on the high
windowsill and held her face in her hands, already trying different words in her mind for
writing about this in her diary. Maybe Mom
would write in the diary about it, too. Now
and then Mom's trowel glinted. The long narrow garden, in the space between the sidewalk
and the street, trailed out behind her like the
train of a wedding dress, and there were little
piles of gray-green weeds along the curb. Mom
didn't look up, but Lucy could tell she knew
she was there, and that they loved each other
very much.

Suddenly she saw what Mom was doing.
She was cutting the heads off all the flowers.
Bright blue and yellow blooms grew in the
rows ahead of her, round like marbles, but the
plants behind her were bare.

She raced down the stairs and out the front

door. She had to get to her mother. She had to stop her.

The early-morning air was cool and she shivered in her thin nightgown. Sharp little stones here and there on the sidewalk hurt her feet. But when she rounded the corner, she saw Mom in the middle of the flower garden, lit by the sunrise that was spreading across the sky now, snipping and snipping, and she saw the pile of flower heads on the ground at Mom's side, and she ran faster, calling out, "Mom! Don't!"

Mom looked over her shoulder and smiled, but the clippers didn't stop. "Good morning, honey. You're up early."

"Why are you killing the flowers?" Lucy stopped before she got too close.

Mom looked at the clippers in her hand, opened her palm to look at the squashed blossoms she'd been holding there, looked back at Lucy, and laughed gently. "I do this so they'll grow better."

Lucy didn't know whether to believe her or not. "You do?"

"Come here."

Lucy hesitated. Then she put one foot into the grass. The dew was cold and she jerked her foot back, shivering violently.

"Come here, honey. Let me show you."

Lucy high-stepped over the wet grass until both feet were on the dirt of the garden, which was warmer. Her toes sank in; she liked that. Mom was still on her knees, so that Lucy was taller than she was, and the early sun made silver streaks shine all over the top of her head. Lucy wanted to touch it, to cover them up.

"If you kneel down," Mom told her quietly, "I can show you better. Come on down here with me."

Lucy knelt in the dirt between the rows of plants, some of them with pretty flowers on them and some of them ugly and bare. Her mother took her hand, guided it to one of the plants that still had a yellow head.

"These are marigolds," Mom said, and her voice was soft and soothing, like a lullaby, or a reverse lullaby, since it was morning and they were supposed to be waking up. "The blue ones are ageratum. If you let them bloom too early, the plants get spindly, and they'll stop blooming altogether before the season's over."

"What's spindly?"

"Thin. Weak. Kind of sickly. The energy of the plant goes into the flower, and not into the stem and the leaves and the roots, where it belongs."

Mom moved Lucy's fingers so that she could feel the stem, the hairlike leaves, the too-fat flower on top.

"Sometimes I talk to them. I say things like, 'You're just too *young*. Let yourselves get stronger first. Later, I promise, I'll let you keep your flowers, and then everybody will say how beautiful you are all the way through October, if we don't get a heavy frost.' "

"You talk to the plants?"

Without warning, Mom pinched Lucy's thumb and forefinger together, and the head of the flower popped off. Lucy gasped and tears welled into her eyes. She tried to pull her hand away, but Mom held it, and the yellow ball of the marigold lay dying in both their palms.

"Sometimes plants get—spindly anyway," Lucy said carefully, looking at the decapitated marigold and not at her mother. "Sometimes plants die no matter what you do, huh?"

"Sometimes a wind comes along," her mother agreed sadly. "Or a hailstorm. Or somebody takes a shortcut through the flower bed and crushes all the plants. Or a dog digs them up. Or some animal eats them—rabbits supposedly like the taste of marigolds, and deer, too. There are all kinds of dangers."

Abruptly Lucy's knees gave out and she sat down in the damp grass, pulling her hand away from Mom's and dropping the flower head into the dirt. She found a rock and set it over the fading yellow ball, ground it down, left it there. "You're supposed to keep them safe," she said, half under her breath. When Mom didn't answer right away she thought

maybe she hadn't heard her, so she looked up
and said out loud, "You're supposed to keep us
safe. You and Dad. You're the parents."

The sunrise was full in Mom's face, making
her look older because it brought out the wrinkles and at the same time younger because it
was a soft peachy color. The tears in her eyes
and on her cheeks were peach-colored. Lucy
wanted to wipe them away, stopped herself by
thinking deliberately, *Serves her right*, and
then felt guilty. Mom said, so softly that Lucy
could hardly hear her and anyway she didn't
want to, "I know. That's what I always
thought, too. But sometimes things happen to
kids that parents can't help. Sometimes—"

Shut up, Lucy thought furiously, but all she
dared say was, "Then why bother?"

"Because it's the right thing to do." Mom
spread her white-gloved hands.

"Doesn't it bother you to have to do all this
stuff? Like pull the heads off plants?"

"Yes. But it's the right thing to do."

"What do you do with them when you break
them all off?"

"You're supposed to leave them in the garden so they'll decay and add their nutrients to
the soil. That's what Grandpa does. But I can't
stand to see them lying there, so I put them in
a bag and throw away."

"There's Jerry Johnston," Lucy said before
she knew she was going to. He was halfway

down the block, his big square head turned to look up at their house.

"Where?" Then Mom saw him, too, and dropped Lucy's hand.

Jerry kept coming closer, passed the side steps, seemed to be looking at them now. The brightest part of the sunrise was at his back, so it was hard to see his face.

"Jerry?" Mom said out loud. "Jerry Johnston? What are you doing here so early in the morning?"

"Hello, Carole." He stopped on the sidewalk between them and the house. He nodded to Lucy but didn't say hello to her. "You're up early."

"I—couldn't sleep," Mom said.

He was standing over them with his arms folded across his big chest. Rings glinted from his hands where they were tucked under his elbows. His white shorts and striped shirt were huge. From where Lucy crouched on the ground next to her mother, he looked like a giant in a fairy tale. He was frowning at them. "It's kind of an odd time to be working in the garden, isn't it?"

"I—it's hard to find time to do this during the day," Mom said. "With the kids and school and everything."

He nodded, as if he understood something that Mom hadn't said. Jerry Johnston was a smart man.

"How's Rae doing in the group?" Mom asked. Lucy thought it was a weird question to be asking him before the sun was even up, and she was embarrassed for her mother.

"She's doing fine," he said. Lucy could tell from the tone of his voice that he and Rae had secrets, even from Mom.

If Mom hadn't asked again, "What are you doing here?" Lucy would have.

"My aunt lives a few blocks away." He gestured vaguely. "I always take early-morning walks, especially when I'm not in my own neighborhood."

"I didn't know you had an aunt who lived around here."

"Oh, I believe I mentioned it when we first met and I saw your address. Aunt Alice. She's eighty-three, and things around her place tend to pile up, so every once in a while I spend the weekend with her and help her catch up."

He was talking a lot, Lucy thought uneasily. Usually he just sat and nodded and maybe said, "Uh-huh," taking in everything you said —and everything you didn't say, everything he saw about you that you didn't see—and putting it to his own use inside that enormous body and mind. She had a feeling he was taking in and using everything about herself and Mom right now, but talking so much that you wouldn't notice it. Lucy noticed.

"We were just—weeding," Mom said. Lucy

didn't see why she said anything at all. "I was showing Lucy about dead-heading."

"Uh-huh." His big pale head bobbed.

There was a long pause. Lucy cupped her hands around a little ageratum plant, fuzzy with blue flowers, and savagely snipped them all off with her nails, one by one, until there was a pile on the ground. The sun was bright enough now that they didn't look quite blue. Mom was sitting back on her heels, staring at Jerry Johnston and fidgeting her hands in the little white gardening gloves. Lucy was afraid she was going to invite him into the house for a cold drink, or suggest they walk to 7-Eleven together for coffee.

"Well," he said, and had already started to move away before he'd finished the sentence, "I guess I'd better go get Aunt Alice's breakfast started. Say hello to Tony and the other Brills for me. . . ." His voice trailed off. He was walking very fast, almost running. He didn't go all the way to the end of the block but turned into the alley instead. Lucy watched him curiously, warily, realizing how little she or Mom or anybody knew about this man who knew so much about their family.

Lucy and her mother finished pulling the flowers off the plants. The sun was all the way up now. More and more cars went by. The lady across the street was calling her dog; she did that every morning, and Dad always complained because she woke him up. Lucy glanced up at the bedroom window and wondered if he was awake now; it made her feel funny not to know. Birds were chirping so furiously in the trees that she looked around for Patches or some other cat, but there wasn't any; they must be singing because they were happy, or just because it was morning.

The dead heads looked like scraps of cloth on the ground. Mom stuffed them and the gray weeds into a black plastic garbage sack and stood up. Lucy heard her knees crack. "I'll go put these in the trash," Mom said. "Why don't you go on in, and we can start breakfast. Cory's probably awake by now."

He wasn't. The house was still very quiet. Lucy was sitting in the kitchen with Patches on her lap, feeling quiet and peaceful like the morning as long as she didn't let herself think about Jerry Johnston and what he'd been doing outside her house, when she heard somebody scream.

Priscilla. In the upstairs hallway, outside Rae and Lucy's room, Priscilla was shrieking. Patches cocked his head and twitched his ears. Lucy sat there for a moment, not knowing what to do. She heard running footsteps upstairs, and lots of voices. Mom ran past her. Lucy hadn't even known she was in the house.

After a minute, Lucy pushed Patches off her lap and followed Mom because she had to, so scared she almost collapsed when she first tried to stand up, had to hold on to door-frames and dining-room chairs as she passed by.

When she got to the top landing, she saw Dad at the end of the hallway in his baggy yellow pajamas, and Pris in his arms. Her crutches were on the floor, blocking the bedroom door. She was crying. "It's Rae! Oh, Daddy, something awful has happened to Rae!"

Dad pulled away from her so roughly that she almost fell. Mom grabbed her shoulders and leaned her against the wall, bent to pick up the crutches and prop them under Priscilla's arms. Molly and Dominic had come sleepily out of their rooms, and Cory was wailing in the big-boy bed. Lucy made herself take a step toward her room, then another.

"Shit!" she heard Dad say. And then: "My God!"

He was pressing against the doorjamb with both hands and Lucy had to duck under his arm to see. She went all the way inside, and nobody stopped her. When she raised her head inside her own room, she screamed and clapped both hands over her mouth.

Rae's bed was all messed up. The top sheet and the green blanket were bunched on the floor. One corner of the fitted bottom sheet had been pulled loose, exposing the gray mattress. The head of the bed had been pulled away from the wall, crookedly. The cords of Rae's radio and headphones and speakers looked like spiderwebs, like thin black bones. And the whole bed was soaked with blood.

13

"Are you all right, ma'am?"

The detective leaning over Mom had a little mustache and a certain way of talking. Lucy thought he was gay. Rae would know. Rae wasn't here. Rae said you could tell if guys were gay but not girls.

Rae was missing. Chills raced through Lucy. Ethan was dead. Her family was changing. Her family was falling apart. She was the next-oldest kid. Maybe she was next.

"Ma'am, are you all right?"

Mom was on her stomach on the hallway floor. She hadn't fainted; Lucy had watched her deliberately kneel, then curl up on her side, then stretch out and lay her cheek and the palms of her hands and her stomach and her thighs on the wooden floor.

She wasn't dead either, though it wouldn't have surprised Lucy if she was. She was panting, and her fingers kept moving across the floorboards like the legs of helpless bugs, like a mother's hands helplessly trying to hold on.

She hadn't fainted. She wasn't dead. But she was on the floor and she wouldn't get up, and that really bothered the gay detective. Lucy had a hard time imagining gay sex. She had a hard time imagining any kind of sex.

She didn't know why it bothered him so much that Mom was on the floor. Let her stay there. "Mom, please get up," Lucy tried to say. But she must have been whispering it, or saying it just to herself, because nobody even looked at her and Mom didn't move, except that her hands kept opening and closing across the slippery, dusty wood.

Lucy tried to make her thoughts into words, black letters marching across the troubled white spaces of her mind, like something written into her diary and there forever. She tried to send the message straight to her mother: *Can't you tell there's nothing to hold on to? Why don't you quit trying? You look really stupid.*

Rae had been gone a whole day now, and there was no sign of her. The cops had taken her bloody sheets. Things that had belonged to her already didn't feel as if they belonged to anybody; no matter how long Lucy sat and held her sister's pink robe or how heavily she smeared her sister's silver lipstick across her own lips, there was no presence in anything, no message, no clue. Lucy wasn't allowed to wear makeup yet, but nobody even noticed.

"Ma'am?" the detective asked one more time. "Are you all right, ma'am?"

Suddenly Mom was up on her knees, clawing at the man, screaming at him. "No, I'm not all right! My son is dead and my daughter is missing! I'll never be all right again!"

You still have us, Lucy thought fiercely through fierce embarrassment. *You still have me*. But she understood that it wasn't enough.

The detective had caught Mom's wrists and was holding them easily, but the forward motion of her body as she attacked him threw him off balance and he sat down hard. Now he didn't look like a detective anymore, and it didn't matter whether or not he was gay; he was an ordinary man sitting on the floor in Lucy's house holding her mother in his arms.

They were not alone. They were part of other people, and other people had had people die. Nobody could change what had happened or keep other bad things from happening to them. But there were people who could help them stand it, help them get through. Not just Mom and Dad, not just Lucy herself, the oldest child left. But people like Jerry Johnston, and Stacey who'd lived through her parents' divorce when she'd thought she never could, and this detective holding Mom who was sobbing so hard she could hardly catch her breath. Lucy wanted him to hold her, too. She wanted to cry like that while he was holding her so she wouldn't go flying off in bloody little pieces into the wind.

She looked away, embarrassed, and tried to listen to Dad on the phone, but the detective murmuring to Mom was louder. "We'll do everything we can to find her, ma'am. And the rest of your family is right here. Your family needs you, ma'am."

Mom beat weakly at his chest and her crying turned to coughing. "My family is slipping away! I can't keep them safe! They'd be better off without me!"

Lucy looked around frantically. Priscilla had taken the three youngest kids into the kitchen for breakfast. Dominic, Molly, Cory. If you named them, it would make them real. Even though Lucy knew where they were, it was easy for her to believe that she'd never see them again.

This day had passed like any other day. They'd all eaten, slept some, gotten up, breathed, had mites on and in them, petted the cat, brushed their hair, touched things. Molly and Cory had watched cartoons. Dad had watched the news. Lucy had gone swimming at Stacey's house. A day like any other day, except that nothing was the way it had ever been before.

They were hunting for Rae. Just like they'd hunted for Ethan. A lifetime ago. A moment ago. This time Lucy helped, but it wasn't making any difference. They couldn't find her. Mom drove all over the neighborhood, was gone so long that Lucy thought she must have had an accident, or driven off the edge of the world. On her way to and from Stacey's house, Lucy asked every kid she saw: "Have you seen my sister? Have you seen Rae?" Nobody had. Some of them didn't even know who her sister Rae was. Dad called all her friends, Jerry Johnston, the other kids in the therapy group, teachers. Nobody knew anything.

Now Lucy sat quietly at the big dining-room table, where she'd sat hundreds of times before. This was Dad's chair; it had arms. There was a smudge on the shiny wood; she rubbed at it and it got bigger. The sunshine coming in the bay window had the same shape and color it had had on other late-summer mornings, as if everything were the same. But she knew there were invisible feeding mites in the sunshine and that anything bad could happen at any time, in the next minute or the next year or at any time during her life. Time was rushing around her like a cyclone, and it had also stopped.

Anything bad could happen, and would.

Anything good could happen too, which was the truth but wasn't real.

Mom was crying so hard now that Lucy could hardly understand her. She didn't want to understand her, but she couldn't help it. "I was their—*mother*! I was supposed to—*keep them safe*!"

Mom pulled away from the detective and curled up again on the floor, curled up her knees, curled her arms around her legs. But she didn't cover her face, and Lucy stared, mesmerized, at the plain terror and anguish there.

The detective was taking notes in a blue spiral notebook like the ones Lucy used in school. "You'd had some trouble with both of them, hadn't you?"

When Mom nodded, her head slid up and down on the floor.

"What about the other kids?"

Mom didn't answer.

"How many other kids do you have, Mrs. Brill?"

Mom still didn't answer. Finally Lucy said, "Five," and shuddered.

"Have you had any trouble with any of them?"

Lucy stiffened. Mom moaned, "No! What difference does it make?" All her words were stuck together. The detective waited, pen poised over the notebook.

Dad hung up the phone, strode across the living room into the hall. To Mom he said, very firmly, "You can't just lie there on the floor, Carole. Come on, now, get up."

"Why not? This is as good a place as any." But she let him pull her to her feet and lead her to the couch. The detective followed at a short distance, writing something down. Lucy got up, took a few steps after them, stopped.

She wasn't holding on to anything. She couldn't reach anything to hold on to. All the voices and other sounds came and went and crisscrossed and tangled, like hundreds of radio stations interfering with each other. Colors got brighter and dimmer, brighter and dimmer: the golden-brown patches of sun across the floor, the green vine on the outside of the bay window, a red book open on the arm of the couch. She thought she was going to throw up. But the sickness already belonged to someone else's body, because she didn't have a body anymore, or a place in the world to be in.

"Nobody's seen her," Dad told them again. "A couple of her friends said they talked to her on the phone the evening before she disappeared and there wasn't anything out of the ordinary."

Just like Ethan, Lucy thought, and Mom said her thought: "Just like Ethan." Then Lucy's thoughts went on: *Just like me. I'm next.* She waited for Mom to speak that, too, but she didn't.

"I went through her address book," Dad said wearily, passing his hand over his eyes as if they hurt, as if everything hurt. "I called everybody I could think of."

"Has Jerry found out anything?" Mom's voice was shaky, but the terrible sobbing had quieted. Lucy relaxed a little. The side of her neck hurt. She put her hand there and discovered a knot, proof of the inside working of her own body.

"He says she never gave him any reason to suspect she was planning to run away or involved in anything dangerous."

"Who's this Jerry?" the detective wanted to know. Lucy had almost forgotten he was there, but now that he'd spoken up she was convinced that he would always be here in her house.

"Jerry Johnston." Mom said the name as if she hated it. Lucy wondered why. "Her therapist."

"Where can I get in touch with him?" Dad gave him Jerry Johnston's address and phone number. The detective copied it down in his notebook, nodded, then asked, "Why did she need therapy?"

"To help her with things we couldn't help her with."

"What things?"

Lucy's mixed-up thoughts suddenly came together. *Don't tell him,* she sent in silent warning to Dad. The detective was an outsider. The Brill family was falling apart.

But her father didn't hear the warning, or didn't believe it. He took a deep breath. "Shoplifting. Lying. Moods. Generally being unhappy and hard to get along with."

"Sounds like every teenager I know," the detective said, with a little laugh that made Lucy instantly furious.

"Things with our oldest son went too far before we took them seriously enough. We wanted to head things off with Rae." Dad laughed a little, too, but Lucy didn't think he thought anything was funny.

"How long had she been having problems?"

"For a while. A year or so. But it got worse after Ethan died."

And then Dad was crying, tears were streaming down his face, Mom was rushing to hold him, and Lucy couldn't stand it anymore. She ran into the kitchen and slammed the door.

All her younger brothers and sisters sat around the sunny kitchen table eating cereal. They were giggling and squabbling as if this were any other morning, as if nothing had happened and nothing was going to happen, as if Ethan weren't dead and Rae weren't missing and Dad weren't crying in the living room and Mom hadn't been lying flat on the floor with no good reason to get up, as if there weren't cops in their house. Even Priscilla, who was old enough to know better, was reading the jokes on the back of the cereal box and laughing out loud.

Lucy stood there for a few minutes, watching and waiting. Then she sank to the floor, pressed her cheek against it like Mom, and let herself be drowned by the horror of what had happened and what was happening now and what might happen at any time.

"Lucy?" Priscilla asked. Dominic laughed. Molly ran to get Mom or Dad.

"Where do you think Rae is?" Pris wanted to know.

It was late afternoon now, hot, and the western sky was clouding up. Lucy saw that the plants out here on the porch were getting dry. She stuck her finger into one of the pots, then pulled it out and wiped it off in disgust. It was Mom's job to take care of the plants, not hers. If they all died, it would be Mom's fault, not hers. "How would I know? Nobody knows."

"Well, I think she's dead. Just like Ethan."

"Well, where's that?"

"Huh?"

"Where's dead?"

Pris slid all the way to the other end of the swing. "You're weird, Lucy."

"Don't you ever wonder? Don't you ever want to know what it's like to be dead?"

Priscilla got down from the swing, even though Lucy was pushing hard with her feet against the concrete floor and making the swing go high and wide. She had to get her crutches before she could run away into the house, and that slowed her down.

Lucy had time to say, "Someday I'm going to find out."

Priscilla couldn't get away from her fast enough to keep from bursting into tears. "Everybody's gonna find out someday!" she wailed. "Everybody's gonna die someday! I don't wanna die! I don't want Rae or Ethan to die!"

"Too late," Lucy said, not quite under her breath, wondering why she was being so mean to her little sister, who was going to die someday.

Pris went clomping into the house, yelling, "You're mean! I'm telling!" As soon as she was out of sight and earshot, Lucy felt terrible. She made the swing go as hard as she could, then drew her knees up under her chin and wrapped her arms around her knees and made herself very small. As if that would keep bad things from finding her. She knew it wouldn't.

She hated it that cops were in her house again, the gay detective talking some more to

Mom and Dad, and a bigger guy, half-bald, old, with a big stomach. Right now he was in Rae's room, which was also Lucy's room but nobody seemed to remember that, going through their stuff. When she'd gone in to rescue her diary, he'd pulled it right out of her hands, flipped through the pages a couple of times, read a few things, then handed it back to her without a word. Lucy had been really embarrassed. But the fat old balding cop hadn't cared about either her diary or her embarrassment.

Now she took the diary out of her pocket and flipped through it from the back. Page after page was blank. It was weird to think what words might end up on them, whether she'd write them or somebody else would. Rae had known all the places where Lucy'd ever tried to hide the diary. You couldn't keep a secret from her if she wanted to find it out. Maybe she'd write Lucy a message.

Lucy kept turning pages. The gold edges glistened; she kept running her fingers over them to make sure they weren't wet. The more blank pages she turned, the more her heart hurt. Her arms and legs hurt, too, like in those TV commercials for pain medicine where there was an outline of somebody's body hollow except for pain. There was pain in her ears. There was pain in the tips of her fingers.

She had to go through a lot of blank pages

before she got to the last thing she'd written, which was about the two cute guys in the apartment across the street who were not too old for her even if they were in their twenties. Rae hadn't written her any messages. Mom hadn't written her any messages. The stuff she'd written herself was stupid.

Lucy closed the diary and closed her eyes. The swing kept moving back and forth. She could just barely feel the concrete porch floor under her toes as she pushed on it, scraped across it, pushed on it again. She could just barely feel the slats of the swing under her thighs, the hot afternoon air with mites and dust and oxygen in it all over her skin and up and down her nose and inside her lungs like fear.

She was so afraid.

Rae rose out of the bushes in front of the porch. Lucy stared. Rae's hair was a mess, and her makeup looked like bruises and blood.

She scrabbled up the porch wall. Her nails made screeking noises on the brick, and Lucy cringed to think of how they must be breaking. One leg came over the wall toward Lucy. Her black shoe and thick rolled black sock looked way too hot to wear in this weather.

Lucy wanted to pull back away from her as far as she could. She also wanted to grab her wrists and help her over the wall onto the porch beside her. She didn't do either one. She stayed where she was and whispered urgently, "What are you doing? Where have you been? You're in a lot of trouble! Everybody's looking for you. The cops are looking for you and Mom and Dad and it's been in the paper—"

"Oh, shut the fuck up," Rae said softly and clearly. "You're such a baby."

Lucy answered back, "You think you're such hot shit." She felt tears in her eyes but she didn't wipe them away because she didn't want Rae to think she was crying or anything. She didn't dare blink or the tears would come loose. "You always think you know everything about everything."

"I know a helluva lot more about life than you do. You are such a baby. Why don't you grow up?"

Rae was still trying to climb over the porch wall. Now she was stuck halfway, as if she was too weak to push herself the rest of the way over. The way she straddled the wall looked painful, and she teetered. When her hands grabbed at bushes and the brick wall and the air, her long red nails flashed like drops of blood and she couldn't grab hold of anything.

There was a noise from inside the house, somebody coming, and Rae fell over backward. Lucy heard branches snap inside the big rosebush in front. Mom would be mad about that.

She got up off the swing. It pitched forward

and almost tipped her off. She went and looked over the wall, leaned way over to see down to the ground through the thorny bush. Rae wasn't there. Rae was gone again.

Lucy was still bent way over, clutching her diary against her and trying to find some proof that Rae had really been there, when Priscilla screamed from right inside the front door, "It was her period!"

Lucy jumped. Her heart took up her whole body, beating hard and fast. She stumbled backward until she felt the swing against the backs of her thighs, then collapsed onto it. The swing careened wildly, then stopped moving altogether. She squeezed her eyes shut tighter and didn't look at Priscilla, who was balancing on her crutches in the doorway. "What?"

"The cops just got a phone call on our phone. That was blood from her period all over her bed."

Lucy pressed her hands over her face, but sobs came out anyway, like big hot stones, tearing out of her chest and smashing back into it again. Priscilla came and sat beside her, crying, too, and after a while they were holding hands.

14

"I hate you!"

Running up the stairs, Lucy bumped against the suncatcher Ethan had made in the third grade. The day he'd brought it home, it had seemed magical; she'd been just little. But all it was was a plastic lid with the face of a sun drawn on it in magic marker. She didn't know why Mom kept the stupid thing. The edge of the lid was cracked now all the way around, and the magic marker was smeared. She swung her fist at it, hit the leaded glass window behind it instead, threw herself off balance, fell to one knee.

"I don't want to be part of this family. I *hate* families! This isn't even a family anymore!"

Priscilla was just coming out of the bathroom. When Lucy stumbled past her, she stuck out one of her crutches, trying to trip her. Lucy saw it in time, though, and kicked it out of her sister's hand. Pris howled.

"You're terrible parents! You don't know how to take care of kids! I don't want you for my parents! You let your kids die!"

She slammed her bedroom door and flung herself, shrieking, onto her bed. The door jumped open again. Lucy looked over her shoulder to see if Rae was there, or Ethan. If they might have followed her, might have come back. Might never have gone away at all, and everybody had been wrong or lying. That wouldn't surprise Lucy.

They weren't there. Nobody was there, come to comfort her or bring her secret messages. She'd made the door open herself, by trying to shut it too hard.

"I'm gonna run away!"

They'd grounded her for two days just for talking back to Dad about chores. Lucy didn't see what was such a big deal about talking back. She was just expressing her opinion. She had a right to her opinion. Stacey talked back to her mother all the time and didn't get in trouble for it. Or if she did, all she had to say was she hated her mom and she wanted to go live with her dad, and pretty soon her mom would give in and Stacey would be back to doing whatever she felt like doing.

Lucy's mom and dad never gave in. They

were strong. They held on. Even now, when a lot of the time they didn't pay much attention to any of the kids who were still alive. When they looked at you or talked to you or listened to you, you knew they were doing it through the smeared, multicolored presences of Ethan and Rae, who were always there and more real than anybody else. Ethan Michael Brill. Rae Ellen Brill, Peeled off the Brill family like strings off string cheese.

Lucy pounded the pillow, kicked the wall, yelled, *"I hate you"* as loud and as mean as she could. She hoped they could hear her. She hoped the whole world could hear her. It wasn't *fair*. This was the last week before school, and she and Stacey had plans. Go to the library—Mom and Dad almost always would say yes to the library, and lots of times Jeremy Martinez was hanging out in the park with his friends. Ride the roller coaster a hundred and one times. Spend the night at one of their houses and watch scary movies all night, then at the other one's house and watch love movies all night.

There weren't very many days left before school. There weren't very many days left, period.

Just ask Ethan. He'd spent a long time trying to hurt everybody else because he was hurting, even though, as far as Lucy could tell, that was his own fault. He'd tried to take stuff from other people that wasn't his, and he refused to use what they did give him.

Lucy thought about Ethan's huge, stinking mouth that got bigger and smelled worse every time she saw him because the flesh around it and inside it was rotting away. She thought about his wild empty eyes. She thought about him getting smaller and smaller and finally going back inside their mother where they'd all come from.

Lucy couldn't look at her mother now without thinking about Ethan possessing her, haunting her from inside her own body. Sometimes when she let Mom close to her, when she touched Mom, she was sure she could feel her brother inside her mother's belly, kicking and feeding and curling tighter and tighter around himself.

Just ask Rae, who'd started her period and then disappeared. Lucy put her hand down between her legs and felt a suspicious moisture there, but when she looked at her fingers, there was no blood.

She didn't see what the big deal was about chores, either. What difference did it make if the tables got dusted and the trash got taken out? Keeping the house clean was just another trick to make you think it was a safe place when it wasn't. Yesterday she'd heard Mom yelling over the noise of the vacuum cleaner, yelling and yelling as she pushed it back and forth across the living-room rug. "No! No! No!" she'd yelled, apparently thinking nobody could hear her, but Lucy heard.

Lucy had better things to do. For one thing, she'd keep herself safe. Nothing bad was going to happen to her anyway; she didn't seem to be afraid of stuff anymore. Today she'd done a bunch of things she never would have done before: crossed Federal Boulevard without a light, stuck her hand through the fence to pet the big white dog that always acted as if it was going to attack you, waded out into the lake till the water was up to her armpits. Stacey had said, "Lucy!" a lot, but the green pickup had slowed down in time, the dog had finally started wagging its tail, and she'd fed a whole family of ducks or geese out of her hand. Their beaks had felt like rubber across her palm.

Still crying, still trembling with rage, even still kicking at the wall, she reached with one hand into the dresser drawer where she kept her diary. She couldn't find it. She sat up so quickly that it made her dizzy, pawed through underwear and tapes. The diary wasn't there.

Rae. Rae had stolen her diary and was going to write in it. Lucy pulled her knees up to her chest and shuddered with excitement.

There was a knock at her door that made it open even farther and she could see Dad standing there. She turned her head away from him, pressed her cheek against her knees, and snarled, "Go *away!*"

He came in anyway. He shut the door behind him, made sure it stayed shut, said her name. "Lucy."

"Go *away!* Leave me *alone!* I *hate* you!" Suddenly she saw her diary, on the floor behind her closet door. There wouldn't be any messages in it, from Rae or from anybody else. Lucy said again, "I hate you."

He sat down on the other bed. Rae's bed, piled high now with Lucy's stuff. She shouldn't put her stuff there; Rae would be mad. He had no right to sit there. "Well, regardless of what you feel about me, I love you."

"No, you don't."

"I love you," he repeated.

"All you care about is homework and chores. You don't care anything about me. You wish I was the one who was dead."

He leaned forward and slapped her. Not hard, but enough to make her cheek sting, and he'd never slapped her before. Lucy screamed.

Her father grabbed her. She tried to fight him off, but he was bigger and stronger than she was, and he was her father. For a minute she was scared of what he was going to do. She'd gone too far and he was really mad at her; she deserved whatever he did.

She could also feel his sadness, and that scared and disgusted her more than his anger.

She imagined the hollowness of his bones, the hollowness of his veins, all of his internal organs like sacks. Like the Visible Man in biology class. She was going to throw up.

What he did to her was hug her. She twisted and yelled to get free, but he held on. Underneath the anger and sadness and fear, inside the hollowness that those feelings made, she had no choice but to feel her father's love. It didn't take much of a struggle before she gave up and collapsed against him.

"I'm sorry, Lucy," he whispered. "I shouldn't have hit you."

"That's all right."

"No, it's not all right. But you have to expect me to react like that when you say I don't care about you. That's going to be hard for me to take for a long time. Maybe forever."

"Because of Rae and Ethan." He nodded. "Everything's changed! They've ruined everything!"

"A lot of things are changed, yes. But not everything. And it's up to each of us whether our lives are ruined."

"Where do you think they are?"

"I don't know. Ethan's dead. I don't know where he is."

"What about Rae? Do you think she'd dead, too? She's been gone a long time. Almost a month. She must be dead."

"No," he said. "She's not."

"How do you know?"

He didn't answer. Lucy sat up away from him and looked up at his face. When she examined it up close like this, it was the face of a stranger, torn apart into pieces, into bones and flesh and tears.

"Do you see her?" she breathed. "Like Mom used to see Ethan?"

She could tell that he was surprised and not too happy that she knew about that. Parents thought you didn't know anything.

She could tell he considered lying to her, or pretending he didn't know what she meant. But he decided to be honest. As far as she knew, he and Mom were always honest. Sometimes she was glad and proud. Other times it drove her crazy.

"I think I've seen her," Dad said. "I'm not sure. I don't know what's going on."

"Me, too," Lucy breathed.

Dad looked at her sharply, as if she'd done something wrong. As if it was her fault that Ethan and now Rae had run away. It wasn't her fault. She didn't think it was her fault. "You've seen her, too?"

"Maybe I just dreamed it," Lucy lied. "Maybe I just thought I saw her because I was thinking about her so hard."

"Maybe." Dad didn't believe it, which gave Lucy an uncomfortable little thrill.

"How come Ethan came to Mom and Rae comes to you? What do they want?"

"I saw Ethan a few times. Or thought I did."

"Did he try to hurt you?" *Did he try to go inside you* was what she wanted to ask, but she couldn't bring herself to say something like that out loud. She could only hope he'd know what she meant. Parents were supposed to always know what you meant.

He didn't know. He answered only what she'd asked. Lucy was disappointed and irritated by her father's stupidity. "No. He never attacked me or anything. Not after he ran away. He did a few times while he was still living at home, but you remember that, don't you?"

"That's not what I mean."

"I know. Twice I saw him, or thought I saw him, in the doorway, and once I thought he was looking in the living-room window. That's all."

"So how come he—how come Mom saw him more and talked to him and—touched him and stuff?"

"I don't know, Lucy. I don't understand any of this."

That was a lie, and it infuriated her. Parents understood stuff, and they could always explain it to you if they wanted to. She tried to pull away from her father but there wasn't enough room on the bed.

"Maybe," he said, more to himself than to her, "it has something to do with teenagers' ambivalence toward the parent of the opposite sex."

Now he was using big words and weird sentences on purpose so that she wouldn't know what he was talking about. So that she'd feel dumb. Lucy was getting madder and madder.

He wouldn't say any more. His hand was still on her knee and he was still looking in her direction, but she could tell that Rae had come between them again. The fact that Rae was gone was more important than the fact that Lucy was still here.

He looked so miserable that Lucy snuggled back against his chest so she wouldn't have to see his face, so he'd have to protect and comfort her from his own pain. At first he didn't say anything. Lucy felt the terror and hurt getting big again. She started thinking of terrible things to yell at him so he'd deny them and hold her again.

But she didn't have to. Dad sighed, put his arms around her, kissed the top of her head. "We'll get through this, honey. It's a terrible time for our family, but we'll get through it together."

She pressed her ear against his heart and adjusted her breathing to match his. His body was warm. Some of her coldness and some of the pain in her chest started to go away.

"And," he said to her, gently, "you still have to do chores."

"I know."

"And I'm still not going to let you get away with talking to me like that."

She laughed a little, embarrassed. "I know. I'm sorry."

"And you're still grounded till Wednesday."

"That's not fair! Stacey's mom—" She stopped, then said, "I know."

He kissed her again and stood up. "Mom's making hamburgers for dinner. You want to help her?"

Lucy fell over onto her bed in the same curled-up position she'd been in while he was holding her. She was so tired.

"Lucy?"

She opened her eyes. "No. I've got stuff I want to do."

"Okay, we'll call you for dinner. I love you."

"I love you, too," she managed to say, and waited until he'd left the room and shut the door before she moved. Then she sat up. Her body ached. She stood, made her way across the room, and checked that the door was latched. They weren't allowed to have locks on their doors because there might be a fire or something might happen to them. Rae and Ethan hadn't had locks on their doors, and something had happened to them anyway.

Lucy retrieved her diary, found a pencil

with enough of a point to write, and turned to the next blank page. The diary was thick with blank pages that she would have to write in. She caught her tongue hard between her teeth and wrote, experimentally, "I hate you."

She paused, then read it aloud. "I hate you." She didn't know whom she was writing it to, and now she wasn't even sure that she meant it, but it was better than the empty page. She wrote "I hate you I hate you I hate you" until the whole page was full.

It was still hot when Lucy went back up to her room around nine o'clock. She might as well go to bed early; she couldn't do anything fun anyway. She turned the fan on high and, before she could stop herself, was thinking with guilty satisfaction that now she didn't have to fight about it with Rae, who'd hated the noise.

Lucy put on Dad's old white T-shirt that she liked to sleep in. The tail came down to her knees and the sleeves almost covered her elbows. She liked the way it smelled.

She crawled under her sheet, turned on her radio, settled the earphones over her ears. She stared out the window at the pine tree and the streetlight and the telephone pole. In the daytime, squirrels ran up and down the pole and drove Patches crazy. One summer Ethan had nailed a tunafish can as high as he could reach and kept it full of Rice Krispies and Cheerios for the squirrels. That was before they had Patches. Before Cory was born. Before Ethan died.

Lucy rolled over, punched her pillow, changed stations. This was going to be one of those nights when she had trouble getting to sleep. It had always taken her a long time to fall asleep, even when she was little, and she always woke up two or three times, because of dreams or noises or having to pee. It had never bothered her, being awake when everybody else was asleep; in fact, it had been kind of exciting, her own dark quiet time.

But lately the hours she tossed and turned seemed longer than those she slept, and she'd just start to doze off when something would jerk her awake again. The big house with all those sleeping bodies in it had turned haunted and scary.

A pretty love song was playing on the radio. Tracy Chapman, she thought. She listened to it and tried to think peaceful thoughts. But the sunny field of flowers where Mom had taught her to go in her mind for one-minute vacations now had weird things living in the tall grass. She kept trying to find hidden messages in the music, like those people who played records backward and heard the devil's voice. Finally she turned the radio off before the song was over. Then she heard the crickets.

They were like one huge beast with its mouth open around her house, and she was afraid of them.

School would be starting in one week. Sixth grade. She was allowed to wear panty hose in the sixth grade, makeup in the seventh. Rae had left behind a drawerful of panty hose, all different colors. Her bedtime would be ten o'clock. Ms. Haeger would have had her baby by now. Lucy wondered what it would be like to have a baby. Next year she'd be going to Pruitt Middle School. Next year was too far away to even imagine.

She must have fallen asleep without knowing it, because somebody opening her door woke her up. The rush of fear gave way almost at once to an equally strong rush of relief; it was Dad, come to check on her. Lucy pretended to be asleep, because the magic only worked if parents thought the kids were sound asleep.

Dad came in and shut the door behind him. He didn't usually do that. Lucy heard him moving, but he didn't seem to be coming any closer to her. Finally, she slitted her eyes. His white T-shirt, a newer version of the one she was wearing, glowed silvery blue in the streetlight and moonlight.

He hadn't come in to check on her after all. He wasn't anywhere near her. She doubted if he'd even noticed she was there. He was sitting on her sister's bed.

"I don't know what you want from me," Lucy heard her father whisper. "Oh, God, Rae, I don't know how to keep you safe."

15

The bell rang again, and Lucy jumped. Bells were always ringing. You'd just get settled in one room for math and then the bell would ring and you'd have to go all the way to the other end of the hall for social studies. The halls were crowded. Kids yelled and pushed. Lucy kept thinking she saw Rae, coming the other way in the hall or watching her from halfway up the stairs; Rae hadn't gone to this school in two years. If you were late to class, you got your name up on the board.

Only the sixth graders had to change classes. The little kids didn't have to. Lucy remembered when she was a little kid; it didn't seem that long ago, but her whole life had changed. The teachers said it got you ready for real life, for middle school. Lucy hated it. She was nervous all the time, and she hated school more than ever, and she had nightmares about bells.

Somebody pulled her hair and pinched her hip. She whirled. It was Justin Tagawa. She knew it was, even though he was clear over on the other side of the hall by now pretending to talk to his friends. She yelled, "Slimeball!" at him and kept going. Justin was kind of cute, even if he did get straight As. Maybe he liked her. Maybe she liked him.

The principal was walking beside her. Behind them, Stacey and Tammy hooted because the principal was walking with Lucy. Lucy's face got hot. She tried to ignore them and the principal, just kept on walking to social studies. They were having a test. She hadn't studied. She hadn't even told Mom and Dad they were having a test. Since Rae had disappeared, they tried to act interested in her schoolwork, but they weren't really.

"So how's it going, Lucy?" The principal was trying to be friendly.

"Fine." She hugged her book against her chest and didn't look at him.

"School going okay?"

"Yeah."

"How are things at home?"

"Fine."

"Any word yet about your sister?"

The bell rang right over them and kept on ringing in her head, making her vision blur for a minute, making her dizzy. She tried to brace herself on the wall without being obvious about it. At least the bell saved her from having to answer Mr. Li's dumb question. She ducked into her classroom and he went on down the hall, probably to talk to some other kid about stuff that was none of his business.

"Hey, Luce, you in trouble *again*?" Stacey demanded out loud in front of everybody. She was laughing. She was supposed to be Lucy's best friend.

"Nah!" Tammy yelled. Tammy was always yelling. At the moment she was squatting on top of the desk. Even when she got caught doing stuff like that, even when they called her parents, she never got in trouble. "Nah, Lucy's the principal's pet. Maybe she's his *girl*friend!"

Everybody in the whole room, including Justin Tagawa and Jeremy Martinez, was laughing at her. They were laughing at her because her brother had died and her sister had disappeared and who knew what was going to happen in her family next. Nothing was normal or the same or any good anymore. The Brill family was weird.

Once Mr. Michaelson got Tammy off the desk and Justin and his friends away from the windows, he started talking about report cards. With a few exceptions, he said, grades were going to be pretty good this first time. He was proud of them. Lucy sank down in her chair, then pulled herself up straight and tried to stare at him defiantly. She was one of the exceptions. He'd warned her last week that if she didn't finish the report on South America, she'd get an *F.* She hadn't even started it. South America was dumb.

Then he passed out the test. Lucy just looked at it. The questions didn't make any sense. She filled in all the multiple choice with *A, B, C,* or *D;* it didn't matter, and when she tried to read one or two of the questions, the words didn't go with each other. She finished before anybody else and then sat there with her head down, pretending to write, remembering to move her pencil once in a while, pretending to think.

Lucy had no place to put her thoughts that was safe, and she seemed to have more thoughts than ever before in her life. If she thought about school, there were bells and reports and tests and sisters in the hall who couldn't possibly be there and who disappeared again and again, scaring you every time. If she thought about home, there were Mom and Dad and Ethan and Rae and danger and sadness and her little brothers and sisters and fear. If she thought about her friends, there were all kinds of things she didn't even understand, like boys and makeup and AIDS and college and French kissing and drugs. If she thought about herself, there was a headful of strangers.

So she tried not to put her thoughts anywhere. She tried not to have any thoughts. But they rattled around inside her head as if she'd broken something in there, and her stomach hurt all the time. Maybe everybody was lying to her and you could get pregnant without having sex. Maybe she had cancer. Kids got cancer. Maybe she was going to die.

"Time's up," Mr. Michaelson said from right beside her, and she wondered how long he'd been there. She passed her test paper in with the others. After it was gone, she couldn't remember whether she'd put her name on it.

They were starting a unit on Mexico. Angela Garcia went up to the map to point out the place where she visited her cousins every Christmas. Angela was fat, but she had straight thick black hair that she could sit on. Angela and Mr. Michaelson said some things back and forth to each other in Spanish. Lucy squirmed. What they were saying didn't make sense. They shouldn't talk in words that didn't make sense. Maybe they were talking about her.

She stretched noisily and turned her head to look out the window, hoping to make them shut up. Rae was looking in.

Walking around the room to keep everybody involved in the conversation, Mr. Michaelson stopped between Lucy and the window. He held up a picture in a magazine that he said was Mexico City and asked her some stupid question about it. She just shook her head and didn't even try to answer. When he finally moved out of the way, Rae wasn't there anymore.

Stacey passed her a note. *Let's go to the store after school. I have money.*

Lucy frowned and shook her head. She always had to go straight home after school. Stacey knew that. Stacey was just trying to make her feel bad. She had to finish her homework before she could do anything else. Probably now she could say she didn't have any homework and they wouldn't even ask her about it. She crumpled up the note, making as much noise as possible, and threw it across the aisle at Stacey.

The bell rang. Everybody headed for the door except Tammy, who was on her hands and knees under a desk barking, and Justin, who was tugging at the tie on Tammy's blouse and yelling, "Here, doggie! Here, doggie!" He was calling Tammy a dog and she didn't even know it; she thought he was paying attention to her. Any minute, Lucy thought, the tie would come undone and you'd see Tammy's boobs; she didn't wear a bra yet. That was probably what Justin wanted. It was probably what Tammy wanted, too.

Mr. Michaelson stopped Lucy at the door. "I want to talk to you for a minute."

"I have to get to gym."

"It's important. If you're late, I'll write you a note."

Detention again, she thought as she followed him to his big desk at the front of the room. Until this year she'd never had detention in her life. Now she'd already had it three times in the first six weeks. She'd thought her parents would be mad, but they didn't seem to care much. Dad said he knew she was having a hard time. She wasn't having a hard time. It was just that school was so dumb.

Mr. Michaelson sat on the corner of his desk, like he was trying to bring himself down to her level or something, and said, "Sit down," but she didn't. Noise came like mosquitoes from the open windows behind him and the halls behind her. There was a lot of noise everywhere these days; that was what made it so hard for her to concentrate. The first and second graders were going out for recess. Rae wasn't out there anymore. Or maybe she was; Lucy thought Rae could probably be anywhere, feeding, like mites, whether you could see her or not.

"I'm worried about you, Lucy," Mr. Michaelson said.

Surprise made her look at him. She caught herself and looked away again. "I'm fine."

"No, you're not 'fine.' Nobody would be 'fine' in the situation you're in."

Lucy made herself shrug. What she wanted was to bury her face against him. Maybe he knew how to take care of kids, since her parents didn't. In as smart-alecky a tone as she could muster, she said, "Oh, well."

"It's been a terrible year for you and your family, hasn't it?"

If she said anything, she'd start to cry, and then she'd never stop, she'd go crazy. She was going crazy anyway. Her whole family was crazy, or dead. Mom didn't have tears running down her face all the time, but Lucy knew she never stopped crying, and Dad wasn't the same anymore.

Three big beautiful trees had stood in front of Stacey's house for as long as either of them could remember, for years and years before either of them had been born. It used to make Lucy feel safe to think about how old those trees were, to lean against them and imagine how deep the roots went if it was true that there was as much of a tree underground as you could see above ground.

Then last spring two guys from Public Service came with a saw that sounded like a giant dentist's drill and cut down all those trees. They said the trees were diseased. They said they were dead inside.

Lucy and Stacey didn't believe that. The

trees had leaves and branches. Every year they turned green. Every year they seemed a little bigger. They couldn't be dead. But then they'd looked inside the stumps, which had been full of some disgusting brown pulp that must have been dead tree. So all those years, when she'd leaned against those trees and walked under them and felt safe because they were so old and tall and deep, all that time they'd been rotting inside, and dead, and they could have fallen on her at any time and crushed her. It was dumb to feel safe.

"My sister isn't dead," she heard herself saying.

Mr. Michaelson nodded. "Sometimes it's harder not to know."

"I kept saying my brother was dead even when I didn't know whether he was or not, and then he was. Dead."

Mr. Michaelson walked over to the board and started erasing it really hard, around and around in the same spot, even though he'd already erased everything he'd written on it about Mexico. Mites probably loved chalk dust.

She saw little bones twitch in the back of his hand as he rubbed and rubbed. She saw little crisscross threads in his blue shirt where sunshine fell across his shoulder. He stayed at the chalkboard for such a long time that she thought he was done talking to her and she was late for gym for no good reason.

He said, "When I was just about your age, my little brother was struck by lightning. He was watching me play soccer. It was a clear blue sky. Not a cloud."

Lucy held her breath. It was awesome that a teacher would be telling her something like this, that Mr. Michaelson had been her age once, that he'd lived through something awful, that his little brother had been struck by lightning longer ago than she'd been born. "Did he die?"

"Instantly."

"What was his name?"

Mr. Michaelson put the eraser back in the tray and slapped his hands together. Dust flew. "Brian."

"He was struck by *lightning*? And it wasn't even *raining*?"

"And for a long time I felt terribly guilty."

"Why? You didn't do anything."

He shrugged. "Oh, let's see. If I hadn't been playing soccer, he wouldn't have been where the lightning was going to hit at that moment. Or if I'd been nicer to him, he wouldn't have died. Or if I hadn't cheated on the spelling test that morning. I tried every way I could think of to believe it was my fault."

Lucy stared. "You *cheated*?"

"Looked at somebody else's paper."

"But that didn't have anything to do with *lightning*," she protested. "Did it?"

"Guilt is a natural part of grieving. If we don't really have any reason to feel guilty, we'll make one up."

"Did you get an *A*?"

His face got a little red. "The point is, Lucy, most people would rather believe they're bad people who caused something bad to happen than believe they're totally helpless, even when they are. The truth is, I was helpless to keep my brother from dying and you're helpless to stop what's happened to your brother and sister. Sometimes shit just happens."

He'd said "shit" to her. That was another present, like the story about his little brother Brian who'd been struck by lightning out of a clear blue sky. She didn't understand why he was giving her these presents. She didn't know what she was supposed to do with them. She wanted to take them away with her, think about them for a while, put them in her diary.

He didn't stop her as she ran out the door, and she was halfway to gym class before she realized she didn't have a late slip. He'd promised. Another adult you couldn't count on. By the time she got her tennis shoes on, she was rigid with indignation and ready for anything Ms. Holcomb might say. Ms. Holcomb didn't say anything, which was weird, and she didn't make her suit up.

But she did stop her after class, with a jerk of her head and a shout of her name over whistles and bouncing balls. Lucy was getting madder and madder. Now she'd be late for English. She used to like Ms. Holcomb. Now she didn't like anybody. She just wanted them all to leave her alone.

"How are you, Lucy?"

"Fine."

"You seem upset." Ms. Holcomb wasn't much taller than Lucy and wasn't much older than Ethan would be if Ethan hadn't died. She put a hand on Lucy's shoulder. Lucy had to force herself not to run out of the gym, out of the school, out of the world. The teacher didn't take her hand away. "Which is what I would expect you to feel right now."

Lucy didn't say anything, because she couldn't think of anything mean enough to make Ms. Holcomb leave her alone, and because she was afraid of what she might think of to say. All grown-ups could think about was death and being sad. All her friends could think about was boys and movie stars and who was whose best friend. Lucy didn't want to think about anything. Last night she'd filled a whole page of her diary with Os, big and little looped Os that got blacker and blacker till near the end of the page she'd torn the paper.

"They're going to start a group after school for kids who—who have things they need to talk about." Lucy hated it when grown-ups were so careful about how they said things. As if they thought she'd break, or explode. She might. "I recommended you."

"What do you mean? What kind of group? I don't have anything to talk about! I don't want to stay after school! That's not fair! I didn't do anything wrong! Just because I was late one time and I didn't suit up—"

Ms. Holcomb put her other hand on Lucy's other shoulder. "Calm down, Lucy. It's not a punishment. A social worker will be coming in once a week to help kids with problems, that's all. Mr. Li is going to ask your parents for permission. We all think it would be good for you. Give you somebody to talk to who understands."

"What social worker?"

"Nobody you know. He did an inservice for the teachers a couple of weeks ago about the transition from childhood to adolescence. He seemed real knowledgeable, and he seemed to really like kids. So when he approached Mr. Li about starting this group, we all thought it was a good idea."

Lucy looked frantically out the window for Rae. Instead, she saw her little brother Dominic climbing too high on the jungle gym.

"What social worker?" she demanded again. "What's his *name?*"

Ms. Holcomb looked at her funny and said, "Jerry. Jerry Johnston."

16

 "Halloween," Jerry told them, "is the celebration of angry spirits."

He looked around the circle lingeringly, as if he loved them all, and Lucy followed his gaze with her own. That was why she liked sitting next to Jerry: you looked where he looked, saw things the way he saw them, and sometimes you could feel his words in your mouth, his thoughts in your head.

Lucy hadn't been in the group long enough to recognize people under their masks. She didn't think Jerry could, either, so it must not matter. In group they hardly ever used each other's names. She remembered Stephanie, Mike, Billy, and she wondered if they remembered Lucy.

There was a witch with long silver nails and

eyes that glowed in the dark. There was a ghost, but you couldn't see through it. Stretching out through the circle was a slimy green snake. On the other side of Jerry was some kind of animal with big teeth. On the other side of Lucy was a spider.

"How angry are you?" Jerry was asking.

Nobody said anything. The snake wriggled and the witch clicked her nails against the floor.

"How angry is your spirit?" Somebody in the circle moaned a little, and the animal with the big teeth growled.

Lucy was supposed to be a zombie, but she didn't think anybody could tell. She'd made up her costume herself, and she didn't really know what zombies were supposed to look like. Black pants, a black shirt of Rae's, white makeup on her face and hands, fake blood on her teeth. She'd told Mom she was too old to dress up for Halloween.

"Halloween is also," Jerry said quietly, "a celebration of sorrow, and fear, and loneliness, and guilt. A celebration of troubled spirits."

The room behind the school cafeteria, where the group met, was decorated for Halloween. A black cutout skeleton danced from strings overhead. Spiderwebs hit you in the face when you came in the door. Black cats with yellow eyes perched in all the windows, ready to jump on you at any minute; even though it was dark outside, you could see their silhouettes. Patches was a black cat, but he had white on him, too; at Halloween, Lucy didn't know what that meant.

"Who's sad in this room? Is anybody sad?"

Nobody said anything, but the witch was crying.

"Who's afraid?"

"I am," said the fuzzy voice of the spider, right at Lucy's ear, and she jumped. One of its hairy spiderlike legs brushed against her cheek.

"I am, too," said the ghost, and then, Lucy guessed, couldn't stop saying it. "I am, too. I am, too. I am, too."

"Who's lonely?" Jerry asked softly, lovingly. "Who feels guilty?"

"I do," said the snake, writhing and coiling on the floor.

"I do, too," Lucy heard herself say.

Jerry was nodding and smiling just a little; she'd pleased him. He had a nice smile, beautiful eyes, pretty rings. He wasn't wearing a costume, Lucy noticed for the first time, even though he'd said this was a costume party. But he did look different.

He looked sick, she thought with sudden panic. Or hurt inside. Or about to be hurt if somebody didn't do something.

He was as big as ever—huge arms, huge

thighs, enormous shoulders and neck and belly. But he didn't feel solid. She leaned against him. There were flat places all over him, thin places, holes covered just by skin and cloth. She thought about caves, and mites, and hungry water under ice.

On the side of his head closest to her, just behind his ear, was a depression the size of her fist. She could touch it, put her fist there and fill it up. She started to lift her arm.

But she was afraid. It was like the soft spot on the top of a baby's head. She'd been afraid of the soft spots on the heads of all her little brothers and sisters, afraid she'd accidentally or on purpose stick her fingers through and touch their brains, handle their thoughts. She'd had a spot like that, her brain open to the world. So had Ethan and Rae. So had Mom and Dad.

She thought about Ethan, not moving when he seemed to be moving, alive when he seemed to be dead. At first she didn't want to think about him, but she couldn't help it. Then she kept thinking about him because, for some reason, it made her feel a little better, a little stronger, not quite so confused. Halloween was a time to remind yourself that things were never only what they seemed.

All over Jerry's head and shoulders and neck were sunken places, as if something had collapsed, as if something inside him had bro-

ken or shrunk. His stomach, which usually
stuck way out in front of him and made him
sit and walk leaning a little backward, now
actually curved inward, and he hunched over
it as if it hurt.

He took her hand.

Lucy's blood pounded in her ears and
throat, but it didn't seem to be her blood.
Maybe, she thought confusedly, she really was
a zombie.

Then she saw that Jerry was also holding
hands with the kid on the other side of him,
the one dressed up like an animal with big
teeth. Jealousy made Lucy try again to see
who that was, but the animal suit covered the
whole head and neck, and the hand Jerry held
was a paw.

"Celebrate what you feel," Jerry said.

His voice cracked, and he seemed to be having trouble breathing. Lucy squeezed his
hand, and he squeezed back.

"Feel it as much as you can. As deeply as
you can. Don't run away from it. Run *into* it."

He moved her hand to the inside of his
knee. He arranged her hand palm downward
and covered it with his. She felt the indenta-
tion in the massive flesh that he wanted her
hand to fill, but the hole was bigger than her
hand.

"Feel as furious as you can. Feel sadness everywhere. Feel loneliness in every part of your

body, every part of your being. Feel guilty about everything. The world is full of things to make you feel that way. You're right to feel that way. Feel the unfairness of it. Celebrate it."

"It hurts," somebody moaned.

"It only hurts until you work it through," Jerry told them. Lucy didn't know what "work it through" meant.

"You make it worse!" somebody accused him.

"I only ask you to get in touch with what's already there. If you don't acknowledge it and face it, it will eat you alive, and you'll be no use to anybody." Jerry chuckled. Lucy didn't see what was so funny.

"I can't stand it! It hurts too much!"

"Use it," Jerry urged. "Give it away."

Lucy saw that everybody else around the circle was holding hands, and the spider took hers. It was a human hand—a girl's, long sharp nails and soft skin—coming out of a spider's leg. Lucy shuddered but held on tight enough that her fingers started to tingle.

"Pass it around the circle," Jerry murmured. "Take the black energy from your neighbor and add yours to it and pass it on."

Lucy's nose itched. The floor was hard. She had to go to the bathroom. She was feeling a little silly. This was stupid, a bunch of people in dumb Halloween costumes sitting in a circle holding hands and trying to feel as bad as they could.

Across the circle somebody sneezed. The snake took off its mask, and Lucy recognized it as a girl named Debra. Somebody else laughed and said, "This is *dumb*," and got up and left the room. Lucy let out her breath.

The tension in the room erupted into noise and chatter. The ghost went over and turned the stereo on; you could see jeans under the sheet. The spider started to dance a funny dance, all eight legs keeping time.

Lucy looked at Jerry. He had fallen back against the wall, as if he couldn't support his own enormous weight anymore. He was sweating and his face was pale; his cheeks were so sunken that they looked like broken bone.

She wanted to ask him if he was all right. She wanted to make him feel better. Instead, she scrambled to her feet and went to get a jack-o'-lantern cookie from the table in the corner.

17

It was the second week of November, and it hadn't snowed yet. Another two days and the record would be broken; TV weather forecasters spoke as though that would be their own personal triumph, and tension gathered like unshed snowflakes in the bright blue sky.

On Wednesday Lucy came home late from school because of the group; it was already getting dark, and lights were on in the house. Mom had all the other kids' pictures spread out on the dining-room table. Hers, Ethan's, and Rae's were missing. Lucy thought about saying she'd forgotten hers at school or lost them somewhere, but she pulled them out of her bag and handed them to her mother.

"Oh, Lucy, you look beautiful."

"I look *terrible*. Look at my teeth! I'm smiling too much."

Mom smoothed Lucy's big picture with her hand, kissed it, laid it down with the others in the space she'd been holding for it. Then she picked up one of the others—Dom's, Lucy saw—and did the same. Lucy watched her closely, to see how this was done. Mom wasn't crying.

Lucy could hardly stand to look at any of the pictures, especially her own. There was something weird about people being caught forever in one position, one shirt, one smile. As if they really were like that. As if they'd never die or disappear or grow up.

It wasn't the teeth that bothered her so much. It was the breasts. She'd tried to hunch over so they wouldn't show, but the photographer had kept hassling her to sit up straight, she was such a pretty girl she should sit up straight and show it off, and finally just to shut him up she had, and now forever everybody would be looking at her breasts, even under the baggy sweatshirt she'd been sure to wear for picture day.

"You look so beautiful," Mom said again. "So grown up."

For the first time, it occurred to Lucy that with Rae and Ethan gone, she was the oldest child. "Where is everybody?" she demanded.

"Pris is upstairs working on her homework.

Dominic is at a friend's house until six. Molly and Cory are outside. I just checked on them."

Mom still knew where everybody was. Lucy was surprised by that, both comforted and offended. *Where are Rae and Ethan, if you know so much? Where am I?* It wouldn't do any good or even make any sense to ask those things, so instead she asked, "How's Dad?"

Mom was holding Molly's preschool picture. Worriedly she glanced up at Lucy. "He's been sleeping off and on all day, so be quiet when you go upstairs."

"What's wrong with him?"

"Oh, nothing serious, honey." It hadn't crossed Lucy's mind that Dad might really be sick. Now that Mom said that, she was worried. "He just didn't sleep very well last night, that's all, and he woke up with another bad headache this morning, so I called him in sick again."

"Is that okay? To call in sick?"

"He gets ten sick days a year."

"He's stayed home four or five times just since—just in the last couple of months."

Mom looked at her over Priscilla's picture, which she was holding against her chest. Lucy suddenly found herself wondering what Pris would look like and act like when she was a teenager. "He's having a really hard time, honey."

"Are you having a really hard time, too?"

"Sometimes. Some days are worse than others. I'm going to be all right. I used to think I couldn't stand it if I lost one of you kids or Dad. I used to put a lot of time and energy into doing things so I wouldn't lose anybody I loved ever. But now I have lost one child and maybe another one, and in some ways it's even worse than I thought it would be. But I'm going to be all right. I don't understand it, but I'm going to be all right." She shook her head a little. "I think now that I could stand it if I lost everybody."

"Everybody?" Lucy breathed.

"I don't understand it, but yes. Everybody."

"You wouldn't care if I died?"

"Oh, Lucy, of course I'd care. I've been amazed both by how terrible the pain is and by how much a person can stand. It would break my heart to lose you, just like it's broken my heart to lose Ethan and Rae. But it wouldn't destroy me. I always thought it would, but it wouldn't."

Lucy wasn't sure she liked this. If you really loved somebody, you never got over losing them. Especially parents never got over losing their children. It was how you knew they were parents, how you knew they'd really loved their kids. "Is Dad going to be all right?" Her neck and shoulders hurt from holding herself so still.

Mom hesitated just a split second before she

answered. "Of course. We have to help him through it. We all have to help each other through it. That's what families are for."

"I thought families were to keep you safe."

"There are some things families can protect you from." Very gently, Mom laid Priscilla's picture back with the others on the table. "Some things nobody can protect you from."

"I don't like that."

"I don't either."

Mother and daughter gazed at each other for a long moment across the table littered with photographs. Lucy felt something pass from her mother to her, some cold wisdom that hurt, but that made her feel filled up. She blew her cheeks out with all the pent-up breath and said, "I'll take Dad a cup of tea."

"That would be nice, honey. But don't wake him if he's asleep."

Lucy started for the kitchen, then asked, "Any news?"

She didn't know why she kept asking that. As always, Mom shook her head. "I called the police again this morning. Nothing. The first person I talked to wasn't even familiar with the case, didn't even recognize our name."

Has she been to see Dad? Is that why he can't sleep and why he stays home from work? Is Rae here now?

"How was group today?" Mom was gathering all the pictures together and putting them into one envelope. Soon they would all appear in frames in the living-room shelves.

"Fine," Lucy said automatically. Sometimes that satisfied them when they asked, and then she was sure they weren't really interested. Sometimes they kept on asking her stuff and that made her mad. One week they hadn't asked at all. That was the week Jerry had talked about how parents couldn't really understand you because they were parents and she'd seen that he was right.

"Well, what'd you talk about?"

"Nothing much."

They'd talked about anger. They always talked about anger. "Anger is the most powerful force in the universe," Jerry'd told them, and Lucy could tell from the way he'd said it, from the look in his eyes and the set of his huge body at the head of their circle, that he knew what he was talking about. "And it's nothing to be afraid of. Anger is the form of energy most accessible to us, most usable. It's a high-energy food. One of the things you'll learn in this group is how to use your anger in nourishing ways."

"Mom?" Pris came tromping downstairs with her science book. She didn't use crutches anymore, and she didn't even limp. If you hadn't known she'd broken something inside her body, you couldn't tell. "What's the difference between an earthquake and a volcano?"

"Ask Lucy. I bet she knows."

It was an old trick. Get one kid to teach another kid something, and they both learned. But even though Lucy could see through it, she still liked being smarter than Pris, so she explained. "A volcano is when all this melted rock comes out of a hole in the ground. Lava. An earthquake is when pieces of the ground move." She looked at Mom. Mom nodded.

Priscilla frowned. "You mean pieces of the ground *move*? And rocks *melt*?"

"Someday California is going to fall off into the ocean," Lucy told her smugly. "There's this big giant crack in the ground and there are earthquakes all the time and someday it's just going to break off and sink."

"What about all the buildings?" Priscilla's eyes were wide. "And the people? And the cats?"

"They'll die," Lucy said flatly.

"Oh, you lie."

"And you know what else? Once upon a time there was this city called Pompeii, and it was right by a volcano and all the people knew but they lived there anyway because they did all the things the gods told them to do and so nothing bad could happen to them. And then one day the volcano blew up—"

"Erupted," Mom said.

"Erupted, and the whole city got covered

with lava, and people and houses and cars and everything got buried alive."

"Lucy," Mom said, laughing a little, "there were no cars then."

"You mean, they died? Everybody in the city just died?"

"They were all just stuck in it, and years and years later scientists found them. Like, whole families would still be sitting at the dinner table or something. There was this one little boy and his dog. Or they'd be looking at school pictures and doing homework."

"Lucy, come on," Mom objected. "Don't tell her stuff like that. There were no cameras then, either."

"You *lie*," Priscilla said again.

Lucy looked to their mother for confirmation, and Mom said gently, "No, Pris, she's right. Not about cars and cameras, but she's right about the volcano in Pompeii and the fault and the earthquakes in California."

"Yuck," said Pris.

"It's weird to think of the world not being solid, isn't it?"

Lucy had known about volcanoes and earthquakes, but she hadn't realized they meant the world wasn't solid. Thinking about that made her skin crawl. She went into the kitchen to make Dad's tea.

She'd never made him tea before, so she didn't know what he liked in it, or what kind.

She picked orange spice because it smelled sort of good in the little packets, and she stirred in a spoonful of sugar and a lot of milk.

Dad was asleep. At first, Lucy was disappointed. But she stood outside the bedroom door and listened to him snoring, and was comforted by the pleasant, even sound. She wondered about his dreams. She wondered about her own dreams. She'd been afraid she'd have really bad dreams after Ethan had died and then after Rae had disappeared, but so far she hadn't. She thought maybe dreams lived inside you all the time, like mites, and fed off stuff you'd have thrown away if you'd known it was there.

Something smelled funny. Lucy looked around but didn't see any cat poop. It was coming from Mom and Dad's room. Not a real strong smell, but kind of sickening, like something half-dead or really really dirty.

Lucy eased the bedroom door open. Hot tea sloshed onto the back of her hand, but she didn't jerk or make any noise. Dad gave a little gasp as if he'd just dreamed something that hurt him, then said something that didn't seem to be in words. Lucy stood still and held her breath, afraid she'd awakened him, hoping she had. She'd never watched her father sleep before.

Dad rolled over, pulled up the sheet, started

snoring again. Lucy let out her breath. She didn't see anything in the room that would make that smell. Maybe Dad had on dirty socks. She wrinkled her nose.

She took the tea into her room. It smelled bad in here too, so maybe it was coming from outside. Her math homework was spread out on the floor and she sat down among the papers. Pre-algebra, spotted now with tea stains. She didn't understand any of it and didn't know why she should. The idea of letters standing for numbers made her nervous; why couldn't they just mean what they seemed to mean? She went through the first couple of problems and wrote down letters and numbers, but she didn't know whether they stood for each other or not, whether underneath the surface they had anything to do with each other. Then she folded up all the papers and stuck them inside the book and put the book on her dresser. School was dumb. She hated school. If it wasn't for the chance to see Jerry, she wouldn't go to school at all. She could count on seeing him every Wednesday after school in group, and lately he'd been showing up a couple of times during the week, waiting for her after class or to walk her partway home.

She opened her diary and, blushing, read what she'd written last night.

He's so cute. He's not really fat, he's just big. He's got big brown eyes and his skin is pink and soft. I know it's soft. I haven't really touched him yet, but someday I will. He still thinks I'm a little kid but someday he'll look at me and he'll see that I'm not. Sometimes I worry about him. He looks sick. He acts like he's really tired and doesn't feel good. But after the group his cheeks get all rosy and his eyes sparkle. I think he likes us. I think we make him happy. I want to make him happy.

She turned the page.

The whole two pages open before her were covered by two words written in huge, fat, very faint letters, so that she had to turn the diary at just the right angle to the light to be able to read them.

BE CAREFUL

And at the bottom, smaller and fainter and shaky:

LOVE, YOUR SISTER, RAE.

18

 "Hi."

"Hi, Lucy."

He recognized her voice. He didn't sound surprised that she'd called. He seemed glad to hear from her, as if her being alive was more important than other people being dead. "What're you doing?"

"Oh, thinking about you."

He didn't laugh to show he hadn't meant it. Her throat tightened.

"And about everybody else in the group," he said. "Wondering how everybody's Christmas is going."

She fingered the heart locket Pris had given her; she could tell that it was really pretty, but she didn't like it much. She wriggled her toes inside the fuzzy red slippers from Mom and

Dad; they were exactly what she'd asked for, even pointed out in K-Mart, but somehow they weren't what she'd wanted, and Mom and Dad should have known what she wanted. "It's okay," she said.

"Christmas can be pretty depressing."

She nodded. They'd talked about this in group, but she wanted to hear him say it all again, just to her. She wanted to hear anything he had to say; the sound of his voice pulled something out of her that hurt.

"Because we're expected to be loving and happy and at peace, and because a lot of us don't really feel that way, Christmas can make us feel even more sad or angry or just plain pissed off."

"I hate Christmas," Lucy whispered.

"What did you say? I couldn't hear you."

"I hate Christmas," she said aloud, as loud as she dared with people right downstairs.

"Good," he said. "Good for you, Lucy."

She was talking on the phone in the upstairs hall, her face to the wall and her free hand cupped over the receiver. They wouldn't give her a phone in her room, because they were afraid it would make her even more isolated from the rest of the family. They were right. It would. A phone in her room had been at the top of her Christmas list.

Downstairs, the little kids were yelling and squealing over their new toys. It scared her and made her mad that they could get so happy about such dumb things. A month from now they'd find something else to make them happy. Why bother liking anything when it was just going to get broken or die or disappear?

But she liked stuff, too, and that made her even madder. She *liked* the noise of the little kids playing. She liked the fudge Mom had made this year like every other. She liked Christmas.

Last night, late, she'd found Mom sitting alone in the living room with just the Christmas-tree lights on and Christmas music playing on the stereo so quietly you could hardly hear it. Lucy had stood silently in the doorway for a long time, thinking how beautiful her mother looked, even with the white streak like glitter in her hair. How sad she looked. How fragile, like the glass angel hung on the tree with gold thread that you could see through her body and her wings. Lucy had been afraid to go in, afraid she'd spoil something or make something break.

Then Mom had looked up and seen her and held out her hand to her. Lucy had gone to her, snuggled beside her. Mom was warm, as she'd always been, and she'd held Lucy lightly, so they could both look at the lights and the snowless night outside the windows, both listen to the music. Lucy wished it would snow.

"Life is so *full* of things," Mom had finally whispered. "So *abundant*." Lucy didn't exactly know what that meant, but it was a word people used a lot at Thanksgiving, and, warily, she liked the sound of it.

She'd sort of fallen asleep there, and had wakened gently when Mom had told her it was time to go to bed so Santa could come. She'd walked up the stairs holding her mother's hand, and still feeling absolutely alone, but filled with wonder that she and her mother were in the same place at the same time, and touching.

"I hate Christmas," she said again, to bring herself back.

"A lot of people hate Christmas," Jerry assured her. "There's a lot to hate."

"What about you?" It seemed awfully bold to be asking this. Nosy. She plunged ahead. "Do you hate Christmas?"

"Yes."

A terrible thought struck her. "You were with somebody today, right? Your family or somebody?"

"I don't have a family."

"You have an Aunt Alice," Lucy said suddenly. "She lives in our neighborhood."

There was a pause, and when Jerry answered, she could hear the smile in his voice. "I don't have an Aunt Alice. I thought you knew that, Lucy."

Lucy blushed at her own stupidity. He'd sent her a secret message, and she'd missed it. "I'm sorry," she said.

"I don't have any family. You kids are my family."

Neither of them said anything more for a while. The smells of turkey and ham that had filled the house all morning got stronger, as if somebody had opened the oven door. Suddenly frantic that Jerry had faded away, that it had been dumb in the first place to believe she could actually talk to him on something like a telephone, Lucy asked him, "So are you all alone for Christmas?"

"Not exactly. But I am—lonely."

"That's awful."

"Yes, it is pretty awful. I hate Christmas, too."

"Come over here."

"I don't think that's a good idea, Lucy. I don't think your parents would like it."

"It's my house, too," Lucy protested.

"I'm really not feeling very well."

"I could come visit you."

"That would be nice." She could tell by the change in his voice that she'd said the right thing.

"I could bring you some turkey and stuff."

"I'd like that. I'm really hungry. I can't seem to get filled up." He chuckled.

"But I don't know where you live."

"How about if I meet you and bring you here? At that little park by your house, the one with the slides?"

"I thought you were sick," Lucy said, at the same time that Dominic yelled up the stairs, "Lucy! Dinner!"

"At about four o'clock?" Jerry insisted.

He'd been expecting her to call, she knew. And, somehow, the idea of meeting him and taking him some Christmas dinner had been his all along, not hers. "Okay," she whispered quickly, and hung up.

Christmas dinner was the same as it had always been. That bothered Lucy. If she died, if she disappeared, wouldn't anybody care any more than this? Would they still put on red napkins and the tablecloth with the holly on it?

At the same time, Christmas dinner was totally different and never would be the same again. It wasn't fair that things you loved could change. It wasn't fair that good things didn't last.

She didn't know which to believe, the differentness or the sameness. She didn't know whether it was the inside that had changed and the outside that was the same, or the other way around. Her stomach hurt when she tried to imagine what Christmas would be like next year and for the rest of her life, who might go away, how she herself might change inside and out.

Mom always fixed both turkey and ham, wheat and white rolls, apple pie and pumpkin pie, because different people in the family liked different things. Lucy hated ham. She wondered who knew that. She'd never even noticed what Rae and Ethan liked. Maybe if she'd noticed stuff like that, they'd still be here. Last year Rae had thrown a fit over the whole-wheat rolls—they were like rocks, they stuck in your throat—even though there were white ones, too.

Today she would watch what everybody ate, and right after dinner she'd run upstairs and put it down in her diary, and next year she'd compare it with what they ate then. But she got confused. While she was paying attention to Dominic's plate, Cory and Molly finished and left the table to go play with their new toys some more. And Dad didn't eat much of anything. Mom kept looking at him worriedly, and once, while he was in the bathroom, she sneaked a spoonful of peas onto his plate, but he didn't eat them.

Dom was taking a long time over his second piece of pie. He'd had one of each kind. Mom and Priscilla were talking about whether the pink and purple socks Grandma had sent her from Texas would go with the flowered pants Santa had brought her, when Dominic put his fork down, looked around at everybody and nobody in particular, and announced at the top of his lungs, "I miss my sister!"

Why not Ethan? Why not your brother, too? Lucy was awash in a furious sense of injustice and danger, even though Dom had been really little the last time Ethan had been home for Christmas. She herself could hardly remember what that had been like, and her own forgetfulness was unfair and dangerous, too. *You better remember everything. You better miss them all.*

"I know, sweetheart," Mom was saying to Dominic. "We all miss her."

Pris declared, "I don't."

"Oh, Priscilla, you don't mean that."

"She was mean and grouchy and she never let me borrow her Garfield shirt and it's *Christmas* and I'm not gonna miss *anybody*!"

"It's bad not to miss people," Dominic said solemnly.

"Missing people hurts," Pris argued. "It spoils things."

"If you don't miss them, they go away again." Lucy hadn't known he thought such things. She stared at him, then looked away. His baby face looked the same as ever, but now she couldn't trust that. Stuff went on inside his head that she didn't know about.

Pris was out of her chair and halfway around the table toward Dominic before Dad caught her. "You stupid baby! You had to spoil everything!"

"Shhh." Dad held her and patted her hair. Pris struggled to get loose, feet and fists and braids flying, and Lucy was relieved to see that Dad was still stronger. "Dom didn't do anything wrong. It's okay to miss the people we love who aren't here."

Pris gave up and collapsed against her father's chest. *"I hate them!* They ruined my life! They ruined Christmas!"

Dad should have said something back to her, but he didn't. He was staring off over her head as if somebody else had caught his attention. For a minute Lucy was afraid to look. Then when she did follow his gaze, there was nobody in the window. There was no snow, either, and the sun was shining.

Finally Mom said, "Christmas is *different.* Our lives are *different.* It's up to us whether they're ruined or not. We can learn to love the life we have now, instead of hating it because it's not the one we had or the one we wanted."

Lucy couldn't stand it anymore. "Mom," she interrupted, "can I take a plate of turkey and stuff over to Stacey?"

Mom kept looking at Dad and Priscilla and Dominic, and Lucy didn't think she'd heard her. She was just about to say it again when Mom got to her feet—slowly, holding on to the edge of the table as if she was very tired—and started clearing the table. "To Stacey? Why? Didn't she have Christmas dinner?"

The truth was, Stacey was having two Christmas dinners, one at her mother's and one at her father's. Twice as many presents, too, and her dad was taking her on a ski trip tomorrow. "Her mom said there's no point in making a big dinner when there's just the two of them," Lucy lied.

"That's too bad. That's a big mistake, I think."

"Well, you know, she's real upset about the divorce. She says it ruined her life." That part was true. Stacey's mother said that a lot, and Stacey told Lucy, and neither of them ever knew what to say next.

"Of course you may take her a plate," Mom said. "There's plenty." And once again, with a crash, the conversation had come round to Ethan and Rae: because they weren't here, Mom had cooked too much, and for the rest of the week, whenever they had leftovers, they'd have to be reminded of what they'd lost.

Lucy carried her dishes into the kitchen and put them on the counter. The clock on the microwave said 3:17. Was Jerry getting ready to meet her now? Getting his house ready? What would he have to do to get ready for her?

Realization struck her of what she was about to do. Sneak out of the house on Christmas Day. Lie to her parents. Go somewhere she'd never been where nobody would know where she was. She didn't understand why, but she couldn't tell Mom and Dad the truth. All of a sudden she was scared. What would happen if she didn't go? Would he stop liking her? Would he track her down?

She calmed down a little by reminding herself that this was Jerry Johnston. She knew Jerry. Ethan and Rae had known Jerry. All she was doing was taking him food and wishing him Merry Christmas. She wasn't running away with him or anything.

Patches was rubbing around her ankles, holding his tail straight up in the air and talking. Ever since Rae had told her that cats only meowed to communicate with humans, not with each other or other animals, it had bothered Lucy that she couldn't always understand what Patches was saying in the language he'd made up just for her. She could guess what he wanted now, but he couldn't have turkey bones because his teeth might break them and then the sharp pieces might stick in his throat and kill him.

She started picking meat off the bones for him, and got so fascinated by how the meat and bones and skin all fit together and came apart that she jumped when Mom came in and said her name. "Lucy, I want you to know how proud I am that you're thinking about somebody else."

Lucy ducked her head guiltily.

"Shall I help you fix a plate?"

"That's okay."

Lucy could hear in her voice that she was frowning a little. "Does that mean yes or no?"

"You broke it!" Molly yelled behind the closed door of the family room, and Dominic yelled back, "I did not!" and there was the noise of pushing and hitting. Mom hurried to investigate, and Lucy was left to fix the plate by herself. That was what she'd wanted, but now she felt abandoned. Somebody was always coming between her and her mother.

Turkey, dressing, ham, potatoes, gravy. She arranged the plate as everybody brought the serving dishes in from the table. Dom and Molly were still mad at each other; Mom told them two or three times to cut it out, settle down, and swatted Molly's bottom when she stuck her foot out in front of Dominic while he was carrying the gravy in Grandma's gravy boat. "It's *Christmas*!" Molly wailed. "You're s'posed to be nice to me on *Christmas*!" and Mom said, "Even on Christmas you're expected to treat each other decently."

On a second plate, corn and peas and cranberry sauce and both kinds of rolls and butter. She needed another plate for two pieces of pie and three pieces of fudge. Jerry had said he was hungry, and she'd seen how much he could eat. She covered each plate with foil and stacked them with the pie on top.

"Do you need help carrying those?" Mom was rinsing the dishes for the dishwasher. Dad always helped, but he wasn't here now. "I was just going to call Pris to help me here, but I could spare her for a few minutes if you want her to walk over to Stacey's with you."

"That's okay," Lucy said, and then quickly added, "No. I'll go myself."

All of a sudden Mom was crying. She kept on rinsing and stacking and putting leftovers into smaller containers and finding places for them in the refrigerator, but she was crying. Lucy knew it was because of Rae and Ethan, and because she herself was about to do something bad. She didn't know what to do. She didn't want to get any closer to her mother's pain than she had to.

It was 3:46. "I'm going now," she said. "To Stacey's," and left the room balancing the stack of plates under her chin.

"What time will you be home?" Mom's voice was shaky, but she'd been asking that question ever since Lucy got too old to be told what time to come home.

"I don't know."

"Well, you aren't going anywhere unless I know when you'll be home."

"Eight o'clock."

"Eight o'clock!" Mom glanced at the clock.

"Lucy, that's over four hours. And it's after dark."

Lucy stayed stubbornly quiet, head bent over the plates. The bottom plate warmed her hands.

"Be home in an hour," Mom told her.

"Oh, Mom!"

"One hour. Five o'clock. It's Christmas. You're supposed to spend Christmas with your family."

"I don't have a family anymore." She hurried out of the kitchen and Mom didn't come after her, proving that Lucy was right.

She was on her way out the door with the food when she thought of something. She set the plates down on the bottom step, yelled at Patches to stay away, and ran up to her room.

At first she couldn't find her diary, and she was sure Priscilla had stolen it. Pris would just love to read all her secret thoughts and then tell everybody.

But there it was, bunched up in her bedspread at the foot of her bed. Had it been moved? She thought so, but she couldn't tell for sure. Gingerly she picked it up, imagining her own fingerprints on top of somebody else's. It was weird to think that there was stuff on your fingers that you couldn't see or feel or taste, but that left a part of you on everything you touched. She stuck her fingers in her mouth. She wondered if Rae would still leave fingerprints. Or Ethan.

She turned the diary upside down and flipped through it backward. There were still a lot of blank pages. She went through them till she got to the last thing she'd written, right after Rae's last message. There were no more messages.

Lucy went back downstairs, slid the diary under the plates, and carried the whole stack outside. Nobody noticed.

It was cold out. The sky was bright blue, like metal, the color of Mr. Li's new car. The ground was khaki-colored and spongy under her feet. It was starting to snow.

Walking down her street toward the park, counting pale Christmas trees in sunny windows, knowing that nobody in any of these houses was going to meet Jerry Johnston or had lost a brother and a sister and maybe a father so far or was sad on Christmas, Lucy wished hard that it would snow. Wished for a blizzard, when the shapes of things changed and you couldn't see where you were going and angels you made in the snow filled in almost before you could stand up. Maybe then this awful feeling that something was going to happen would go away. Of course, it really didn't matter what she wished, but it was snowing harder.

If the park had a name, she didn't know it. It

took up one block, and there was a hill in the middle of it so you couldn't see from one side to the other. It had swings and a spiral slide and two picnic tables. A row of little trees climbed the hill, tied to sticks with thin white rope; the trees had always been here, and Lucy didn't think they'd ever been any smaller than they were right now. The white rope was hard to see against the snow.

But one of them had fallen over against the sharp sky. Stick figures in a row, one after another like always, and then one broken, the bottom half still sticking straight up and maybe even still growing, the top half dragging the stupid rope that hadn't kept it safe after all.

She followed the sidewalk to the top of the hill. The cold air hurt in her lungs. It was hard to believe that air really went into your lungs and then came out again, and that while it was in there you took something out of it. It was hard to believe you really had lungs, with all those little hairs and pockets. But the air was cold in there and hurt, and her hands were so cold she could feel their bones, and it was gross but the little hairs inside her nose were cold. From the top of the hill she could see the whole park, and she was the only person in it.

She stood up there a long time. The wind had secret snow in it, snow you couldn't see but you could feel along with all the snow you could both see and feel. She was shivering and her eyes were watering. She wished she could just go home and everything would be the way it used to be. She wished Jerry would show up. Maybe he wasn't going to come. She wished Ethan would show up, or Rae, and tell her what to do.

A sidewalk went catty-corner across the park. The pine trees and bushes along it looked like a Mohawk. The sidewalk took you to the corner of Pruitt Middle School, where she'd go next year.

She didn't believe that. She didn't believe she'd ever be anywhere but on this cold hill in this stupid park, waiting. Waiting for Jerry, for Ethan, for Rae. She herself next in line and then her little sister Priscilla.

In the corner of the park toward the school was a swing set and slide. She'd played there lots of times, and so had her little brothers and sisters. She couldn't remember if Ethan and Rae ever had, and Pris was already starting to say she was too old for stuff like that. From up here the swing set and slide looked like a giant bug, the way a mite would look if you could see a mite, or a germ.

Right at this very second, thousands and thousands of her cells were coming off. If anybody noticed anything, those cells would just look like snow. Nobody would guess they'd once been part of Lucy Ann Brill.

The snow in the park and on the streets was starting to look blue because the sun was going down. Lucy was cold and lonely. There were blue-gray streaks in the snow. Footprints, she thought, and then worried about who might have been here, who might still be here that she didn't see.

Suddenly she realized that the streaks made letters. An *E*, with the middle arm crooked and longer than the other two. An *R* with a too-long tail. Way off to the left, toward the school and the swing set that looked like a bug, a *D* was sliding off into the street.

The letters made a word. The word was a message for her.

She was shivering so hard that her legs wouldn't hold her, and she had to sit down in the snow. But when she did that, she was wet and colder, and the message just looked like streaks again because she couldn't see how it all fit together.

She pushed herself up onto her knees. There were sharp, invisible pieces of ice in the wind now, and every time one of them hit her she lost more cells. Slowly, she turned her head from left to right in order to read the message. It was already getting fuzzy and hard to read, filling in with more ice and snow till pretty soon it wouldn't be there at all.

DANGER

Rae was here, or had been not long ago. Rae was trying to warn her about something, but Lucy didn't know what. What was the use of somebody getting you all upset about some dumb message if you didn't have any idea what they were talking about? Rae was just being mean.

She squatted, and the top plate almost slid off. When she caught it, she was sure she squished the pie. She peered at the broken tree. It was the same dead gray color inside as out.

It was windy on top of the hill. She put her plates in a row on one of the picnic tables, one, two, three, lined them up with the edge of the plank. She laid her hand on the foil that covered the one with the pie on it, trying to tell if the pie was squished, but she didn't look inside. She couldn't take the food home. If Jerry didn't show up, she'd just leave it here for the birds or the poor people. She hoped Stacey didn't call while she was gone. She wondered what time it was, how much of an hour had passed.

She went and sat on a swing and pushed off. The chains were so cold that she had to keep moving her hands up and down. One winter when she was little she'd put her tongue on the iron fence and a piece of skin had torn off. Until then she'd never thought of tongues having skin. She'd checked a lot of times to see if her skin and blood were still on the fence somewhere, but she'd never found anything and her tongue had healed, so sometimes she wondered if that really had happened.

She pumped and pumped. The chains were stiff and made loud creaking noises. When she was as high as she could get, she jumped. It seemed to take a long time before she hit the ground. The air hurt as she passed through it. The ground hurt, even though it wasn't hard.

Lucy lay down flat on the ground, even though it had hurt her. She spread her arms and legs and tried to feel the curve of the earth, tried to feel it spinning, tried to feel the hot lava that they said was deep down under her wherever she walked or sat or lay. Snow didn't cover the whole ground yet. Yellow-brown blades of grass that weren't growing anymore crisscrossed under her nose. She didn't understand growing, what happened inside. Or not growing.

She was grabbed.

"Rae!" she cried, not knowing why.

Somebody had grabbed her by the waist and was pulling her up, so that now she was on her knees. There was an awful smell, like really bad halitosis, and panting close to her ear like somebody who couldn't catch their breath to say what they wanted to say. Lucy threw her fists back and twisted around to look. Nobody was there.

She sank back on her heels, then stood up shakily and looked around. In front of her was the lake, but you couldn't tell it was there if you didn't already know; all you saw was trees. On her left were houses with Christmas lights on their porches that faded out against the sky.

Jerry was coming from her right. He was hurrying, bobbing up and down like a big balloon. He was wearing a red jacket. He was stumbling.

Lucy turned. Behind her, running down the hill toward home was Rae. Wearing Lucy's pink sweater that she hadn't even missed, and no coat. Rae was panting and her hands were in fists, as if she were running hard. But Lucy saw that really she was barely moving at all.

Lucy tried to run after her. But she took only a couple of steps before she slipped on the snowy grass and fell. She slid partway down the other side of the hill, away from Rae and toward Jerry, and she couldn't think how to get up again.

Jerry was beside her. When he knelt, he lost his balance and almost fell on top of her. He braced himself on his hands and around her. "Lucy. It's okay. I'm here."

"Rae." Lucy couldn't catch her breath.

Jerry stiffened a little, brought his arms and legs closer around her like the four corners of a cage. "What about Rae?"

"I—saw her," Lucy gasped.

"Oh, darling, I don't think so. I know how much you wish you'd see her, but the truth is she's not here."

She couldn't say any more. Her breath was being pulled out of her. She wriggled forward just enough to get herself out from under him, then scrambled to her feet and ran away down the hill, the top part of her body way ahead of her feet so that she almost fell again.

"Lucy! Come back here!"

"I brought you your food!" she shouted back to him, and kept running.

It was getting dark, the light was weird and everything looked a little different, but she knew her way home. Jerry didn't follow her. She didn't think he was strong enough. She was a little afraid of what would happen once he'd eaten her food, but right now she had to catch up with Rae, had to get both of them home. As she ran across King Street the street-light came on right over her head.

Rae and Dad were on the side steps together. Lucy looked twice, and they really were there. The yard light had come on, making them both a sick pink. The snow was pink, too. She could see Dad right through Rae, all wrinkled and funny-shaped, as if her sister were made of wax and melting, or lava hardening into rock you could sort of see through (*translucent,* she remembered) trapping Dad inside forever, making him into a fossil.

Rae's arms were around Dad's neck. He was bent over her. Lucy thought: *Everything's going to be all right.* Then: *She's too old for him to hold her like that.* Then: *I wish it was me.*

Then she realized that Dad and Rae weren't hugging. Rae was attacking him. He was trying to protect himself from her. Her fists were swinging. Her nails glittered like little red knife blades. Her arms were around his neck not because she loved him but because she hated him. She wasn't kissing him; she was biting and sucking. She was trying to hurt him.

Rae's legs went up around Dad's waist like a little kid's. Dad staggered and cried out.

"Rae!" Lucy yelled, and ran toward them, as if to warn them, to stop something from happening. But when she got there, Rae was gone, and it was only Dad, shivering, waiting for her at the top of the steps.

He put his arm around her and they went into the house together. Lucy didn't know what she'd say if he started asking questions about Stacey; Dad could be a real detective when he thought you were trying to get away with something.

But he didn't say anything.

He didn't tighten his arm around her in a hug. He didn't kiss the top of her head or wish her Merry Christmas. When they got inside, he just stopped and she just kept on walking, so that they moved apart without either of them really meaning to.

Lucy went upstairs. From Pris and Molly's room came the little beeping of Pris's new Donkey Kong Junior game. From Mom and Dad's room came jazz, the tape Dad had given Mom for Christmas; Lucy paused to listen. She didn't like old people's music, but it was the first time her mother had listened to music since Ethan had died.

Her diary was on her bed. She didn't think she'd left it there. *Rae,* she thought giddily. Rae had left her a Christmas message.

She flipped to the last stuff she'd written, suddenly afraid that she'd put in there that she was really taking food to Jerry today. But she hadn't been that stupid. The last entry was about Jerry, but all it said was:

I love Jerry Johnston. I love Jerry Johnston. I love his eyes. I love how we make him fuller and stronger and healthier. I love his hands. I love how he says FEEL IT CELEBRATE IT FEEL BAD MAD SCARED AS HARD AND HOT AS YOU CAN THEN GIVE IT TO ME I love Jerry Johnston I love Jerry Johnston.

It excited her just to read it. Maybe Rae'd read it, too. Maybe Rae's fingerprints were on the diary but they were invisible unless you had that special stuff, that dust. Lucy tried to be careful where she touched her diary.

She turned the page. Mom had written a long message, filled up the whole two pages. Irritated, Lucy didn't read all of it; it was like being lectured, only in writing. She did see that Mom had written, "Don't give those feelings away. They belong to you," and "You'll love other boys and other men," but that last just proved what Lucy already knew, what Jerry had taught her: Mom didn't understand.

Quickly she turned the page, wondering if she could just tear out the pages Mom had ruined without hurting anything else. On the back of Mom's second page was a message from Rae, the writing fainter and shakier but the same words as before:

BE CAREFUL
LOVE, YOUR SISTER
RAE

19

 Lucy wrote *DARLING* into her diary as many ways as she could think of.

Catty-corner, with giant letters and spaces so that it filled up almost the entire page. When you broke a word up into its pieces like that, any one of them could fall right off the page and then the word wouldn't make sense anymore. She wrote it twice catty-corner, because the first time she didn't have room for the *G*.

Tiny, with a really sharp pencil, and all squished together. It took up only about half an inch in the exact center of the page; she measured. From an arm's length away, it looked like a solid line. Or a mashed bug, except that she couldn't wipe it away with the side of her hand, and there wasn't any blood.

In her best looping cursive, the *D*s and *G*s connected like paper dolls.

He'd called her darling.

She didn't know what that meant.

It wasn't like the gorgeous guys on the soaps or in the romance books Rae used to read. It wasn't like when Grandma gave you a little box of raisins for the ride home, or when the lady at Target called everybody darling, even Dad.

Darling she wrote, stretching out the connections between the letters and twisting the diary so that that one word went around all four edges of the page. Then she started on the next square inside it: *darling.*

"Lucy, you're not paying attention," Mr. Michaelson said. "Again."

Hastily she closed the diary and put her hand over the word *DIARY* on its cover. She should have known better than to bring it to school.

Everybody in the class was laughing at her. Even Stacey, turning around in her seat. Stacey had on lots of purple eye shadow today, and a really short skirt. Lucy wasn't allowed to wear makeup till next year. She was so sick of being treated like a baby. Jeremy Martinez said, "Uh-oh, Lucy's in trouble *again!*" and made a noise like a siren. He was so immature.

"Give it to me," Mr. Michaelson said.

Stunned, she looked up at him. He was holding out his hand. She stared at his face, which all of a sudden was the face of an enemy, and at his hand, close in front of her face.

"Give me the diary."

She was so embarrassed that her whole body was hot. The thought of Mr. Michaelson reading her innermost thoughts—about Jerry Johnston, about Ethan and Mom, about Rae and Dad—made her shiver. It was always either too hot or too cold in this dumb school. She'd heard Mom say a million times that that was one reason why kids got sick, especially in the winter. Lucy thought sure she was getting sick now. She managed to whisper, "It's—private."

He just took it from her. She knew she couldn't stop him, so she didn't even try. He just reached down with his bigger, stronger hands and took it away from her and carried it to the front of the room. She'd never see it again. All the stuff she'd written in there was gone forever. In her mind she tried to make it not matter, tried to make herself not here.

Jeremy and Justin were yelling, "Read it! Read it out loud!" If he did, she'd fall apart, or she'd squish together till she looked like a mashed bug, or a line so solid that nobody would ever get inside her again.

"No," Mr. Michaelson told them. "I'm not interested in embarrassing anybody. I'm just trying to get Lucy—and the rest of you—to pay attention. I'll lock it up in my desk until after school, Lucy. You can come and pick it up then."

I can't. I have group. I have to see Jerry. But she didn't say anything. She'd already said too much.

Mr. Michaelson went on teaching the class then, as if history was the most important thing in the world, and even though she didn't want to, Lucy actually heard some of what he said. About the explorers with weird names that didn't even sound like names: Vasco da Gama. Amerigo Vespucci. Ponce de León, who kept looking for the Fountain of Youth. What a dummy. Just because you stayed young forever didn't mean you wouldn't die.

In science they were studying forces. Gravity and centrifugal force and centripetal force and magnetism. In gym she saw Rae, standing in the doorway by the hall, shimmering in the weird light that came down from the high windows and up from the shiny floor. Lucy left the volleyball game and ran toward her, fully expecting her to vanish and not knowing what she'd say to her anyway.

But Rae stayed there and stayed there and stayed there, shimmering, until Lucy was almost to her, and she was just going to say hi over the echoing noise of the game when Ms. Holcomb caught up to her, grabbed her by the shoulder, spun her around, and snarled, her shiny face and sweaty body right up close to Lucy's, "What do you think you're doing, young lady? You think you can just walk out of my class whenever you feel like it? Your teammates are depending on you. Who's supposed to take your position now? Who do you think you are?"

Lucy would have said, "There's my sister," but she had other sisters, and she understood by now that most people didn't see Rae. And anyway by the time Ms. Holcomb had finished yelling at her and giving her a week's detention of shooting baskets after school for half an hour every day, Lucy glanced over her shoulder and of course her sister wasn't there.

They met as usual in the hot little room behind the cafeteria, but they were going to Jerry's house today. He'd said last week that the exercises they'd be doing from now on were easier to do at his house because they'd have more privacy. Lucy couldn't wait to see where he lived. She'd missed her chance on Christmas; she'd chickened out.

Actually, she couldn't imagine him *living* anywhere. Did he do all the things she did in her house? Did he sleep? Did he go to the bathroom? Did he take showers and get dressed and undressed? Did he cry and laugh and get scared and love people and hate people? She couldn't imagine it.

Besides Jerry, she was the first one there. Suddenly shy, she didn't sit down. She walked around the outside of the waiting circle of folding chairs. Circumference. She made a straight path from one side to the other. Diameter. She stood in the center and paced out to the edge, then back to the center and out to another spot on the edge. Radius.

No matter what she did, there was still a circle. But if you took away any of the chairs it wasn't a circle anymore, so it must not have been real in the first place.

Lucy moved one of the chairs, collapsed it, laid it flat on the floor. "So, how are you, Lucy?"

Even though it was a circle so they'd all be equal, the minute Jerry sat down there was a head to it. His big head kept turning to watch her. When she was right behind him, she knew he couldn't see her, and so first she hurried through the blind spot to get into his line of vision again and then she stayed there for a long time but he didn't turn his body in the chair to look at her. His hips on both sides drooped over the metal seat. His gigantic knees were spread a little, like wings, or like a crab's claws.

"Lucy. I asked you a question. How are you?"

He was mad at her. She could tell by his

voice. "Fine," she said at once, and sat down next to him.

"No, you're not. In this group we're honest with each other, remember? How are you really?"

"I'm scared," she whispered, knowing the words he wanted, not knowing whether they really had anything to do with how she felt.

"Of course you are."

"I'm mad."

"You don't have to whisper. There's nothing to be ashamed of. Say it out loud. Say it proudly."

"I'm scared," she said out loud, and it did sound different. "I'm mad."

He would have made her say it louder and louder till she was yelling it, but Mike and Billy came in then and some of his attention turned to them.

Mike did drugs. Cocaine and crack. At least, he said he did; she didn't know whether to believe him or not. She didn't know whether to believe anybody in the group when they talked about their problems.

Then she started to remember stuff about Billy. He had a brother, older than Ethan, who'd been sent to Nubie, too. That's how Jerry knew him; back then, kids didn't get to know Jerry Johnston unless they got in big trouble. She couldn't remember Billy's brother's name. Back then, she hadn't known you should pay attention to stuff like that.

Staring at Billy, she kept on remembering. Before he'd run the last time, Billy's brother had hurt their mother. Beat her up or something. Lucy'd been shocked that anybody would want to hurt their parents. She still wouldn't ever actually do it, of course, but now she could see why some kids might want to.

Billy's brother was in jail now. Or in a mental hospital. Or maybe they didn't know where he was. She wasn't sure if she really remembered all this or if she was making it up. Naturally, Billy didn't talk about stuff like that in group. None of them did.

Suddenly she did remember: Billy's brother was in a nursing home. He couldn't feed himself or anything. He couldn't talk. He pooped and peed in his bed. He'd been in an accident, she thought, or he had some disease. Jerry visited him. That was nice of him. Lucy didn't think she could ever stand to visit somebody like that.

"How are you?" Jerry asked each one of them, and he really listened to the answer. "How are you, Mike? How are you, Billy? How are you, Julia?"

He made them all say the same things, like a password, like a secret code: "I'm sad. I'm scared. I'm mad."

When everybody was there, Jerry said, "The group will meet at my house from now on."

Mike, who complained about everything, complained. "Shit. It's fuckin' *cold* out there."

"The exercises we'll be doing from now on can get rather noisy," Jerry explained, "and we'll need more privacy than this."

"What are they?" Stephanie asked. Lucy suddenly remembered that Stephanie's mom was dying. She remembered that every week. Something wrong with her liver or something. Was your liver the thing that made you live, like a driver was somebody who drove and a printer was a machine that printed? Words were weird. Dying was weird. She didn't like being around Stephanie, once she'd remembered again about her mom.

"They're about trust," was all Jerry would say. "About us trusting each other."

"Well, I ain't walkin' halfway across town for some stupid meeting," Mike declared, and stretched out his legs and folded his arms across his chest.

"It's not very far. You'll come with us," Jerry told him quietly, and Lucy knew he would.

Jerry took a deep breath and tried to stand up. Sitting so close beside him, Lucy felt his muscles tense. It was hard to believe they were under somebody else's skin and not her own. Julia, on the other side of him, must be feeling them, too. That made Lucy a little jeal-

ous. Julia was a nerd, a schoolgirl. She did all
her homework and even extra-credit projects,
got straight *A*s, never got in trouble. Maybe
that was why she was in this group. But Lucy
didn't think even Jerry could help with a prob-
lem that big.

Jerry's chair swayed and creaked. He leaned
way forward with his white hands around his
huge knees and tried again. When he still
didn't make it and sat back down hard, Lucy
was sure his chair was going to break and he'd
collapse on the floor in the middle of them
and then she'd have to figure out some way to
pick him up.

But finally he was on his feet, panting and
towering over them. "Let's go."

His house was only about six blocks from
the school, past Stacey's house, toward the
lake. It bothered Lucy that he'd been living
right there and she hadn't known it. As they
went by other houses, she looked into their
doors and windows and yards, wishing she
could tell who lived there, what they were going to mean in her life someday.

Jerry's house was a lot smaller than the
Brills' house, because there was only one of
him. Lucy wondered what it would be like to
live alone. And whether, if more people got
lost out of their family, they'd have to move
out of their house.

Jerry's house sat back away from the sidewalk, behind a row of bushes. Probably that was a hedge. Probably in the summertime all those bushes grew close together to make a wall. But now they didn't have any leaves on them, and you could see all the branches and twigs and the little feathery tips, like split ends, that were too tiny to be called twigs but she didn't know what their name was. In the summer Jerry's house could hide behind the hedge, but now you could see right through, and it was just a plain little white house with a green roof and a green porch.

There was a step up from the main sidewalk to the skinny one that led to the house, and then five steps up to the porch. The kids all waited for Jerry to go first, except Mike, who made Lucy laugh even when she knew she shouldn't. Mike ran ahead, crashed through the leafless hedge, jumped over the porch railing, and sprang at them like Freddy Krueger, fingers like claws. Everybody laughed except Jerry.

Jerry was having to concentrate to get up the steps. Once when Lucy had had the flu real bad she'd had to concentrate like that, had to *think* about how to eat and walk and turn over in bed. He was watching his feet, as if he wasn't sure they'd do what they were supposed to, and he was gripping the railing on both sides; both his hands and his feet looked awfully small for such a big body, and Lucy had the sudden fantasy that they'd been cut off of somebody else's body and stuck on his.

Twice his foot slipped off the edge of the steps. Without thinking, Lucy held out her arms to catch him, and she saw Billy and Stephanie doing the same thing. He'd be like a fortune cookie if he fell into them—hollow, just a thin shell around a giant hole, with a message inside.

But he made it up the steps, unlocked the front door, and led them inside. First there was one of those entryways where you put your coat. Some of the kids hung theirs on hooks, but Lucy kept hers on. Then there was an ordinary living room—green carpet, white walls, furniture and lamps and pictures that you wouldn't remember from one visit to the next.

In Lucy's house, everything was there to remind you of somebody: the picture Aunt Kathy had painted of the house she and Dad had grown up in, which had been torn down when North Valley Mall was built; the couch where bedtime stories always got read; the old-fashioned red rug Mom had bought when they took that family vacation to Boston the summer before Molly was born. No, Dominic, because he hadn't been with them either.

Anybody could have lived in Jerry's house. Lucy wanted to.

It would be easy for Ethan to be living here.

It wouldn't surprise her at all if he jumped out from behind that door, or crawled out from under that couch, or sort of oozed out from under the kitchen sink.

It wouldn't surprise her, except that he really was dead. She'd touched his body. She'd watched him get buried. He couldn't be living here. He couldn't be living anywhere.

Rae could be. It wouldn't surprise her if Rae was living here right now. Lucy listened hard but didn't hear anything. It was weird how quiet Jerry's house was. It didn't even make the noises that other houses made. No creaks, no motors turning off and on, no faucets dripping or clocks ticking.

It was a hungry quiet. It sucked at you. She felt its teeth and tongue, and the hollow places just under the surface that it wanted her to fill up.

"Come on in," Jerry said, not just to her. "Have a seat. I'll be right back."

He made his way across the room and through a door at the other end. The bathroom, Lucy thought, or the kitchen. Maybe he was going to serve food. She wasn't hungry, but she'd have to eat something so he wouldn't feel bad. Mom felt bad whenever anybody didn't like what she fixed, especially since Ethan and Rae were gone.

Mike started after Jerry, taking great big high steps on his tiptoes. Lucy and some of the others laughed, but Stephanie yawned and said, "Oh, don't be an asshole, Mike," and Mike quit and came to sit on the floor beside her. Lucy guessed they liked each other, and wondered how long that had been going on. She wondered what else was going on in the group that she didn't know about. She hated secrets. She hated Stephanie and Mike. She hated Jerry because he'd known all along. The door Jerry had gone through opened a crack and Rae was looking out.

Lucy blinked. Now the door was shut and nobody was there. But it had been open, just a crack, and her sister had been behind it looking out. She got to her feet.

"Gee," somebody said sarcastically, "this is fun."

"I gotta be home by four-thirty," Julia said. "I gotta go to the dentist. What time is it?"

Somebody else—Mike, probably—farted loudly, and everybody laughed, even Stephanie. Lucy laughed, too, but she was moving toward the door.

"Look at this!" Billy teased. "Lucy can't stand to let Jerry Johnston out of her sight for one minute!"

Lucy flushed painfully. "Lucy loves Jer-ry! Lucy loves Jer-ry!" She was sure that wherever he'd gone in his house, Jerry would hear them. But she was at the door now, and when it opened too easily at her pull, it slammed her in the face.

She gasped and pressed both hands over the bridge of her nose. Her cheekbones ached. Maybe she'd have a black eye. Behind her people were hooting, and she knew she must look dumb. Stephanie said, "She's hurt, you guys. You think that's funny?" but they kept on. She hated them. She went through the door and shut it tight after her, hoping it would lock her in.

She was in a short hallway. There was a ceiling light at the other end, but it wasn't very bright. The carpet was green and the walls were white, like in the living room, and there was nothing on the walls. The only room opening off the hall was at the very end, under the light, on the left-hand side.

Her nose hurt. Her head ached. She wiped her nose on the sleeve of her coat, trying not to think about it because it was gross, and started down the hall toward the closed door.

Voices. She stopped, the backs of both hands pressed against the walls for balance and direction. In Jerry's living room behind her, the kids were talking loud. The wall on her right must be an outside wall, because she could hear somebody whistling to a dog. But she was sure there were also voices ahead and to her left, from behind that door, and that Jerry's was one of them.

He came out of the doorway while she was standing there listening for him. In the split second before he saw her, Lucy stared at him and felt funny in her throat and between her legs.

"Lucy?"

He pulled a key out of his pocket and locked the door, tested the knob. She'd never seen anybody lock a door *inside* a house before.

He was coming toward her. There wasn't much distance between them; it was a short hall, and he was walking fast now, not at all unsteadily. His head and body blocked the light, and she was covered with his big dim shadow.

"Lucy." He said her name again, not a question this time. His voice wasn't very loud and she couldn't see his face, but she knew she'd displeased him. "What are you doing?"

She backed up a couple of steps. "Where's Rae?"

He didn't seem surprised by the question. That surprised her. "You just have to live with the fact that nobody knows, and nobody may ever know." He shook his big shadowy head as if he felt sorry for her. "I'll bet you still look for her everywhere, don't you? Even in my house, where you know you won't find her. That's a normal part of the grieving process, honey. We call it denial."

Honey. "I saw her," Lucy said.

"Where?"

"Here."

Jerry looked from side to side and spread his hands. "Here?"

"I *saw* her," Lucy insisted. "She was looking out that door into the living room." She jerked her thumb over her shoulder, then looked to make sure that she hadn't gotten turned around, that the door she'd come through was still there. It was. She fumbled behind her and rested her palms flat against it.

"Did anyone else see her?"

"I don't think so."

"It's just because you *want* so badly to see her, Lucy. Because it's so hard to accept that death is final."

"She's not dead," Lucy said stubbornly, but now she wasn't sure again.

"We'll deal with those feelings in group."

"No."

"Lucy, everybody feels those things, especially at your age, especially when you've gone through hard times. You don't have to hide them."

"They'll think I'm really stupid," she said, and, just saying that, felt as if she were crossing Federal Boulevard without a light again.

Jerry had taken more steps than she'd realized, and now his hands were on her shoulders and he was pulling her toward him, turning her around. For a second she thought he was going to spank her, or kiss her, or carry her away in his arms. He pulled her back against his big, hard, warm body just enough to reach around her and open the door.

The living room was white and green and noisy. She'd been away from it for so long she wouldn't know what to do once she went back in. But she didn't have any choice. Jerry pushed her through, hard enough that she stumbled. Then he came through, too, and locked the door behind them with another key.

It hadn't been locked before. He must not want anybody else going into the inside parts of his house, where she had just been. Tingling with a fearful feeling of being too special, she sat down beside Julia as Jerry said, "All right, people, let's get started. We have a lot of work to do today."

20

It was darker outside her head than in. Inside her head were all sorts of colors and shapes. She saw them when she closed her eyes, and Jerry had taught her that they were always there, and that they had names. Electricity. Synapses. Terror. Rage. And that they could be used.

Outside her head, when she opened her eyes, almost no light at all was coming through the heavy curtains at Jerry's one living-room window, and there weren't any lights on in the room. She could see just vague silhouettes of the people in the circle all around her, and couldn't tell who was who. That wasn't supposed to matter. You were supposed to trust them all.

"Concentrate," Jerry murmured. "Celebrate what you feel."

She knew where he was. She always knew where he was and what he wanted her to do.

Obediently she held her hands out a little way from her body and closed her eyes again. Red came to her, red with fat fingers and long teeth. She tried to make her breathing even more shallow and irregular than it already was. Pretty soon she'd have to fall.

"Feel it as much as you can. Don't run away from it. Run *into* it."

She'd tried to do this every time since they'd started meeting at Jerry's. Stephanie and Billy could do it, but she was too afraid. Jerry said that was because she put her fear in the wrong place. Today was her birthday. She was twelve today. She'd never be eleven again. Nobody in the group knew that, including Jerry, and she didn't want them to know. But she wasn't a little kid anymore and today, finally, she was going to do this right.

Mike coughed. Somebody's knuckles cracked. Jerry said again, in a singsong voice, "Concentrate."

When she got home, there would be cake and ice cream and presents. Mom was fixing hamburgers and french fries for dinner because she thought that was still Lucy's favorite meal, when the truth was she couldn't care less.

"Concentrate," he said again, so softly that she thought she might be the only one who heard. "Find the rage and go into it."

She hated Ethan. She hated Rae. She hated Mom and Dad and Priscilla and Dominic and Molly and Cory. She hated Stacey. She hated school. She hated herself. She hated herself.

"That's right," Jerry breathed. Lucy thrilled, and redness grew.

"It *hurts*," she whimpered.

"Of course it hurts, honey," he told her gently. "But it's real."

"You're making it hurt worse."

"I make you face what's already inside you. So you can get rid of it."

"You make it worse," she insisted. She could hardly believe she was arguing with Jerry. "I do get mad sometimes, and I get scared, and I miss my sister and my brother. But you make me feel worse than I feel."

"It hurts because you're afraid of it," Jerry told her. She'd heard him say that before. "It hurts because you're trying to hold it in."

"It'll kill somebody," Lucy moaned. "It *hurts*. It'll kill *me*."

"Use it," Jerry urged. "Give it away. Give it to me."

She was falling backward. She tried to stop herself but couldn't think how. She was falling backward and sideways and from the outside in. Redness rose, sank, spread. She was falling.

Jerry caught her.

He'd been standing behind her all the time and she hadn't, after all, known he was there.

He caught her but she kept on falling. She thought she would break right through his body into the hollow inside, which used to be filled with redness, too.

But other hands were on her then. Under her shoulders, under her knees, at her sides just under her breasts. "Put your hands on her," Jerry was saying, and, "That's right, that's right, put your hands on her," and the rage was draining out of her into all of them, into him.

Jerry leaned over her. His face was upside down. He lowered his upside-down face and whispered almost without sound, a very secret message meant only for her, "Happy birthday, darling." Then he kissed her full on the mouth.

21

Lucy lay on her bed. It was the evening of her birthday, almost the end of her first day of being twelve. They'd had the hamburgers and french fries, the chocolate cake and strawberry ice cream. She'd blown out the candles on the first try, and Molly and Dominic had clapped because now she'd get her wish. That was a lie and it made her mad that they were allowed to believe it, but she didn't say anything. Priscilla tried to get her to tell what her wish was, but she wouldn't because then it wouldn't come true.

She'd had to go to school today even though it was her birthday. Mr. Michaelson had said happy birthday after history class. How had he known? He said didn't she want her diary back now and she took it to shut him up, but it wasn't hers anymore.

Maybe everybody would leave her alone for a while now, because they thought she was up here playing with her birthday presents. She wasn't, though. The presents didn't have anything to do with her; they were just somebody else's idea of what she'd like. Nobody knew her.

Except Jerry Johnston. He knew her better than she knew herself. He'd given her the best and most confusing present of all. The kiss.

She could only think about the kiss a little bit at a time. His big face lowering over hers, upside down but fitting. His open mouth, teeth, tongue.

Afterward, she'd been really tired, in a way that had felt sort of good, and Jerry had seemed bigger than before, stronger, with more energy. There hadn't been any sunken places on him. But she could only think about that a little bit at a time.

The books she'd gotten for her birthday were piled on Rae's dresser, and as far as she was concerned they could stay there forever. One was from Pris, about a summer romance, with this truly nerdy-looking guy and girl on the cover. Priscilla didn't know anything about romance yet. She was still a little girl. She didn't know anything about anything. Jerry didn't even know her name. *But he will,*

Lucy thought, and didn't like thinking it. *It won't be long.*

One book was from Mom, about invisible things in the world, because once a long time ago Lucy had asked a few questions about mites; you had to be careful what you showed an interest in around here.

Dom had given her the Tina Turner tape she'd asked for. He kept saying he bought it with his own money. Big deal. It was in the new tape player, her big present from Mom and Dad, and she had the earphones on, but the volume was so low that she could just barely hear the whooshing and clicking of the tape as it turned. Right now the earphones were to keep sound out, not to let it in. Tina Turner didn't have anything to say to her. Tina Turner didn't know Ethan Michael Brill or Rae Ellen Brill. Or Jerry Johnston.

Happy birthday, he'd said with his mouth over hers, and she'd felt the words instead of hearing them. How did he know?

Darling, he'd said with his mouth over hers.

Somebody knocked on her door, and it wasn't the first time. All of a sudden Lucy thought maybe people had been knocking on her door for hours, knocking and then running away.

She wouldn't answer. She'd pretend she was listening to the tape and couldn't hear the knocking. She'd pretend she was asleep.

Lucy looked around her room and was disgusted. It was a little kid's room, a baby's room. From here she could reach the stuffed animals on her shelves, and the big dancing doll Grandma had made with elastics on her feet that fit over your feet so she could dance with you. She stuffed them all under her bed. Then she stood on her bed and ripped all seven pictures of Emilio Estevez off the wall. Little pieces of green paint came off with the tape. Dad would be mad. If he even noticed.

For a minute she stood up there, trying to keep her balance on the bouncy mattress, crumbling the pictures into tighter and tighter balls. The blotches on the green wall reminded her that there was other paint and wallpaper underneath, that other people she'd never even heard of had lived in this room.

She got off the bed and rummaged through her desk drawer till she found the picture she'd cut out of the newspaper a couple of weeks ago of that guy from Libya that everybody thought was so awful. Muammar Qaddafi. His fist was raised and his eyes were blazing. He was so cute.

Smoothing the square of newspaper with her palm, Lucy wondered what it would be like to live in Libya. She didn't know for sure where Libya was, except that it was far away from here.

She got tape and climbed back on the bed.

The picture of Muammar Qaddafi didn't cover most of the places where the paint had peeled off, and she knew it was making more. She didn't care. Muammar Qaddafi was so cute. He didn't let anybody push him around.

There was another knock and then the door opened and Mom stuck her head in. Lucy frowned and turned the volume up, but not before she heard Mom ask, "Lucy? You all right?" Since Ethan died and Rae disappeared, you couldn't get any privacy around here.

Mom came in, uninvited, and stood in front of her. Lucy closed her eyes and listened to the end of "What's Love Got to Do with It?" But that was the last song on the tape and so she couldn't help hearing Mom ask, "Did you have a good birthday?"

"It was fine," Lucy said automatically.

"Next year you'll be an official teenager."

Big deal, Lucy thought furiously, but despite herself she did feel a little thrill.

"I remember when I was twelve."

I don't want to hear it don't tell me. When you were twelve you didn't know terrible things were going to happen in your life. Don't talk about it don't talk about when Rae and Ethan were twelve I don't want to hear it

But Mom said, "Twelve can also be a really confusing time. I remember being unhappy a lot."

Lucy lay rigid with the earphones still in her

ears. What was she being asked to admit to? She watched her mother's face and could see the twelve-year-old girl there, could also see the old lady with all white hair.

Mom bent and kissed her forehead. When Mom kissed her, nothing left Lucy's body or mind; nothing was taken from her and used. Lucy put her arms around her mother's neck and held on tight, and Mom lifted her a little off the bed to cradle her.

They stayed like that for a few minutes. Lucy said into her mother's shoulder, "I'm too old for this. I'm not a baby. I'm twelve years old."

Mom chuckled softly. "Nobody's ever too old for this."

"I wish I was all grown up."

"I know."

"I wish I was still a baby."

"I know."

"I wish Rae and Ethan were here." For once, it didn't make Lucy cry to say that.

Mom didn't cry either, but her hug got tighter. "I know."

"Mom?"

"Yes, honey."

"Dad . . . sees Rae."

"I know."

"Do you see her?"

"I think so. I'm so confused and tired by

now that I can't always tell what's real and what's just in my head."

"She's trying to tell me something."

"What do you mean?"

"I get—messages from her."

Mom leaned back a little to look at her. "What do you mean, 'messages'?"

Lucy felt dumb. "Oh, you know. To be careful and stuff like that." *Not to trust you.*

"Have you talked to Jerry about this?"

You don't understand anything, Lucy thought frantically, but out loud she said, "Yes."

"What does he say about it?"

None of your business. "I don't know. Nothing."

"Lucy, listen. This is important. If you actually see Rae, you have to tell Dad or me. We have to tell the police everything that might help them find her."

Lucy made a deliberate decision then that both scared her and gave her a little rush of power: *I won't ever tell you anything.* Out loud, she said, "Okay."

Her neck had started aching, but she didn't want to move and hurt Mom's feelings. She ran her fingers along the stripes in Mom's sweater, trying to follow any one particular strand of yarn as it twisted to make the pattern.

Mom sighed and sat up straighter, then

reached to take the earphones gently off Lucy's head. Now everything sounded weird, as if Lucy'd been underwater for a long time, or underground.

Mom took her hands. Lucy realized how cold her own hands were, and then she was cold all over, shivering. She wanted to turn her electric blanket on high and pull the covers up over her head, but Mom was holding her hands so hard they hurt, and Lucy imagined their cold hollow bones and icy blood.

"There's something really important that I want to say to you, Lucy. Kind of a birthday present."

She paused, swallowed, looked away. It scared Lucy to think what she might be going to say. *Your father and I are getting a divorce,* maybe, or *I don't love you anymore.* Her heart hurt, and she thought about its four chambers, ventricles and another word she couldn't remember. Blood pumping in and out, in and out. Oxygen and stuff in her blood. Those things with the weird name. Corpuscles.

Mom said, "I want you to understand that Ethan's death and Rae's—disappearance are not more important than your life."

Lucy stared at her.

"Not to Dad. Not to me. And most important, not to you."

"Oh," Lucy said.

Mom stood up, then leaned over and kissed her again. "Happy birthday, sweetheart. I love you very much." Her eyes were full of tears, and the streak in her hair was very wide and white, but right now Lucy didn't mind.

She thought about what Mom had said as she fell asleep listening to Tina Turner. Her dreams were about blood and bones and boxes inside boxes, but they weren't scary dreams and they didn't wake her up. On her way to school the next morning she was still thinking about what Mom had said, and it had snowed just enough in the night that the side-walks were glittery and beautiful, and she was feeling good until Jeremy Martinez threw a snowball at her that was mostly mud and it got in her hair and she called him an asshole and he called her a honky bitch. They weren't on school property yet, so they didn't get in trouble, but Lucy was in tears by the time she got to the bathroom and her hair was ruined for the day. Stacey said Jeremy must like her.

It snowed off and on all day. The footprints she'd left on the sidewalks would be gone by the time she went home. She was in math class sixth period, half listening to Ms. Abercrombie talk about how a normal number like 100 could be broken down further and further and further—25×4, 10×10, 2×50, till it wasn't the same number anymore—when she saw Rae flicker past the window like a handful of snow, and she couldn't stand it anymore.

She stood up. Ms. Abercrombie stopped in the middle of another sentence about factors. "Lucy?"

"This is stupid," Lucy said, and walked out. Behind her she heard the class break up into shouts and whoops and catcalls, and she heard Ms. Abercrombie yell her name, but none of it had anything to do with her.

She wanted to run down the hall but she didn't, because somebody might notice and try to stop her, and then she'd have to hurt them or something because she wasn't going to be stopped. But nobody was in the hall. Even when you had a hall pass and were on your way to the bathroom, it felt funny to be out in the hall when nobody else was, as if you were doing something wrong, and now she really was doing something wrong, and it felt really funny. For a minute she thought about just walking the halls forever, walking and walking, but that was too dangerous and anyway Rae wasn't in the school. She knew now where Rae was. And maybe Ethan, too.

She went down the gray steps by the library. She thought the librarian saw her but nobody came after her. The door at the bottom of the steps went out onto the end of the playground. She pushed it open and went outside, pulled it shut behind her. It was as easy as that. The door was locked now. She couldn't go back inside even if she wanted to.

It was cold outside and snowing, and she'd left her coat in the building. She hugged herself and ran. All the way to Jerry's house, she didn't see Rae. She didn't see anybody in any of the houses; maybe nobody lived there. Maybe they were all dead. Maybe houses were for something else altogether, and the idea of people living in them was just a trick to make you miss what was really going on.

By the time she turned in at the skeletal hedgerow, she was shivering violently and panting. No lights were on in Jerry's house, and for a minute she was scared that she'd been wrong. But she couldn't stop now; she didn't know where else to go or what else to do. She ran up the five slippery steps and onto the porch, which thumped under her wet shoes, and before she knocked on the door Jerry opened it to her.

He was huge. He filled the doorway. But he made her think of those fake buildings Dad had told her they used on movie sets, that looked solid from the front but there was nothing behind them. He looked tired and sick. She realized that this was Wednesday and he looked like that every week before group. After group he always looked better.

He smiled at her. His pale eyes were like the

glitter on the sidewalks late in the afternoon. His flabby cheeks seemed to crack and split, but there wasn't any blood.

"Welcome, Lucy," he said.

22

"I'm proud of you," Jerry told her.

Her heart swelled. She had no idea what she'd done to make him proud of her, but it was what she wanted to hear more than anything in the world.

"You know when you need me. You know when you're ready. That makes me proud."

She smiled.

"And you knew to come before the others get here."

"I left school," she said.

He nodded. "You did the right thing."

"Mom and Dad wouldn't like it."

"For quite a while now I've known that you've needed more intensive work than the others. I didn't want to push you until you were ready."

Lucy said again, "My mom and dad—"

"Parents don't always know what their children need," Jerry said. Lucy remembered Ethan needing something from Mom that she couldn't give him, Rae needing something from Dad.

Jerry was having trouble catching his breath. He was panting, and she could see his tongue, coated with some kind of white stuff. Snow, she thought confusedly, or fur. Probably dead skin cells. She thought there was a caved-in place above his right eye.

She peered past Jerry. His house was more familiar to her these days than her parents' house, felt more like home. She didn't see Rae, but she would. Rae must be all right if she was here with Jerry. Lucy would be all right now, too.

Maybe she'd been wrong. Maybe Rae wasn't here. Maybe she was alone in the house with Jerry. Something moved inside when she thought that.

"What does that mean? 'Intensive work'?"

Her voice came out embarrassingly loud, and she didn't know why she'd asked anyway. She didn't need to know what it meant. She trusted Jerry.

The sound of her voice was absorbed right away, soaked up, by the spongy quiet of Jerry's house. Softly, almost lovingly, he answered, "You're not getting what you need from your parents or anybody else right now. The only person you can get it from is me."

That sounded so good. Still standing in the open doorway, still shivering, Lucy blushed and nodded.

He reached around her to shut the door. His arm brushed against her, his chest and belly. She noticed that he didn't have much body heat. Even though she was so cold, she was a lot warmer than he was, and his coldness seemed to be pulling her warmth out of her, so that she shivered all the more.

With the door shut, the house was dim. Fuzzily, she wondered if it could somehow be coated, too, the windows covered with snow or with dead skin.

He must have the furnace turned way up, because the air got warmer and warmer as she followed him into the living room. There was a time when Dad would have had a fit if anybody'd turned the heat up that high in their house. Now Lucy didn't think he'd even notice. Maybe Jerry's house was like the earth: the deeper you went the hotter it got, until at the core things that should be solid weren't, and volcanoes started.

Abruptly Jerry turned and put his hands on her shoulders. They were so lightweight they could have been gloves. He was a whole lot taller and bigger than she was, but at the mo-

ment she was heavier, she was holding him
up.

In one graceful movement, as if they were
dancing, he swung her around and sat her
down on the big red pillow in the middle of
the floor. He was leaning close over her, and
his breath smelled awful.

He lowered himself to sit beside her, hardly
creaking the floorboards at all, and gently
pulled her over backward so that her head was
in his lap. She felt his lumpy thighs under her,
and the hollow between his thighs and his
belly where she knew his penis was, like a
dragon in its cave. His belly in its red plaid
shirt loomed over her; when she turned her
face into it, it indented, as if there were nothing inside.

"Are you comfortable?"

She squirmed around a little, mostly to get
the feel of his lap against the back of her head,
and felt a hardness that she recognized right
away. Jerry had a hard-on. Lucy lay very still
and shut her eyes and whispered, "Yes."

"Now I want you to pay attention to your
body. Are there places where it hurts? Where
you feel tension?"

"My head hurts."

The headache was so deep that she thought
her *brain* was hurting. She imagined her brain
to be an ugly, pulpy brown, with red and

green lights flicking on and off to indicate trouble, but nobody there to see.

Jerry's hands were on both sides of her head, and it hurt worse, pounding at her temples, cutting across the bridge of her nose. She was starting to get sick to her stomach.

"And—my stomach."

He put his hand low on her stomach. Pain and nausea swelled like a balloon, gathered at the spot where his hand was and started spreading all though her. She didn't think she could stand it, but she didn't try to get away.

"It hurts *everywhere*!" She was crying. She'd always been crying, and she'd never stop.

"*Use* the pain!" Jerry hissed.

She didn't know what he meant.

"Make the pain as big and as strong as you can!"

She couldn't. It would tear her apart. It would eat her alive. She couldn't do what he wanted. She couldn't do this right.

"That's right, that's right," Jerry was crooning. "Make the pain as awful as you can, and then give it to me."

All of a sudden, her head didn't hurt quite so much and her stomach wasn't quite so sick. At the same time she realized that Jerry's hands and thighs and face were filling out, so that there was more solid flesh and not so many wrinkles.

"What are you feeling? Right now?"

She struggled for the right words. "I—don't know."

"You're *scared*," he prompted.

Once he'd said it, she was. So scared.

"You're *furious*."

Rage crawled around inside her; it lived there now. Lucy curled up her knees and clenched her fists against her mouth. That way, all of her fit into Jerry's wide, deep lap.

For a minute she wanted to be in her father's lap instead. Her father's lap didn't feel empty, like Jerry's; her father's arms didn't seem brittle. With Dad, she wasn't expected to fill something up or to keep something from breaking.

"You're scared and mad because your parents are lousy parents."

"No," she whimpered.

"*Yes*. They let your brother die. They let your sister disappear. Parents are supposed to keep their kids safe."

"It's—not their fault."

"You don't have to defend them to me, honey. That's not your job."

Honey.

"Your job is to work through your feelings in a safe environment. This is a safe environment. I'll take care of you."

Lucy relaxed some. The fear and fury were, in fact, bigger and stronger now, but not so scary, not so much enemies.

"You're scared."

"Yes."

"You're *angry*."

"*Yes.*"

"Your parents have lost two children, and now you're next."

"No!" *Yes.* Jerry's voice pulled at her, pulled something out of her. His big body was folded over her, and his mouth, pursed to kiss or to suck, was almost on hers.

The doorbell rang.

Somebody to save me. Mom and Dad to take me home.

But nobody knew she was here. And Jerry was right: Mom and Dad were bad parents. They didn't save anybody.

And anyway, why would she want to be saved from Jerry? He was the only person in the world she could trust. She curled up smaller in his lap, around his hand that kneaded her belly like a cat making a nest, way down inside the waistband of her jeans.

"*Feel* it!" he whispered urgently. "*Feel* the anger and the fear."

But she knew she couldn't. Not the way he wanted.

"*See* it. What color is the anger? What color is the fear?"

"Black," she said. "Red." But she was just saying those things so he'd let her stay on his lap.

"Good. Stay with it, Lucy!"

But she'd already failed him.

The doorbell rang again, and they both heard somebody yelling. A guy. Mike. "Hey, Jerry, let me in! It's fuckin' cold out here!"

Jerry kissed her. Lightly, but she felt his teeth and the hollow probing tube of his tongue.

Then he lifted her off his lap and got up off the floor. He was still having a hard time; he had to get up on his knees first, then hold on to the arm of a chair to hoist himself up. But she saw that he was a lot stronger and steadier, and this time the floorboards did creak under his weight.

"Mike's here," Jerry said with a smile. He was towering over her like a papier-mâché giant.

"What's he doing here?" Lucy protested feebly. "It's not time for group yet, is it?" She sat up, stretched, rubbed at her eyes. Moving hurt. Inside her bones was marrow, soft spongy stuff. Inside her flesh was blood. Her headache and nausea were just about gone, but she was so tired.

"Mike's been needing a little extra from me, too," Jerry said over his shoulder. "Looks like he's ready."

He lumbered into the entranceway, where she couldn't see him anymore. She heard him unlock and open the front door, and both the light and the temperature in the room changed. She heard him say, "Mike. Come on in. I'm proud of you."

Jealousy made her private parts ache. The door to the hallway at the other end of the living room eased open. She saw a shiny eye peeking out, heard a faint hissing as if somebody wasn't even strong enough to whisper very loud.

Rae.

Lucy struggled to get to her feet. It was like being in the tub full of plastic balls at the amusement park. She kept slipping and sliding. Everything around her kept moving.

She found she was having to concentrate on stuff that she'd hardly even thought about until now. Like how her hands and knees, shoulders and hips were supposed to work together. Like how the muscles in her thighs were supposed to get shorter in the front and longer in the back so that she could stand up. Like where she and Jerry and Mike and Rae and Ethan and Mom and Dad all were, in relation to each other.

By the time she was finally on her feet, both the outside door and the door to the back hallway were shut again. Jerry came into the living room with his arm around Mike's shoulders. Lucy looked away.

"Lucy's here, too," Jerry told Mike. "Must be

my lucky day." Lucy thought that was a funny thing to say. Mike gave her a dirty look.

Jerry held out his other arm. After a minute, Lucy went to him. His arm around her was like the feather boa she'd worn one Halloween with a blond beehive wig and Mom's high heels; it wasn't very heavy, but it wrapped her up.

"Well," Jerry said cheerfully, "who wants to be first?"

There was a silence. Lucy tried hard to figure out what he was talking about, embarrassed that she didn't know. Then, from the other side of Jerry, Mike said, "First at what?"

"Working on feelings." Jerry's voice was husky and shaking a little. Lucy thought he sounded excited. "Working on rage and fear."

Lucy wanted to say she'd be first because she knew that would please Jerry, but she was afraid to. "Oh, shit, I will," Mike said.

"Good for you, Mike."

I'm sorry, Lucy wanted to say. *I'll be next.* She thought she heard the click and creak of the hallway door opening again, but before she could turn around to see, Jerry sat down on the floor, pulling her and Mike with him.

"You sit at his feet, Lucy. I'll take the rest of his body."

Obediently she crawled over by Mike's feet. Jerry settled Mike's head and shoulders in his lap. Jerry's thin jeans pulled up away from his

socks when he crossed his legs, showing white
pocked flesh.

"Take his shoes off."

Mike laughed shrilly, but he didn't try to
kick her or anything when she pulled his
sneakers off. They were soaking wet, and so
were his socks. Lucy hoped frantically that
Jerry wouldn't make her take Mike's socks off,
too. That would be *so* embarrassing.

"Now don't touch him unless I tell you to.
Just pay attention to what happens. Maybe
you'll be able to do it sometime."

"I'm sorry," Lucy said. "I'll be next."

"Not today." She'd lost his attention. It was
her own fault. She'd missed her chance. "I can
only do one of these a day. I don't want to
OD."

Pushed away, hurt, Lucy sat back. She
didn't want to be here. She wanted to go
home. But she couldn't leave until Jerry told
her to.

"Are you comfortable?"

Lucy started to answer before she realized
he wasn't talking to her anymore, he was talking to Mike. Mike said, "Yeah."

"Now I want you to pay attention to your
body. Are there places where it hurts? Where
you feel tension?"

After a minute Mike said, "I've got kind of a
stiff neck."

Jerry slid one hand inside Mike's shirt on

each side of his neck. Lucy heard both of them start breathing harder.

"Jesus Christ, it *hurts*!" Mike was crying, and his body writhed on the floor. Jerry was holding the top half of him still, but his legs twisted and his feet kicked. Lucy backed away.

"*Use* the pain!" Jerry hissed, his face very close to Mike's, very far away from Lucy. "Don't try to get away from it! Make it as big and as strong as you can!"

Mike groaned. "It hurts everywhere! Down my arms and down my back!"

"That's right, that's right," Jerry crooned. "Make the pain as awful as you can, and then *give it to me*!"

"I can't!"

"What are you feeling, Mike? Right now?" Jerry was bent so low over Mike that they looked to Lucy like one creature. His hands were pressing on Mike's neck and shoulders, and his thick legs were stretched out beside Mike's body, hemming him in.

"Shit." Mike laughed. "How the hell should I know?"

"*What are you feeling?* This is not a game." Jerry could have been yelling, even though really he was whispering. Lucy was glad he wasn't yelling at her.

"Mad," Mike said.

"How mad?"

"Real mad."

"You're furious. Good. You're enraged. Who are you mad at?"

"My old man," Mike whispered.

"Who? I can't hear you."

"My fucking father!" Mike suddenly yelled. His knees drew up and then kicked out straight. Lucy scooted farther back. Jerry bent lower. "My *father*!"

"Yes. Do you hate him?"

"I *hate* him!"

"Do you wish he was dead?"

"I wish he was dead!"

"Yes. He's a lousy father. He hurts you."

"He hurts me!" Mike was screaming so much now that Lucy could hardly understand the words.

"Feel it," Jerry whispered urgently. *"Feel* the anger and the fear."

"It hurts!"

"Yes. Stay with it, Mike. You're doing fine."

Lucy's back was to the hallway door, but she heard it open. It stayed open for a long minute, then closed again. She wanted desperately to look. She wanted to go back there and find Rae. But she was afraid to move. If she left Jerry and Mike alone together now, Jerry would never notice her again.

"Do you wish I was your father?"

Mike didn't say anything. He was sobbing. Lucy was embarrassed to see him crying. She watched his feet in the dirty wet socks, twisting on the dim floor in front of her almost as if they weren't attached to his legs.

"Mike, Mike, do you wish I was your father?"

"Yes!"

"Say it!"

"I—wish—you—were—my father!"

"Then I am. I am your father. I am your father."

Lucy lost count of how many times he said it, and finally lost track even of the sense of the words. Somehow Jerry contorted his huge body until it had slid out from under Mike and over his head like an envelope, like a shroud, until Jerry was on top of Mike, covering all of him except his feet, which kicked and twisted and then relaxed and lay still. There was the loud noise of gulping and swallowing.

"Lucy."

From close behind her, Lucy heard her name. Afraid to take her eyes off Jerry, she whispered, "Rae?"

"Lucy. Go home."

"I can't. He won't let me."

"Get out of here. Go home."

Hardly aware of what she was doing, Lucy pushed herself backward across the carpet. Then she was crawling. Then she was standing up, fumbling with the lock on the front door. Then she was outside, where it was dark and cold and snowing hard, and running down the slippery steps and out through the hedge and along the sidewalk toward home, all the time hearing voices calling her name. Jerry moaning, "Lucy!" because he wanted her to stay, but he didn't really need her because he had Mike, and Rae crying, "Lucy!" because she wanted her to run away, stay away, go home. Lucy ran home.

23

 The door was locked.

The extra key wasn't under the brick.

Panic-stricken, Lucy pressed the doorbell again and again. Feeling it buzz under her fingertip, she imagined the tiny spurt of electricity transforming into chimes that were supposed to tell somebody inside the house that she wanted in.

Some part of all that wasn't working, because nobody was coming.

Lucy leaned on the doorbell again. It played the first few lines of "You Are My Sunshine" again. That was the song Dad had set it on when he'd first brought it home, a long time before, while Rae was still at home. On the box Lucy had read that there were eleven other tunes you could choose from, including

"Happy Birthday" and "We Wish You a Merry Christmas." But Dad had never bothered to change it. Another thing he obviously didn't care about anymore.

It only played as far as "You are my sunshine, my only sunshine, you make me happy when skies are gray." But by that time, Lucy was rigid, from cold and from terror brought on by a series of full-blown fantasies that had come at her like crystals in an ice storm—no two exactly alike, but all of them cold and sharp and hurtful:

They'd moved.

They'd all been killed by a mass murderer. Stabbed. Shot. Raped. And the murderer was waiting by the hall table to get her.

She'd never lived here. She'd dreamed it. She'd made it all up. She'd never had a family.

"Boy, are you in trouble!" Priscilla said as she opened the door. "You're in so much trouble!"

Lucy practically fell inside. It smelled like home. Light from the umbrella lamp made a circle on the wood floor, the way it always did. The stairs still went up to the right. It was warm, except for the cold air that still chased her. "Goddamn you!" she yelled at her sister. "Shut the damn door!"

"Shut it your damn self!" Pris yelled back, and then just stood there with her teeth bared and her arms folded. The door was wide open. Ice crystals were coming in.

Lucy slammed and locked the door, then leaned against it. Her chest hurt from the cold air, and way down low on her stomach, where Jerry's hand had been, there was a weird warm ache that she'd never felt before. "Where's Mom?"

"What makes you think I'd tell you anything?" Pris was staring at her. "God, your face looks awful. You've got zits all over!"

Lucy put her hand to her face and felt a few bumps, but both her fingers and her cheek were too cold to tell much of anything. "Where's Mom?"

"Out looking for you."

"Where's Dad?"

"Out looking for you."

"Oh, God. Who's taking care of the little kids?"

"I am."

"Oh, God." Lucy slid down the door to sit on the floor. Right away, the snow and ice soaked through her pants, so that now her butt and legs were cold and wet just like her feet, ankles, hands, ears, face.

Pris nodded, still grinning. "You are in *so much trouble*."

"How'd they know?"

"Guess."

"Priscilla."

"The school called, dummy. Whaddaya think?"

Molly came running down the stairs. Mom and maybe Dad would say, "Don't run on the stairs." Priscilla didn't say anything. Priscilla was supposed to be in charge while Mom and Dad were out. Out looking for her. So if something happened, if Molly fell and got hurt, it would be Lucy's fault.

Lucy had a sudden vivid image of her littlest sister tumbling all the way from the top of the stairs to the bottom and landing in her lap, dead. There was blood. There was coldness. But at least she and everybody else knew whose fault it was.

She tried to reach out her hand, tried to say something, but Molly was leaning safely over the railing halfway down and kicking at the posts and yelling, "Pris, Pris, he took my truck and he won't give it back! It's *my* truck! Make him give it back!"

"Work it out yourself," Priscilla told her smugly. It sounded a lot meaner than when Mom and Dad said it, and they said it a lot.

"I hate you!" Molly screamed, already on her way pounding up the stairs. "I'm telling Mom!"

Lucy tried to get up, but her feet slipped in the water and she sank back against the door to wait until she was strong enough to try again. She knew she couldn't stay here for the rest of her life, but she really didn't see why not. "How long ago did they leave?" she asked Pris.

Priscilla didn't answer. With an effort Lucy opened her eyes. Pris was still standing there with her arms folded, looking at her and laughing. *Laughing* at her.

"What's so funny?"

"You are!" Priscilla chuckled out loud now, and she unfolded an arm to point at her. "You're sitting there in the water like you peed your pants, and you think nobody knows you're in love with that stupid, ugly, fat Jerry Johnston—"

Lucy flew at her. She didn't know how she got her feet under her, or how she kept from falling back into the spreading cold dirty water. But she managed to throw herself against her sister, and Priscilla's shouts of laughter turned into shouts of surprise and self-defense, and Lucy wanted to kill her. Wanted her dead and broken and shut up. Wanted them all dead.

She had hold of Priscilla's braids. They were both rolling around on the floor now, in the water, knocking over the dish of cat food and the trash can under the table. See how Pris liked getting her fancy new pink sweater dirty.

Priscilla kicked her between the legs. Pain forked upward through her body, and Lucy shrieked. They were both shrieking, "I hate you! I hate you! I hate you!" over and over again until you didn't have to hear the words to know what they meant. Dimly, Lucy was aware that sounds of a big fight were coming from upstairs, too, Molly and the two little boys banging around and yelling, "I hate you!" too.

The house was overflowing with anger. Lucy couldn't keep her footing in it. It was soaking through everything. Pris sank her teeth into Lucy's hand, and Lucy doubled the hand into a fist and rammed it into Priscilla's mouth.

Somebody pushed between them. Dad. And Mom went racing up the stairs. *Don't run on the stairs,* Lucy thought confusedly, and imagined her mother tumbling down the stairs and landing in her lap all broken and dead. At least they'd know whose fault it was, which was better than it not being anybody's fault.

Dad was yelling, "Stop it!" He held each of them away from his body in one-armed bear hugs. Behind his back they both tried at the same time to kick each other, and ended up kicking him. "Stop it! Both of you!" He shook them, hard.

The jumble of noise from upstairs was sorting itself out now into Mom yelling, "Cut it out!" and Cory crying and Molly screaming, "He broke my new truck!" and Dominic yelling, "I did not!" Lucy sagged against her father's arm.

He shook them again, not so hard this time, and Lucy was afraid they might already be wearing him out. "What the hell is going on?" he demanded.

Both Priscilla and Lucy were crying and could only say, "I hate her! She hates me!" Lucy's hand hurt, and she thought she saw blood at the corner of her sister's mouth.

Dad was glaring at her. "Where have you been?"

"At Jerry's," she managed to say. "For group."

"You're lying. You walked out of school at two o'clock in the afternoon. Your group doesn't start until four. We went to Jerry Johnston's house looking for you, but nobody answered the door."

"She's in love with Jerry Johnston." Priscilla sneered, and Lucy wanted to kill her again but Dad wouldn't let her.

"Where were you?"

"At Jerry's!"

"Lucy, don't lie to me!"

Dad was roaring at her. His voice filled her ears. She broke away from him, but then for a minute didn't know which way to run.

He let go of Pris and grabbed both of Lucy's shoulders. She was afraid of him; she thought he was going to hurt her, and she deserved it,

too. But instead he brought his face so close to
hers that she saw only a little part of it, and
for an instant she wasn't sure whether this really was her dad at all. Maybe a monster had
invaded their house. Maybe she'd called the
monster there because she was bad. Maybe—
"You're grounded!" Dad said to her very very
quietly. "You're grounded *to your room* until
you tell us the truth."

"I was at Jerry's," she repeated, but her
heart wasn't in it. "Why won't you believe
me?" But it didn't much matter whether he believed her or not. She knew what was real.

Shaking his head in disgust, Dad turned
away from her to deal with Priscilla. Abandoned, Lucy stumbled up the many stairs and
down the long hall to her room.

She collapsed onto the bed nearest the door,
which was Rae's. She fell right away into a
sort of half sleep where snow covered things
and ice crystals changed how things looked
and most of her body belonged to somebody
else, and none of those were bad feelings.

She woke with a little scream and sat up
straight. For long minutes she didn't know
where she was, because she was on the wrong
side of the room. Her first thought was of
Jerry. She missed him; she was afraid of him.
Her next was that she couldn't have been
asleep very long: she could hear the little kids
still crying, Mom still trying to settle them

down, and she saw by her alarm clock that it wasn't quite six o'clock yet. And her clothes were still sopping wet.

She tried to think. She'd never been grounded to her room before, but Rae and Ethan had, and she knew that Mom and Dad had to let you go to the bathroom. They had to feed you. They made you go to school; tomorrow was Thursday, so maybe she could ditch school and run away.

Maybe she could go to Jerry's.

Maybe Rae was wrong. Maybe Rae was all in her head.

Right now she was tired and cold. She turned on the light, found a flannel nightgown and socks and slippers and her robe, and carried them into the bathroom. Nobody yelled at her. Nobody even noticed.

She shut the bathroom door before she turned the light on. For a minute she stood shivering in the darkness without touching anything. Food smells came up from the kitchen; it smelled like fried chicken. A car went by on the street, tires crunching on the snowpack. Somebody walked by. Jerry. No.

Lucy turned on the light and looked at herself in the mirror. As she started to undress, the usual thought came: *God, I'm so ugly.* But she wasn't. She liked the shape of her jaw, the shape of her breasts.

It was cold. She pulled her nightgown over

her head before she took her pants off, being careful to keep it rolled above her waist so it wouldn't get wet. Her clothes below the waist were stuck to her skin and she worked to get them off, sitting down on the cold edge of the tub. Her socks smelled like a wet dog. She wished she had a dog. She wondered where Patches was, hoped somebody else in the family would think about him on a cold, snowy night like this. She pulled off her jeans and stuffed them into the hamper. The hamper was almost full. It was her turn to do laundry this week, but she couldn't very well do it while she was grounded to her room, could she? Served them right.

She hooked her thumbs into the wet elastic waistband of her underwear and pulled them down. She had goose bumps, but the air felt nice and warm, and she backed toward the heat vent.

It was then that she saw the blood. Her period had started.

Now I can have a baby, was the first thing she thought. Then she thought, *Now I can get pregnant,* which seemed like a different thing altogether. Then she was thinking about Jerry, which didn't make any sense at all.

Hastily she wrapped her wet and blood-specked underwear inside her wet jeans and put them in the hamper, too. On the shelf was a box of tampons and a box of pads; the very thought of putting something up inside her made Lucy shudder, and she took the box of pads into her room, hiding it under her robe in case anybody was in the hallway watching her, as if she was doing something wrong.

Nobody was watching. Nobody knew. She fell asleep with Patches curled against her stomach, helping to ease the cramps. Somebody had let him in out of the snow.

24

She slept fitfully, and woke up twice during the evening to change the pad. Each time she was kind of afraid to look because there'd be so much blood, and each time she was a little disappointed when there was only a thin brownish streak.

The first time she got up, she caught Patches nibbling at the food somebody had set on her desk. She hadn't heard anybody come in or go out, but the plate was still warm.

She used to like fried chicken, but now she hated it, and it bothered her that Mom didn't remember that. The milk clogged her throat. She wasn't hungry anyway. When she took a piece of chicken off the bone for Patches, the sight and sound of flesh and skin and tendons tearing made her a little sick. She set the tray on the floor outside her room and shut the door tight. Chicken bones could kill cats.

The tray was gone when she got up the second time. On her way back from the bathroom, she heard Dad and Mom in their room talking about her. "Lucy," Mom said, and then Dad said something that had her name in it, too: "Lucy." Lucy wasn't even curious. She just went on back to bed.

When she woke up again, it was morning, and Mom was at her door with a breakfast tray, and now Lucy was hungry. "Come in," she said drowsily, and started to sit up. Wetness and itching and aching ran deep between her legs. She shouldn't have to tell Mom her period had started. Mothers should just *know,* a secret message between women.

"Good morning, honey," Mom said. "Here's your breakfast." She settled the tray over Lucy's lap before Lucy was even sitting up all the way, and its legs tipped on the wrinkled sheets. This was the tray you got your meals on if you were sick in bed or on the couch in the family room. The beige plastic had faint stains on it from everybody's cups and plates and hands.

She had to go to the bathroom. Naturally, Mom hadn't thought of that before she trapped her with the tray, and Lucy wasn't about to say anything.

She *itched.* Way up inside where she didn't

think she'd ever felt anything before. Nobody'd told her that your period made you
itch.

Mom stood with her hands in the pockets of
her blue robe. She hadn't set her hair yet this
morning, so the white streak wasn't a streak;
there was white all over the top and front of
her hair. Mom was *old*. Lucy frowned and
took a bite of toast. It wasn't toasted enough
and there wasn't enough butter on it, but she
was hungry. It hurt her throat when she swallowed.

"We were really worried about you yesterday," Mom said.

"Why?" Lucy demanded through a mouthful
of scrambled eggs. She liked her eggs sunny-
side up, but of course it didn't matter in this
family what *she* liked.

"Because we love you."

"You don't love me. All you care about is
Ethan and Rae." Remembering Dad's reaction
when she'd said something like that to him,
she waited to see what Mom would do.

Mom just closed her eyes for a second, then
opened them and said quietly, "That's not true,
but I'm not going to argue with you about it. I
just want you to know that we called Jerry
Johnston last night and he said you hadn't
been at group."

Lucy stopped chewing and stared at her
mother. Then she shrugged elaborately, swal-

lowed, drank some orange juice. Her throat burned. *Why would he say that?* "So?" she said out loud.

"So we know you were lying to us about where you were."

"So? You never believe me anyway."

Mom sighed. "Well, I hope you decide to tell us the truth soon. We all miss you when you're stuck in your room like this. You have about an hour to get ready for school now." She started to leave.

Lucy wanted her to stay. *My period started.* "I bet Pris doesn't miss me," she said sullenly.

Mom kept her back to her, but Lucy could tell she was smiling. "Pris's mouth is fine, Lucy. How's your hand?"

She looked at her hand where Pris had bitten it. She'd forgotten all about it, and there wasn't even a mark. "It hurts," she said, "but that's all right." She *itched*. She squirmed around on the bed and almost spilled the juice but couldn't reach the itch. She itched, but Mom wasn't smart enough to ask about that.

"Let me see." Mom came back to her, and by the time Lucy figured out she was talking about her hand, she was holding it, turning it into the light, kissing it quickly and putting it back down. "I guess you didn't damage each other permanently." She started out of the room again, stopped, and touched the box of pads on the dresser. "Lucy. Honey, did you start your period?"

"What's it to you?"

Mom came over to her, kissed the top of her head, whispered, "Congratulations," and left the room in a hurry. It seemed to Lucy that she'd sounded and looked scared, but that wouldn't make any sense. But then, nothing adults said or did made sense, except Jerry. He was a mystery, which wasn't the same thing.

When you were grounded to your room, you couldn't use the phone, so she couldn't call Stacey to tell her about her period or even to say which corner to meet on to walk to school. She always timed it so she left the house either before or after all her brothers and sisters, so she'd wouldn't be seen walking anywhere near them; this morning Mom wouldn't let her leave until ten minutes before the first bell. "Right now, I can't trust that you'll go straight to school."

"What makes you think I'm going to school anyway?" Lucy muttered, only half under her breath.

She was sorry right away that she'd said it, because Mom looked up from helping Dom with his boots, raised her eyebrows, and said, "Tell you what, Lucy. You'll walk to school this morning with Molly and Dominic and me. That way we can be sure you get there."

All the way to school Lucy held her books against her chest and watched her feet and thought about the blood and the itching from secret places inside her body. At the corner of the playground, Mom stopped and hugged the little kids, but Lucy just kept walking, and Mom didn't call her back.

"You hear about Mike Garver?" Stacey asked her as they made their way up the crowded stairs to homeroom.

Lucy didn't want to talk about Mike Garver. Mike Garver was dumb. She wanted to tell Stacey about her period. She wanted to find out if Stacey had ever been grounded to her room, which she seriously doubted, and to talk about how much she hated her mother and her father and her brothers and sisters. She wanted to tell Stacey about Jerry Johnston, but of course she couldn't do that.

"He died," Stacey said.

Lucy stopped on the stairs. Jeremy Martinez ran into her, called her a dirty name that she didn't even know what it meant, and pushed around her. Ms. Abercrombie yelled at her from the top of the stairs to keep moving, but Lucy grabbed the back of Stacey's sweatshirt, pulled her over to the wall, and said, "What?"

"He died. Last night. Come on, we're gonna be late."

"What do you mean, he died?"

"What do you mean, what do I mean?"

Stacey had on silver lipstick, and when she laughed her lips looked like tin foil. She laughed now and pulled away from Lucy just as the tardy bell rang, right over their heads. The bell was so loud that Lucy didn't hear what else Stacey said, but she thought it was just, "He died," again.

Some people said he'd OD'd. Some people said it was AIDS. Some people said he'd frozen to death in the snow. There was going to be a special assembly fifth period, right after lunch; some people said Mr. Li was going to tell them what had happened to Mike. Some people said it was a vampire, or a werewolf, and Mr. Li wouldn't tell them the truth about that.

All morning Lucy kept feeling worse and worse. The cramps and the itching had spread all through that hole at the center of her body, the hole that was left when they'd taken all the different-colored plastic layers off the model in science. The place like a cave where all the organs and stuff with weird names were. Pancreas. Uterus. Fallopian tubes.

Her head ached constantly. Sometimes she was so hot she'd be sweating and faint; then, just a few minutes later, her teeth would be chattering. Every time she looked in the mirror, or put her hand to her face, there were hundreds more zits.

In the rest room before lunch while Stacey

tried to get the flakes of hairspray out of her hair without ruining the style, Lucy said, "I started my period last night."

Stacey tossed her head. Lucy saw admiringly that her glossy hair didn't shift at all. "So? I started mine a *long* time ago." Lucy didn't know whether to believe her or not. If she was lying, that was bad. If she had started her period a long time ago and Lucy hadn't known about it, that was bad, too.

While she was standing in the lunch line, she saw Jerry Johnston go into the office. She knew right away that he'd come for her, and she could hardly eat lunch. It was pizza anyway, which was always disgusting at school because they put anchovies on it, and her stomach was kind of upset, and Jeremy Martinez sat across from her and stared at her the whole time, and she found a big zit on her neck. When the monitor pushed his way between the crowded tables to tell her she was wanted in the office, Lucy didn't even care that Jeremy and his stupid friends started chanting, "Lu-cy's in trou-ble! Lu-cy's in trou-ble!"

Jerry seemed to take up most of the principal's office; he was a lot bigger than Mr. Li, and he was wearing a bulky red sweater that made him look even bigger. Probably the sweater had been a Christmas present. Lucy wondered who'd given it to him, and was mortified that she hadn't thought to get him anything.

He looked healthy, waiting for her. His cheeks were rosy. He had his arms folded across his stomach, and she knew if he held her against it, it would be firm this time, like a good mattress. He was smiling at Mr. Li; she wasn't close enough to hear what he was saying, but she liked the way his voice sounded. He knew what he was doing. He was in charge. She could trust him.

Mr. Li said something to the secretary, Mrs. Davis, and Mrs. Davis came and opened the gate in the counter to let Lucy go in. Mrs. Davis was looking at her funny. Lucy was suddenly afraid she had blood on her pants, suddenly aware of how ugly her face was all covered with pimples, suddenly acutely shy. She couldn't look at Mrs. Davis or Mr. Li. She couldn't even really look at Jerry.

"Lucy." Mr. Li didn't exactly have an accent, but when he said her name, it sounded kind of Oriental, like Loo Si. "How are you?"

"Fine."

"Well, I know you're upset about Mike Garver. We all are. It's a terrible thing." He was sitting behind the desk, which made him look even smaller than he was. His hands were side by side, flat on the big calendar, which was all covered with tiny writing. Lucy couldn't quite see what it said. She wondered

if he wrote secret notes to himself in Chinese
or Cambodian or whatever he was.

"What happened to him?" she heard herself
ask. She still didn't look at either of them, but
she listened for Jerry to answer.

"That's why I'm here," he answered quietly.
"I want us to process it together."

"Mr. Johnston wants to take you out of
school for the afternoon," Mr. Li said.

"For a special group meeting," Jerry said. "I
think we need to process what's happened."

Lucy moved closer to Jerry, risked glancing
up at him, with a little thrill found him watching her, looked down again. "He's already
talked to your parents," Mr. Li said, "and
they've given permission."

Lucy looked at Jerry again, and he winked.
He hadn't talked to her parents. It was their
secret. She felt honored, chosen, and very
grown up.

"Would you like to go with Mr. Johnston for
the afternoon?" Mr. Li asked kindly.

Lucy forced herself to look away from Jerry
and at the principal. "Okay," she said.

"The rest of the day will essentially be taken
up with the assembly anyway," Mr. Li was saying, as much to himself as to them, and then
he kept talking while he wrote stuff down on a
sheet of paper with the school name on it and
hurried around the desk to the file cabinet and

shuffled through a bunch of folders in there and stuck the paper into one of them.

There must be a folder in there that said BRILL, LUCY ANN. BRILL, RAE ELLEN, too, unless they'd taken that one out already, and BRILL, PRISCILLA CAROLE, and BRILL, DOMINIC ANTHONY, and BRILL, MOLLY ELIZABETH. Maybe even BRILL, ETHAN MICHAEL, although Ethan hadn't gone to this school for a long time. There wouldn't be one for Cory yet—BRILL, CORY SCOTT—but he'd be starting preschool next year.

Mr. Li was still talking to himself, kind of fluttering his hands, when Lucy followed Jerry out of the office, through the gate, past Mrs. Davis, and out the front door of the school. She didn't say anything about her coat because she didn't want to go all the way down the hall to get it, and at first the cold air felt good, but by the time they got to the corner she was shivering.

"Mike died last night," Jerry said.

Of course she already knew that, but she understood it was a way to begin. "He was at your house last night," she said. "How come you told my parents that I wasn't there?"

Immediately she felt guilty. She didn't want him to think she was mad at him. "That's between us. It's private. How come you ran away?"

Lucy was ashamed. "I don't know."

"Did you get scared?"

"I guess so."

He put his arm around her, just for a second. His sweater itched against her skin, but it made her warm and she wished he didn't have to take his arm away. But she understood. They were in public. Somebody might see and think there was something weird going on. "There's nothing to be afraid of, honey. Not with me. I have something special to show you today."

She nodded. They crossed the street and turned left, heading toward his house. Behind them, still not very far away, the bell rang at the school. Lunch was over. In a few minutes they'd be going into the auditorium for the assembly, where they'd hear what had happened to Mike. But she'd know a lot sooner and a lot truer, because Jerry was going to tell her.

"I wish you'd stayed," Jerry said, "because what happened between Mike and me was beautiful. He really worked through a lot of that rage and sadness. He felt better than he had in a long time." Jerry chuckled a little. "So did I."

"He died," she said, confused.

"It was beautiful," Jerry said again. "Brief, but beautiful." He shook his head and sighed. "Now it's over and Mike is gone and the rest of us have to go on."

Her back itched between her shoulder

blades. She reached up under her shirt as far as she could, gasping as the cold air swept across her skin. Her back was covered with zits. Her breasts itched under her bra. The insides of her mouth and nose itched.

As they passed through Jerry's prickly hedge, it broke off against her elbow and left little bits and pieces of wood on top of the hard snow. She felt blood spurt between her legs, and she burst into tears. The tears felt as if they were turning to ice before they even got out of her eyes.

Now that they were in his yard, on his porch, Jerry could do what he wanted without anybody seeing, and he picked her up. She put her arms around his neck and held on tight. Behind her back he put the key in the lock and turned it, his hand moving across her hip. Then they were inside his house where it was warm and dim, and he'd shut the door behind them, and Lucy was dizzy and crying, and Jerry was holding her and saying her name over and over and over as if it meant something else, as if it wasn't about her anymore but about him, as if it meant love.

He laid her on the big pillows on the living-room floor. He brought a blanket to cover her, but she was sweating now and she kicked it off. He lay down beside her and held her against him. Even though that was hot, too, she stayed there, and all she could see was the twisted red yarn of his sweater moving up and down as he breathed and talked.

"Mike wouldn't let me take him home," Jerry was telling her. "It wasn't very late, and he always took the bus back after group. That's part of what we teach in this group, how to take care of yourself in a dangerous world. Kids learn—" He stopped, laughed a little. "I guess you don't care about theories of adolescent development, do you? Anyway, he'd been gone a couple of hours, maybe three, and I was just—uh, reading, pottering around the house, making progress notes, when his foster mother called and said he'd never made it back. We figured probably he'd run away, and she said she'd call the cops if he didn't show up by midnight. He'd run lots of times before."

Dreamily Lucy wondered why he was talking so much. Right now she didn't feel anything bad or mixed up. What she felt was feverish, a little dizzy, a little sick to her stomach, and she itched. She loved the sound of his voice deep deep inside his body, the way his chest rumbled and his throat purred under her ear.

"But I was worried, so I went out looking for him. And I found him, under the hedge just outside my yard. That's as far as he'd made it. I called an ambulance and the foster family, of course, but I knew it was too late."

"What did he die of?"

"We won't know for sure till they get the autopsy results back, but they think it was a heart attack brought on by drug use."

"What's an autopsy?"

His hand rubbing her back stopped for a minute; until then she hadn't even really realized he'd been massaging her, under her shirt, and now she wanted nothing more than for him to start doing it again, even though she was embarrassed to think of all the zits he'd feel. "That's where they look inside a body," he said, "to see why a person died."

Lucy stiffened in amazement. He started rubbing again, but she still had to ask, "They look *inside*?"

"Yes."

"They cut you *open*?"

"Yes."

Waves of nausea spread through her body, hot and then cold. Sure she was going to throw up, she rolled away from Jerry and tried to sit up, but she was too dizzy. "Everybody *dies*!" she wailed. "I *hate* it that everybody dies!"

He encircled her in his arms again and eased her back down on the pillow, then wrapped his heavy legs around her too. "Not everybody, darling," he murmured. "Not everybody."

He was scaring her. She didn't want to be

scared, but she was. Her head was spinning and her ears were ringing and she felt dizzy.

It was embarrassing. Here she was, alone with Jerry Johnston and getting his attention in a way she'd dreamed about. Here she was, as close to him as she could ever get without actually getting inside him or him getting inside her: his lips sucking at her neck, his teeth nibbling. Here she was: something was about to happen to her that would change her life forever and she was such a baby she was making herself sick.

When Jerry murmured, "It's okay, honey," his mouth moved across her flesh like some little live creature.

She heard herself say, "You lied to the principal. My parents never said it was okay for me to be here."

He chuckled and stroked her hair. "Sure," he admitted. "I'm on your side, remember? If it takes lying to the grown-ups to do what's best for you, then I'll lie."

Amazed by his daring and by her own complicity in it, she whispered, "They'll find out. They always find out."

He shrugged. His whole huge body seemed to move in sections, as if the pieces weren't totally connected. "It doesn't matter," he told her softly. "They can't stop us now. It's too late. We've come too far."

He tightened his arms and legs around her.

She wanted him to do that, ached for him to do it, but then she couldn't breathe and she was going to be sick for sure. The terrible itching was everywhere now—inside her throat, under her arms, inside her vagina. She struggled to turn her face out of the hollow of Jerry's body.

He held her a little away from him to look into her face. Cold and abandoned, she whimpered. After a few seconds he shook his head sadly and let her go. "Oh, dear," he said kindly. "You're not quite ready for this, are you, sweetheart?"

Lucy saw how much she'd disappointed him, and she could hardly stand it. But she was desperate not to faint or throw up, and desperate to scratch in very private places.

Jerry sighed, lay back, and said carefully, "I don't know how long I'm going to be able to wait for you, Lucy."

She didn't want to lose him. She didn't even know what it would mean to lose him. "I'm sorry," she managed to say, but he didn't say anything back.

She didn't know where the bathroom was. She struggled to her hands and knees, then to her feet, and barely made it to the porch before she was throwing up. She leaned over the railing and tried to keep her eyes closed so she wouldn't see the ugliness she was making all over Jerry's clean white snow.

He followed her out onto the porch. At first he just stood behind her while she threw up, and she was embarrassed but she couldn't stop. "Damn," he said, almost under his breath. "So much for our plans for today."

"No," Lucy gasped. "You said—something special. You promised—"

"You're in no shape for anything like that today." From the tone of his voice, she knew she'd let him down.

"I'm—sorry."

"We've still got time," he assured her, and put his big hands on her shoulders.

She threw up again over his porch railing, and he held her head till she was through. Then, gently, he turned her around and tilted her chin up and peered at her face in the bright afternoon sunlight that hurt her eyes and must be making the zits on her face look hideous. She was ashamed and excited, and she was going to throw up again.

"Lucy, my dear," he said, "I think you've got chicken pox."

25

Lucy spent the next six days under a quilt on the family-room couch. People brought her things: orange juice, vegetable beef soup, tea. She watched TV for hours and hours, till *Married with Children* and *The Equalizer* and *All My Children* and the six o'clock news kind of blended together and made a weird kind of sense. She listened to music till the earphones and then the music itself started to hurt her ears. She itched, and for a while she bled.

The doctor said she had chicken pox all over her body, including inside. Inside her ears. Inside her nose, up higher than she could reach. Inside her vagina. Priscilla said at least it wouldn't matter if she got scars. Lucy tried to stick her tongue out at her, but it was swollen and her lips were cracked. So she settled for a dirty look; with her eyelids all red and puffy, Pris probably couldn't even tell where she was looking.

Sometimes Mom would come and sit with her, stroke her hair and wash her with a warm washcloth when Lucy could stand to be touched, read to her when she could stand noise, just sit in the room with her when she couldn't. It had been a long time since Lucy'd been home with just Mom and Cory. It didn't even feel like the same house. "Poor baby," Mom kept saying. Her voice was gentle and singsong, like a lullaby, but she was also laughing a little. "Talk about 'the curse'! I promise you, it won't be like this every month."

How does she know? Lucy thought groggily. *She thinks she knows everything. Maybe it will be like this every month for me.*

A lot of things happened during those six days. Despite herself, Lucy saw that life didn't stop, life had lots of stuff in it, even when you were sick, even when people you loved died, even when you were in love.

The guy on the news, the cute one with the dimple even if he was almost as old as Dad, said there'd been an earthquake in Austria. Or Australia. Or Armenia. He had pictures of people digging and yelling. Lucy didn't completely understand why they were so upset.

That was the day the itching was the worst, bad enough to make her cry.

Dad had to take Rae's dentist records to the police station again, because they'd found another body of a girl about her age. If they had to identify her by her teeth, that meant her body was decayed. Lucy tried to think about that. She ran her tongue over her teeth, and it wasn't quite so swollen now. She hadn't brushed her teeth in days. Guiltily she wondered if they'd be able to tell that she hadn't brushed her teeth if she died of the chicken pox and her body decayed and they only had her teeth and bones to tell that she'd been Lucy Ann Brill. It was weird that they could tell it was a girl and how old she was, without hair or makeup or breasts or a vagina. It must not have been Rae again, because when Dad brought the records home there was just a little bit of crying, Mom and Dad holding on to each other in the kitchen. She didn't like that. They were still crying about Ethan and Rae, when *she* was the one who had chicken pox *inside* her.

Dominic got spanked for lying. Cory broke a glass but he didn't get hurt. There was a mouse in the family room. Patches ran around with it wriggling and squeaking in his mouth, and Dad couldn't get him to take it outside, and then she woke up and there was the back half of a little gray mouse on the floor in front of the couch, and she screamed even though her throat hurt and Dad came with the dustpan and scooped it up and threw it under the lilac bushes in the backyard. The tail had been moving, she was sure of it. Mice were so *tiny*. They were cute, but she hated them when they were in her house, but she hated having them die, too, and hated Patches for killing them, even though Dad said it was a cat's nature.

Jerry came. More than once she heard his voice. She sat up against the arm of the couch and tried to comb her hair with her fingers. Nobody came to tell her he was there. The first time she asked about it, Mom said without looking at her, "You're too sick for visitors." Later Mom told her, "We'll discuss Jerry Johnston when you're feeling better."

Something's wrong. "I am feeling better! I want to see him!"

"No," Mom said, and Lucy was too weak and confused to argue.

The third time he came—maybe it was more than that; maybe he'd come to see her lots of times and she'd been too sick to know it and they wouldn't tell her—Lucy wrapped herself in the quilt and stumbled as fast as she could to the front door, which was just shutting behind him. Both Mom and Dad were standing there. Mom's arms were folded. Dad's fists were clenched, as if he'd been fighting somebody off. "How come you guys didn't tell me Jerry was here?" Lucy cried. "He's my friend!"

They both turned to look at her, and Dad said, "What are you doing up?"

"I feel fine."

Before Lucy could get her feet untangled from the quilt enough to step back, Mom had reached out and put her hand on her forehead. Smiling at her, Mom said, "Well, it looks to me like you can go back to school on Monday. That gives you the weekend to catch up on your homework. Pris has been bringing home your assignments for you. I know you have a book report due in English, and there are three or four pages of fractions—"

"I want to see Jerry!"

They looked at each other over her head. She hated that. It made her look back and forth between them like Patches watching people play ball. Then Dad said to Mom, "I guess now's as good a time as any to tell her."

Mom nodded. "Lucy, come and sit down. We need to talk."

Something terrible is going to happen something terrible is going to happen something terrible

Tripping over the ends of the quilt, Lucy followed them unwillingly into the living room and sat on the arm of the brown chair. It was true that she didn't feel queasy or feverish anymore, and her period was done, and there were only a few scabby places in her hair that still itched. But something terrible was going to happen. Right now.

Dad kept standing. He was really tall. He said, "Your mother and I have decided that until things settle down a little you won't be seeing Jerry Johnston anymore. We've pulled you out of the group, and we've told him not to come by the house or the school for you."

Lucy had caught her breath and pulled the quilt tight around her. *"Why?"* she wailed.

"Because we think he's a bad influence right now. He upsets you more than he helps."

"How do you know that? You think you know everything!"

"Oh, honey." Mom shook her head sadly. "It's obvious from the way you act."

It's my fault "He doesn't upset me. You guys upset me. You're the ones somebody should protect me from!"

"He lied, Lucy." Mom was leaning forward in her chair and looking hard at Lucy. Lucy didn't want to see her ever again, and so she pulled the quilt across her face. But that didn't stop her mother. "He told Mr. Li that he had permission to take you out of school last Thursday, and that was an out-and-out lie. He had never talked to either of us."

"Well, he had to say that. You'd have said no."

"You're damn right we'd have said no." Dad

was mad. His voice was tight and his eyes were all squinched at the corners. She told herself that she didn't much care whether he was mad at her or not. But, trembling, she lowered the quilt just enough that she could watch him.

"The point is," Mom said, "he *lied*."

What's the big deal about lying? Lucy thought furiously. *Things aren't what they seem anyway. Everything's a lie.*

"That kind of behavior," Dad said, "is absolutely unprofessional, and I won't stand for it."

"*We* won't stand for it," Mom said quietly, looking at him.

Dad said, "We. And your principal won't stand for it, either. He's canceled Johnston's relationship with the school and reported him to the social work licensure board. No more groups. No more contact with kids. He's called all the parents."

They're trying to kill him, Lucy said to herself. It didn't come as a surprise.

"And," Mom said, "some of the stuff you've been writing in your diary about him and about what you do in the group is pretty scary."

Lucy gasped. "You've been reading my diary?"

"You know I have been. Don't pretend to be morally offended or something. You and I

have been writing things to each other in your
diary ever since Rae disappeared. That's how I
know you wanted me to know something was
wrong about Jerry. That's how I know—"

All of a sudden Dad swiveled and slammed
his fist into the wall. Lucy's heart beat so fast it
hurt. Mom said in a shocked voice, "Tony?"

Dad was roaring. "That son of a bitch knows
something about Rae! I know he does!" He
stomped out of the room, out of the house,
and a moment later they heard the harsh
noise of the station-wagon engine revving up.

Mom pressed her fingers to her cheekbones,
like she did when she was getting a headache.
From behind her hands she said, "We just can't
trust him with you, Lucy. You're too important for us to take chances."

"He knows what's best for me—"

"No. We're your parents."

"You're awful parents!" Lucy was whispering now. "You don't know how to be parents.
You shouldn't be allowed to have kids. You let
my brother die and you let something bad
happen to my sister, we don't even know
what, and now Jerry says I'm next, and he's
right, I know he's right!"

She shouldn't have said that. It would just
make them not trust him even more. But it
didn't make any difference anyway. Once
they'd made up their minds, they never gave
in.

Mom sighed and stood up. Thinking she was going after Dad, Lucy was already plotting her escape. She'd run out the front door when Mom went out the back door, and she'd hide someplace until they got tired of looking for her, and then she'd run to Jerry's, where it was safe.

Maybe, it dawned on her, that's what Rae had done. Maybe she really had seen Rae at Jerry's. Maybe Ethan was there, too, and Mike Garver. Maybe nobody had died after all.

But Mom stayed where she was and said softly, "I'm sorry, Lucy. I know this is hard for you. But we need to pull together as a family, now more than ever, and Jerry Johnston works against that. I'm sure he believes he has your best interests at heart, but—"

"I *hate* this family!"

"Lucy, don't."

"I *hate* this fucking family!" Lucy yelled into the bunched-up quilt that smelled of calomine lotion and her own sweat. "I'll leave! I'll run away! Just like Rae! You'll never see me again! As soon as I get the chance, I'm running away!"

Mom stood very still for a few minutes. Then she said, "Well, then, I guess you'll have to go with me to take Priscilla to her dance class."

"No."

"Yes. I can't leave you here and take a

chance on your running away, and it's not fair for Pris to miss her class just because you're behaving like this. You will come with me."

Lucy said, as nastily as she could, "It's against the law to leave little kids alone. You have to leave me here to watch the little kids. You really are a terrible mother, you know that?"

"It'll only be for a few minutes. They can watch cartoons. You don't leave me any other choice."

So if something happens to them, it'll be my fault. That's okay. This is all my fault anyway. "I've been sick, remember? I've got chicken pox. I can't go outside."

"You're not that sick now. It'll do you good to get some fresh air."

"You're trying to kill me. You want all your children dead."

It was a mean thing to say and Lucy hated herself for saying it. But she hated her parents more. They were trying to keep her away from Jerry.

Mom had gone pale. She and Lucy stared at each other for long minutes across a teeming shaft of sunlight that angled in the windows. Then Mom turned and said evenly to Pris, who'd been standing behind her all this time with her duffel bag full of dance stuff in her hand, making faces at Lucy, "Let's go. You don't want to be late."

It struck Lucy that some kind of power was shifting in her relationship to her mother, because if she really refused to go, she was probably too big for Mom to force her. Knowing that gave her a dangerous, heady feeling.

But she'd give in on this one. It wasn't worth it. She had other things to think about. She had to figure out some way to get to Jerry.

Priscilla said something snotty to her, but Lucy didn't even hear what it was. When Mom came back from getting the little kids settled with snacks in front of the television, she didn't look at Lucy at all. Lucy just shrugged, wrapped the quilt around herself some more, and followed her mother and sister out to the car. She didn't put a coat on. Mom didn't tell her to. To her disappointment, it wasn't all that cold outside.

Priscilla sat in the front seat with Mom and they chatted all the way there. Huddled in a corner of the backseat, Lucy might as well not have been there. That was fine with her. She stared out the window and tried to fill her mind with nothing but thoughts of Jerry. After Pris got out, Mom didn't invite her to move up to the front seat. That was fine with her. She felt like crying, but not because of Mom. She didn't care what Mom thought.

She found herself staring at the back of her mother's head and neck and shoulders as they drove home. There wasn't any gray yet in the back of her mother's hair, but there would be. Someday her mother would be old. Someday her mother would die.

They didn't say anything to each other all the way home, until they turned into the driveway and the station wagon was there and Mom said, "Oh, your father's home," as if Lucy'd been worried about that.

Dad was there, and so was Jerry. They were standing in the entranceway by the front door, under the dusty umbrella lamp. Dad's shoulders were all hunched up and he was breathing hard. Lucy thought Jerry looked like a blown-out eggshell, like Humpty Dumpty.

Mom said, "Tony?"

Dad said, "Lucy, go into the family room with the other kids," but she didn't, and he didn't make her.

Jerry said, "Hi, Lucy," and she said hi back.

"I've told Mr. Johnston that he's not to have anything to do with Lucy anymore," Dad said to Mom, "but he doesn't accept that."

Mom said, "You told Mr. Li that we'd given you permission to take Lucy out of school when you'd never spoken to us about it. That alone would be reason for us to terminate her therapy, let alone—"

"Lucy is a very disturbed child," Jerry said. His voice was hollow. He sounded sick, or very tired. Lucy was afraid she might have given him chicken pox. "She needs both individual and group therapy."

"We'll make that decision," Mom said. "We're her parents."

"He says we're unfit parents," Dad said. Lucy caught her breath.

"You've been through a great deal in the last few years," Jerry said quietly. "Losing two children would put a tremendous strain on anyone."

Dad grabbed the collar of his shirt. It was a green shirt, one Lucy had never seen before. "Where's my daughter, you filthy bastard? Where is she?"

Dad had lifted Jerry off his feet. She saw the surprise on Dad's face when he realized that, and he set Jerry back down.

"Take your hands off me, Mr. Brill, or I'll file assault charges as well," Jerry said, and Dad took his hands away.

"What do you mean 'as well'?" Mom demanded. "What are you threatening us with?"

"When I got here, the three small children were here by themselves. That's child neglect."

"It was just for a few minutes," Mom protested. "Priscilla—"

"That combined with Ethan's problems and Rae's mysterious disappearance and Lucy's behavior problems in school indicates to me that this is a highly dysfunctional family."

"We tried to get them help—"

"Stop it, Carole," Dad snapped. "We don't have to defend ourselves to this—buffoon."

"Well, actually, you do," Jerry said reasonably.

Lucy noticed that he kept standing up on his tiptoes and then putting his heels down again, up and down, up and down, as if he were about to float away. She didn't want him to float away. She wanted to float away with him. She wondered what a buffoon was. Dad had no right to call Jerry names.

"Because, you see, if you insist on preventing Lucy from participating in therapy with me, I will report child abuse and neglect to the Department of Social Services. They would be required to investigate. Chances are good that they would remove the children, at least Lucy, in her own best interests. I do, after all, know most of the workers down there."

"I can't believe anybody would think we're abusive parents." Mom couldn't seem to stop shaking her head.

"Ever spank your kids?"

"Dominic got spanked yesterday for lying," Lucy said. "I heard it."

Jerry just nodded.

"Get out of this house!" Dad thundered.

He didn't touch Jerry and he didn't move toward him, so Lucy was disappointed when

Jerry turned to go. "Wait!" she cried, and ran after him.

"Don't worry, honey," Jerry said, just to her, at the same time that Dad caught her from behind and wouldn't let her go.

26

"Can he really do that?"

"Jesus, Carole, I don't know. He is a social worker, and because of Lucy we're clients again. That gives him power. Makes him dangerous."

"If he heard you saying that, he'd use it as more evidence of how 'dysfunctional' we are. He'd probably write it down somewhere."

"Well, I think we'd better proceed on the assumption that he isn't bluffing."

"What are you saying, Tony? That we ought to allow him access to Lucy again because of what he might do to the family if we refuse?"

"No."

"Good. Because if anything, we have more reason to protect her now."

"I'm saying we can't afford to underestimate

the enemy. We have to understand the risk we're taking."

"Well, I don't understand. Why is Jerry Johnston our enemy?"

"I don't know. But there's more to Jerry Johnston than we know."

"There's something—I don't know—desperate about him," Mom said. "Like an addict who can't get a big enough fix."

Dad agreed. "I don't trust him. I can't say exactly how, but I think he's dangerous. It has something to do with other people's turmoil. He needs it somehow. He stirs it up, exaggerates it, especially in teenagers when they're in so much turmoil anyway, and then somehow he uses it for his own purposes. But I can't pin it down to anything more specific than that, and that's all intuition and—metaphysics."

Lucy had never heard the word *metaphysics* before. More adult secret code. The older she got, the more of it she thought she learned, but there was always a whole bunch of stuff that grown-ups kept hidden from her.

"This is the farthest thing from metaphysical," Mom was saying. "One of our children is dead. One is missing. Lucy's in danger. If there's any pattern to this at all, Priscilla is next. Tony, we have got to do something. We can't just stand here and let our children be— taken. Used, one after another."

Lucy waited for Dad to say something that

would make sense out of all this, but he didn't.
She should have known better than to think
he would.

Finally Mom asked him, "Do you still think
Jerry knows something about Rae and
Ethan?"

"Yes."

"Then you should tell the police."

"Tell the police what? All I have is a hunch,
and that's probably just me looking for an-
swers and reasons when there aren't any."

"They really are gone, aren't they? Our babies really are gone. I always thought I'd die if
anything happened to any of my children.
Now I've lost two, and I'm amazed at how
much pain a human being can stand. But God,
Tony, I don't want to lose Lucy, too."

Then Mom was making that noise again that
she'd made so long for Ethan and then for
Rae. Lucy wouldn't have thought a person
could make a noise like that. It sounded like
one of those dolls from the olden days that
you tipped backward and it cried. Just a really
short cry and then it stopped, and when you
tipped it again, it made another short sharp
cry. Lucy'd almost gotten used to hearing it. In
the night, in the middle of a sunny Sunday
afternoon with the football game on, when
she came into the house after school. Now
Mom was making that awful rhythmic noise

for her, the noise that took the place of breathing.

The sound changed. First it got kind of muffled, as if Mom had hidden her face in something soft. Then it got softer and the rhythm changed; it wasn't just Mom's breathing that made the sound now, but some kind of movement, like dancing or swinging on a swing. Dad said out loud, "I love you, Carole," and then Lucy, crouched in the hall outside their bedroom with her duffel bag under her elbow, knew what was going on.

Her parents were having *sexual intercourse.* Maybe they were making another baby. Maybe she'd have another brother or sister whose life was starting right this minute, and she was there. At the same instant that she was getting ready to run away forever.

For just an instant, she wanted to stay here. But she didn't see how she could. She turned away from her parents' door. Of course, they didn't notice.

Patches followed her downstairs, meowing loudly for food. She filled his bowl and patted his head a few times, feeling sad. But he just kept flicking his ears and tossing his head and eating, and so finally she left him alone.

Very quietly she lifted the phone receiver and dialed Jerry's number, wincing at the beeps the numbers made when she pressed them. He'd been expecting her, because he an-

swered in the middle of the first ring. With her
hand cupped over her mouth, she whispered,
"Jerry?"

"Are you ready, my love?"

It was hard for her to talk then, but she
managed to say, "Yes. Can you come get me?"

"I'll meet you in front of your parents' house
in twenty minutes. It's a gray van."

Your parents' house. That made her feel
funny, but he was right; it wasn't her house
anymore. "Okay," she said, and nodded, and
carefully hung up. The receiver made a tiny
click when she set it back on the hook, but she
didn't think anybody had heard.

Twenty minutes. What would she do for
twenty minutes? It was too cold to wait outside. She put on her heavy coat. Last spring
she'd gone shopping with Dad, Priscilla, and
Rae, and they'd all bought coats on sale, and
her sleeves were already too short. She put on
her boots and scarf and gloves. The red scarf
and gloves had been a Christmas present from
Molly. Lucy felt tears hot behind her eyes, but
she was tired of crying, tired of everybody crying, and she held them back.

She picked up a *Time* magazine from the
arm of the couch and flipped through it. There
was a picture of some old Russian guys, and
pictures of that earthquake. She didn't care. It
had nothing to do with her. She was running
away from home. Jerry was on his way to get

her. She looked some more at the picture of the mother crying in the grandmother's arms, and then put the magazine back down.

Patches squatted right in front of her and peed on the living-room carpet. Lucy stared at him in disbelief. When he was done, he arched his back and stretched his tail up straight with just a kink at the very end, then rubbed himself once back and forth across her ankles and walked away. She ought to clean up the puddle, but she didn't have time to go find the ammonia and a rag and, anyway, it wasn't her house anymore.

She hadn't been watching a clock or anything, but it must be time. Making sure to step way over the wet spot on the rug, she carried her bag to the front door, and started to go out. Then she unzipped the side pocket and took out her diary. Holding it away from her as if it were a mouse by the tail, she carried it gingerly back to the dining room and left it on the table. She wouldn't need it once she was out of here. She wouldn't be able to keep secrets from Jerry anyway.

Patches tried to go out when she did. It was too cold for him, and she shut the door quicker and harder than she meant to. But if anybody heard the door slam it was too late anyway, because there was Jerry Johnston's gray van waiting for her in front of the house. Lucy ran down the steps, slipped and almost fell, ran through the snow to the curb, and climbed up into the high van beside Jerry.

He didn't say anything. He didn't have to. When he put his arm around her and drew her to him, she felt herself sink into his down jacket and then into the soft side of his rib cage and belly. He kissed her cheek. His lips were cold and she hardly felt his breath. It was warm and dark in the van, with little bursts of light here and there where street-lights and snow reflected off metal.

By the time they got to the end of her street, Lucy realized they weren't headed toward Jerry's house. "Where are we going?" Her voice was loud and echoey, and she was embarrassed to even be asking the question.

"I have another house in another part of the city." He glanced over at her; she saw the quick blue flash of his eyes. "You'll be joining others there."

"Others?"

That was a funny way to put it.

She didn't want there to be any "others."

Maybe he meant Rae. She thought about that for a minute.

She didn't even want it to be Rae.

They went around another corner. In the dark and snow and from the van's high seat, Lucy couldn't recognize any landmarks. She didn't think they could have gone very far away from her neighborhood yet, but she had no idea where they were.

It didn't matter. She was with Jerry. "Other troubled kids," he explained. "Other people your age who are angry and sad and scared, like you."

"Who?"

Jerry reached over and patted her knee. Her jeans were stiff, her legs so cold they burned, and even though his hand rested there for a minute or two, her knee was no warmer than it had been before. "We're being followed," he said suddenly, and put his hand back on the wheel to turn the van hard around another corner. Lucy slid away from him across the seat and scrambled to right herself.

Like a little kid, she pulled her knees up under her and peered over the back of the seat. The back window was a small, steamed-up, grayish rectangle at the far end of the gray box that was the van, and she couldn't see much of anything through it except headlights.

But when Jerry stopped for a red light, swearing under his breath, the other car pulled up on his side. It was weird to be looking down like this. Lucy recognized the dented white body and blue-gray top of her mother's car. Behind the wheel—leaning way far forward to see up into the van, gesturing frantically with her mouth and hands, the white

streak glittering like ice all through her hair—
was Mom.

"That's my mother!"

"Shit, I know that. I thought you'd have
enough sense not to let anybody know you
were leaving."

He was mad at her. Lucy couldn't stand it.
Suddenly she wanted more than anything to
be in that car with her mother, on her way
home. She grabbed the door handle.

She couldn't do that. She couldn't leave
Jerry.

She dropped to her hands and knees between the seats. The gearshift pressed into her
thigh. She pushed past it and crawled through
the long, dim, empty van to the back window.
She sat on her knees and leaned her forehead
against it. It was cold and wet between her
and her mother. Her mother couldn't reach
her, to punish her or rescue her or tell her
what to do. She was alone with Jerry in the
closed van, on the nighttime street, in the
whole world.

"God*dammit*," Jerry said, and Lucy knew he
was swearing at her. She pressed the side of
her face hard against the window glass, for the
moment understanding that she was in as
much danger here as anywhere else.

The van shot forward through the intersec-
tion while the light was still red. Lucy grabbed
the metal ridge around the window to keep

from tumbling backward, and thought how easy it would be to get your fingers stuck in there. A car on the other street passed barely behind them and in front of Lucy's mother's car, honking its horn wildly, and then there was a whole stream of cars.

A busy street for this time of night, Lucy thought. Maybe it was Federal Boulevard. If it was, she'd have some idea where she was.

By the time there was a break in the traffic and the blurry headlights that were Mom's car could start after them again, they were almost a whole block ahead. Mom ran the red light, too. Lucy hugged herself in surprise. This must be really important for Mom to break the law.

Jerry turned the van sharply to the right and Lucy fell against the wheel well, hitting her shoulder and the side of her head. When she sat up again, they were hurtling down an alley. She saw garbage cans, parked cars with snow on their roofs, a couple of garage doors with words spray-painted on them that she couldn't read.

Mom's car nosed into the alley after them. There must have been a hill, because Lucy slid toward the window as the van went up and then toward the seat as it went back down, and for a few seconds Mom's headlights weren't there. But before they came out of the other end of the alley onto the street, the dented and dirty old white and blue car was there again, and gaining. It always embarrassed Lucy to be seen in that car.

They sped along streets she was sure she'd never seen before, careened through neighborhoods she couldn't quite picture anybody living in. Houses and trees hardly looked like houses and trees as they streamed out behind the van like ribbons, like tin cans tied to the bumper of a newlyweds' car.

They jumped over curbs, into and out of parking lots. Lucy bumped her knee. They squeezed through alleys so skinny that she thought sure they'd smash into one wall or the other. Mom stayed with them. Lucy hadn't known Mom could drive like that.

Then, all of a sudden, they were in a park somewhere, and Mom's car wasn't behind them anymore. Tears of abandonment flooded Lucy's eyes, hot at first and then prickly cold on her cheeks. If Mom really loved her, she'd have caught up with the van.

It excited her, scared her, made her mad to see so plainly that there were things her parents couldn't do for her no matter how much they wanted to. That was what Rae and Ethan must have learned before she did. That was what it must mean to grow up.

There were lots of tall dark trees here, and open snowy spaces, and they'd lost Mom. Jerry still drove fast for a while on the road that spiraled deeper and deeper into the park. Then he slowed down. Then he came to a stop in a grove of blackish pine trees taller than the van and close together, with snow on their branches like the streak in Lucy's mother's hair. Jerry turned the engine off, and in the silence she could hear him panting. "Come here," he said.

She hesitated, staring out the back window. There was no one else in the park.

"Lucy," he said. His voice was weak, and he was slumped back in the seat. "Please, sweetheart, come here."

He needed her. When she crawled to him, the van shifted a little under her weight. She pushed between the seats, between the gearshift and Jerry's thigh; Jerry's thigh gave, as if it were making itself hollow to take her in.

He put his arms around her and she relaxed into him. Then he pushed her down across the seat and wedged one massive leg over her. She struggled to free herself but couldn't; he wasn't very heavy, but he was bigger, stronger, and he needed her to stay where she was.

"It's okay, Lucy, it's okay."

He was murmuring against her ear, against her temple. She felt her own pulse there, and his tongue and teeth against it.

"You feel rage. It's good to feel rage. Rage is nourishing. Feel it, my love. Feel it as big and as full as you can, and then *give it to me*."

Rage.

Rage at Ethan for dying.

Rage at Rae for going away.

Rage at Mom and Dad for not keeping any-body safe, at Mom for coming after her to-night and then losing her, at Stacey for not really being her friend, at the world because it wasn't the way she wanted it to be.

Rage hot and cold, red and flashing silver and every color, bursting out of her ears and mouth and vagina. She was screaming. She was moaning. Jerry pressed his open mouth over hers and sucked.

"That's good, that's good, oh, you're so good, you're so beautiful. Give it to me, Lucy, give it to me."

Then his huge, heavy, growing body stiff-ened and shook on top of her. He groaned into her open mouth, and she knew she was dying or being born again or turning into something she'd never been before.

27

He carried her over the threshold of his secret place. Without words or pictures in her mind, she was aware of his sheepskin coat under her cheek and ear: the different colors of brown in it, the way the plush spread apart, the odor of lanolin.

Vaguely she thought to put her arm up around his neck. She tried, but it wouldn't stay. Even if she couldn't hang on to him, she knew he wouldn't let her go.

She was hollow. Her body was hollow; she didn't think there were any organs left inside. Her mind was hollow. She wasn't scared or mad or hurting anymore, or tired or hungry. She didn't have to go to the bathroom. She didn't miss Rae or Ethan, didn't hate Mom and Dad, didn't worry about the little kids.

Nothing itched or cramped. All she was was with Jerry, in his arms.

He was shaking and breathing hard. He pushed through the door without stopping and it slammed shut behind him as he carried her into the center of the house. He was humming; she felt the vibrations in the hollow of his neck just above the thick coat collar, and the strong beating of his heart almost but not quite loud enough to hear. The humming got thinner and louder, like a teapot getting ready to whistle. Faster and faster, he carried her through rooms and halls. Then they were outside.

Not exactly outside. There was nighttime sky overhead, with a few cold-looking stars and a few snowflakes. There were bushes and a tree. But there were walls on all four sides.

When Jerry set her down, she was on ground, not floor. She staggered and caught herself on a cold, wet metal bar—a fence or a railing. She was in a space in the middle of Jerry's secret house, like a big box with the lid and bottom off, a room with no floor or ceiling.

For a minute she couldn't find Jerry, and she thought maybe for some reason he'd left her here. Then she saw him, squatting over in the corner of the courtyard, big and round and gray as a boulder. He grunted, straightened a little, and moved his arm up and over in front of him. She couldn't tell what he was doing. She didn't care.

Then she saw that he was pulling open a door in the ground and laying it open beside the hole that it had been hiding. Opened like that, it looked kind of like book covers.

Jerry came over and gathered her up again. He was still humming, still panting. This time he laid her over his shoulder and held her there with his forearm across the backs of her legs. Her head and arms hung down his back like the snout and paws of the red fox fur that Rae'd found that time at Goodwill. Its long body had been all skinned and hollowed out.

He had a thick rope in his other hand, and he used it to pull the trapdoor shut after them. When that happened, Lucy's ears felt funny, like when she'd flown in an airplane to Grandma and Grandpa's in Texas. But they didn't exactly hurt this time. She didn't think anything would ever hurt her again.

They were underground, underneath Jerry's house. Lucy had never been under the ground before. They were inside the earth.

Lucy thought of mites and spiders, of worms eating secret tunnels for themselves to travel through. She thought of earthquakes, and those stone plate things that moved around down here; of volcanoes, because this was where lava came from.

After they'd gone down a whole lot of winding steps, Jerry stopped. Over his humming she heard the jingling of keys again, the scraping and clicking of keys in locks. The door he opened this time was in a wall, not in the ground, and it had padding on both sides.

He took her through the door, into a secret chamber deep inside his secret house, and shut the door behind them. He crouched and slid her off his shoulder. Her legs wouldn't hold her, and she collapsed onto something bouncy, like thick foam rubber. Jerry stood up again and ran his hands all around the edges of the door, the way Mom did when she sealed a container for the freezer.

Lucy tried to look away from Jerry, into the chamber. It was so dark that she thought maybe she'd closed her eyes again without knowing it, and she stretched them wide until they hurt at all the corners.

Then she started to see things. Shapes. Movement. On a couch or bed was a boy curled up on his side.

Ethan.

She started to crawl toward him. Her arms and legs were heavy. Her hands and feet didn't seem to belong to her.

But it wasn't Ethan. Ethan was dead. It was Billy Duncan, from group.

Somehow, for some reason, she'd kept crawling across the foam-covered floor, and now she was right next to him. He was asleep.

She raised one hand. That made her tip sideways, but she didn't quite fall over. She touched Billy's shoulder. He opened his eyes. They were flat and white and didn't have any light in them. She didn't think he was seeing her or anything else. She heard herself say, "Hi, Billy," but he didn't say anything back, and he smelled funny.

"Lucy."

Rae.

Rae was coming toward her. Lucy wasn't even surprised. Rae was as dark as everything else in the chamber, but her eyes were little white circles with black dots.

"Lucy."

Then she realized that shadowy figures were coming toward her from everywhere, like fog. They were closing in. One or more of them touched her. Now she couldn't find which one was Rae. Their faces all looked blurred. They were all saying her name.

Hands were under her, inside her clothes, raising her up into the dark air. She was swirling. She opened her mouth to breathe or to cry out. The fog got inside her throat, burning, pulling. The faces and hands and tongues and teeth got inside her body everywhere.

Then she saw Jerry in the center of the foggy circle and heard him calling her name, too. "Lucy," he said. "Lucy."

28

She was naked, but not cold, not embarrassed. Hands were on her everywhere, rubbing, holding her down. Stephanie's nails were digging into her left shoulder, but it hardly hurt at all. Rae was on her knees with one hand on each side of Lucy's pelvis and her head bent so low that Lucy felt breath on her belly, on her pubic hair. That was okay. Rae was her sister. Other teenagers she didn't recognize had hold of her feet, her knees, her hands, her hair. She couldn't move. Part of her mind kept saying, *Get out of here! Fight!* and she knew that if she was ever going to get out of here, if Rae was going to get out of here, they'd have to do it themselves.

She felt like a traitor for even thinking about leaving. She really didn't want to go anywhere. Even if they hadn't been holding her down, she couldn't have moved.

Everybody was humming. She thought she might be humming too. This underground chamber was full of humming, rubbing, sucking.

Her head was in Jerry Johnston's lap, held there by the insides of his giant soft thighs and by his big hands massaging her head and face. She knew it was Jerry by the smell of him, the feel of him; she couldn't turn her head to see.

Jerry was humming. His whole body vibrated, making her vibrate, too. Then his voice broke out into words. "Rage," he said, and the word was big and hollow, hungry, "Rage. Sorrow. Terror. You are scared. You are sad. You are *furious*."

And she was, then, everything he'd said and more. She was more than sad; she was distraught. She vibrated with terror. She was enraged.

She writhed under all their hands. Among all the hands that were on her, she searched in her mind for Jerry's and was able to pick them out right away. They moved all over her body like a massage. Cupping, slapping, pressing, pulling.

"Feel it, Lucy," he murmured to her, just to her and not to anybody else. "Let yourself really feel it all."

Somehow he was inside her, inside her

mind. Dimly she understood what he was doing: he was finding what she already felt and
making it stronger, making it bigger, making
it hotter and thicker and more to his liking
and much more dangerous to her. So vaguely
that it was almost unconscious, she understood that Jerry was using her, that he needed
her hurt and fear and anger in order to stay
alive, that even those feelings wouldn't keep
him going for long and so he'd use her up in a
hurry and she'd be dead and then he'd find
somebody else to feed him.

Jealousy spurted brief and hot, deep inside
her. She felt Jerry reach for it and grab hold.

She would gladly give him anything she
had, everything he could find in her and use
for himself. She would die for him. That was
all right with her.

Rae cried a thin hollow wail, raised her
head, and took her hands away from Lucy's
hips. Lucy couldn't tell exactly where her sister was touching her until she wasn't anymore. Now those spots were cold.

Jerry was so close to her that she couldn't
tell which were her feelings and which were
his, and she didn't care.

She saw a face, part of a face, a figure moving outside the circle. In the same chanting
voice, Jerry said, "Rae," and Rae, sobbing, put
her hands back on Lucy's pelvis and lowered
her head over her again. Now Lucy felt her

sister's tears on her belly, between her legs.
But that was okay, because the circle was
complete again, there weren't any gaps, and
Jerry was going to kiss her, she saw his face
coming down over hers.

His mouth seemed to cover her whole face.
There were teeth in it that sank into the flesh
under her jaw, and a tongue that lapped at her
eyes and nose, but mostly he sucked. Hands
massaged her everywhere, inside and outside.
Humming and chanting rose. Rae's sobbing
was almost a scream. Jerry sucked. Lucy saw
her mother's face, her mother's hands. But it
couldn't be her mother. It was too late for her
mother to be here. She felt herself draining
into him, and understood in a dizzying rush
that she was going to die so that he could live.

"Stop it!"

Light. Cold air. Yelling. Jerry's mouth, face,
hands taken away from her. The hands and
voices of the others taken away from her.
Mom in the open doorway. Mom running into
the room. Stephanie and the others (but not
Rae) surrounding Mom, putting their hands
on her, pulling her down.

"You crazy son of a bitch, you can't have my
daughters!"

Mom was sprawled on the floor now,
against the cot where Billy was still asleep.
She was held down by half a dozen members
of the group (but not Rae, not Rae). Lucy

longed to be one of those with their hands on
her mother, but even though nobody but Rae
was touching her now, she couldn't move.

"Well," Jerry said from somewhere behind
her. He was panting. "Carole."

"You sick bastard!"

"I'm glad you're here." Jerry's voice was
husky with excitement as he moved farther
and farther away from Lucy. A profound terror swept her: her mother was in danger; she
was going to lose her mother.

Jerry was bigger and needier and more
powerful than her mother could possibly understand. Lucy understood.

Jerry didn't try to stand up or even to crawl.
He just scooted across the foam floor toward
her mother. The heels of his hands left little
indentations for a second or two, and his legs
and butt left a faint trail like a snake's. Four
people were holding Mom, although right now
she wasn't struggling. On the cot, Billy still
hadn't moved, and, suddenly, it occurred to
Lucy that he must be dead.

She shivered and tried to hide herself,
mostly from her mother but also from Jerry
and the others. When she was this far away
from Jerry, when he wasn't paying attention
to her, she felt stuff again. Bad stuff, painful
stuff, stuff she didn't want to feel. So sad. Furious. Scared to death.

Rae was sitting on the padded floor next to

the pile of Lucy's clothes. Her legs were spread out in front of her and her hands fell limply onto the mat between them. She was wearing jeans and a sweatshirt that Lucy recognized from before she'd disappeared; they were filthy, and way too big for her now. Her head was up and her eyes were open and at first she seemed to be watching what was going on, but when Lucy motioned to her to hand her her clothes, she didn't move.

Lucy thought maybe Rae was dead. Like Billy. Like Ethan. Like Mike Garver, she realized, who probably really had died of a heart attack or the doctors wouldn't have said so but who, before his heart attacked him, had been full of rage and sorrow and fear, and had been used up.

Jerry had used him up, and now he needed more. More and more and more. Nobody could fill Jerry up anymore. Nobody could make him happy. Maybe she could. Maybe she was the one person in the world who could make him happy. Now he really needed her.

Feel it. Feel it as big and as hot and as hard as you can, and then give it to me.

She'd have to get her clothes herself. She was so tired and weak and confused that it took her a long time to get to them, crawling across the padded floor and trying to hold on to the smooth padded wall. Then it took her a long time to put them on because she could barely remember how buttons worked, or sleeves. The cloth hurt her skin.

"I get so *empty*," Jerry said thoughtfully, reasonably. "I get so *hungry*. It used to be just sort of a small, nagging discomfort, and it didn't take much to soothe it. When I was a kid, all I had to do was befriend screwed-up kids, once in a while see to it that they got in serious trouble or got badly hurt. That was easy."

Lucy couldn't imagine Jerry as a kid. She couldn't imagine anything. Her mind and body were all shapes and colors and loud noises, sorrow and rage and fear.

"But the older I get," Jerry was saying, "the more anxious and agitated I get. Lonely. Out of balance."

He'll fall on me, Lucy thought. *He'll squash me.* She wasn't at all scared by that. In fact, she hoped it would happen.

"Sometimes the hunger is all I am. I get ravenous. It's life-threatening. You understand that, don't you, Carole? I know my kids do. I have to do this in order to survive. It's a matter of simple self-preservation. Basic, primal survival. I have no choice."

Suddenly Mom tried to pull away from Stephanie and the others who were guarding her. They must have been a lot stronger than they looked, because they didn't let her get away. She did manage to kick or punch one of them;

Lucy heard the impact, like a crumpled paper bag.

Then they pulled Mom down. She cried out. One leg was twisted under her. Lucy saw that she was wearing Rae's bright yellow socks and, under her open coat, the Boys' Club sweatshirt Ethan had had years ago. Stephanie lowered herself over Mom and sat on her stomach. Mom cried out again. One of the others slapped her face.

They were hurting her mother. Before she knew what she was doing, Lucy had gathered her strength and was trying to get to them.

Somebody grabbed her from behind. It was Rae. Lucy smelled her sweet-sour odor and remembered now that that was the smell Ethan had always left behind, like a snail, when he'd come on those weird visits to Mom. Lucy sniffed quickly at her own skin to see whether she was starting to smell that way yet.

Jerry had moved himself across the mat to be closer to Mom. He had a hand on her neck, under her collar, and was trailing the fingertips of his other hand down her cheek, around inside her ear, through the white and dark strands of her hair. In the movies and on the soaps when the cute guys did that and pretty music came up, you knew they were going to kiss somebody and then make love. Lucy'd often wished there'd be music in real life to

warn you when somebody was going to kiss
you or when the murderer was nearby.

Jerry cupped Mom's face in his hand. She
jerked away but he got it again, in both hands
this time. Was he going to kiss her? Jealousy
stirred in her, and moral outrage. This was
her *mother*. This was *Jerry*.

Mom's lip was bleeding where somebody
had hit her. Lucy didn't think she'd ever seen
her mother's blood before, or even thought
about it. She started forward, thinking to put
herself between Mom and Jerry, but Rae's
thin arms got tighter around her waist, and
Rae's very thin whisper sounded in her ear.
"Wait."

Lucy sat very still. Her sister's body heat
seeped into her body, and she sent hers back.
They were breathing the same air. She felt the
beating of her sister's heart through her own
rib cage, the coursing of her sister's thoughts
in her own mind as they started to make sense
again.

But there were her own thoughts, too, and
the beating of her own heart. Not daring even
to whisper, she formed a message to Rae in
her mind: *You're so strong*. The answer came
back as if it had been written in red ink across
the pages of her diary: *So are you*.

It was almost as if Lucy and Rae had a plan,
a secret code. They didn't. They'd never talked
about anything like this. But it was clear to

Lucy that if anybody was going to save anybody here, she and Rae were going to have to
do it. Some things your parents couldn't save
you from, or even tell you what they meant.
Some things were yours.

"It's a gift that you're here," Jerry was mum-
bling. "A great good fortune . . ."

"I came," Mom said through clenched teeth,
"to save my daughters from you."

"You're—a good mother."

"Go to hell."

"Anger," Jerry breathed. "And grief . . ."

Mom wailed, "You killed my son!"

"And fear . . ."

Mom didn't say any words then, but she
made lots of noise. Her sobs were swallowed
up by Jerry's padded and locked underground
secret chamber, and because she was trying so
hard to stop them, they kept getting more and
more ragged and painful. Lucy squirmed. Rae
whispered again, "Wait. Not yet."

Jerry was having trouble talking, but Lucy
understood him to say, "Make the circle."

He stayed where he was, hunched over and
panting, while Stephanie and the others
dragged and carried Mom toward the center
of the low-ceilinged room. Mom fought them.
She kicked and scratched and shouted. It
didn't make any difference.

When Mom was positioned and secured on
the mat by all those shaking young hands on

her hands, feet, hips, shoulders, neck, Jerry took a deep breath and, grunting, pulled himself into the circle. He reached out both hands and took Mom's head into his lap. She whipped her head back and forth and spat at him. Grinning broadly, running his pale tongue over his bared teeth, Jerry pressed one huge flat fist hard against each of her temples and made her stay still.

They hadn't undressed her. Lucy was relieved, but she wondered why. Jerry'd taught them that you needed freedom of movement in order to have freedom of thought, that it was easier to uncover your feelings if your body was uncovered. He must be in a hurry tonight. All he did was unbuckle Mom's belt and raise her sweatshirt a little.

Lucy tried to look away. Something awful was going to happen, and it was going to happen fast. There should be drums, creepy music. "Rae," Jerry said. "Lucy. Join us."

"No," Lucy said. But Rae pushed her forward, and one on each side of Jerry holding Mom, the sisters joined the feelings circle.

Watching Mom's face carefully from only an inch or two away, Jerry began. "Ethan is dead."

Mom said nothing.

"Your son is *dead*."

Mom still didn't say anything, but her breathing was getting fast and harsh. She had her eyes and mouth squeezed shut as if to keep Jerry from getting in, but he was bent so close over her that Lucy didn't think she'd have to have her eyes open to see him or her mouth open to taste him. His tongue lapped at her lips, and he matched his breathing to hers, breathing in when she breathed out.

Jerry was chanting now. "Ethan Michael Brill is dead. Your firstborn child is dead. You let him die. You didn't protect him. You didn't keep him safe. Ethan is dead. Ethan Michael—"

"Stop!" Mom shrieked, and the instant she opened her mouth Jerry pressed his over it. There was a slurping sound that seemed to go on for a long time. Under her hands, under Rae's hands, Mom's body shuddered.

Rae's white lips were making motions that Lucy didn't understand at first. Then she saw that her sister was sending her a secret, silent, very important message: "Get ready."

Jerry's chant was so rhythmic and insinuating that other people in the circle had picked it up. *Ethan Michael Brill. Ethan Michael Brill. Rae Ellen Brill. Lucy Ann Brill. Lucy Ann Brill. Lucy Ann Brill.*

Lucy heard herself saying her own name over and over again with him. She tried to stop but couldn't tell whether she did or not.

Ethan Michael Brill. Rae Ellen Brill. Lucy Ann Brill. All your children, one by one. Lost. Dead. You can't keep any of them safe.

Mom was screaming now, no words, just terrible raw noise matched to Jerry's rhythm that made her rise up and fall down under Lucy's hands. Her screams and the movements of her body got mixed up with everything else, and Lucy couldn't tell where one thing stopped and something else started, where she stopped and her mother started and Jerry started, until Rae jumped.

Rae hurled herself at Jerry. He hadn't seen her coming. She broke the circle, stopped his chanting and his feeding. He gasped, choked, and fell over sideways, away from Rae's assault and into Lucy's lap.

As soon as Jerry's hands and mouth were off her, Mom tore loose from the others. She and Rae pulled him off Lucy. Nobody was making any loud noise now. Mom was panting. Rae was making a high-pitched whine in her throat. Around the room everybody was quiet, except for Stephanie, who gave a long low moan and collapsed onto the mat.

Jerry was gurgling. Bubbles came out of his nose and mouth. He lay on his side like a huge baby, or like a mannequin made of light plastic. Afraid to touch him, Lucy forced herself to kick at his arm; it moved as if it didn't have any weight at all. His enormous bloated belly lay ahead of him on the mat. It sank like bread dough as Rae knelt beside it and pushed her fists into it again and again.

29

It was hard for her to climb back up all those stairs, but she did it. Rae was ahead of her, and Mom was behind her with her hand on Lucy's back. Way far behind her were Jerry Johnston and Billy and Stephanie and the others. Way far behind her, under the ground.

When they finally reached the heavy padded door at the top and climbed through it and were in the dark outside again, it was hard for her to know where she was. But she made herself remember: this was the courtyard in the middle of Jerry's secret house, the hole at the core of it that made it hollow.

She heard crackling, and tinny voices. A radio, she realized. A police radio. She heard sirens.

She heard her father's voice.

She stumbled over a prickly bush. She rammed her knee into a wooden box full of sharp dead flower stalks. She heard Dad, calling and calling Mom's name, but she didn't know where he was or how to get to him.

Rae fell.

Mom crouched beside Rae and yelled, "Tony! Tony! We're in here!"

"Car-ole!" Mom's name sounded much longer than it was when Dad called and called it; it sounded almost not like a name at all. Lucy's head swam. She swayed and grabbed onto a branch, but it snapped off in her hand.

All of a sudden there were blinding searchlights and loud voices, and lots of people in uniforms, and Dad kneeling beside and Mom saying over and over again, "I've got them. I've got both the girls," and Dad saying Rae's name and Mom's name and then, "Where's Lucy?"

"I'm here," Lucy said out loud.

Dad came through the lights and knelt in front of her and took her in his arms.

Rae was sitting up. Mom was saying to the cops, "He's down there. They're all down there. Hurry."

"Down where, ma'am? Who's down where?"

"I'll show you." Lucy twisted away from Dad and ran to the spot among the bushes and benches and hedges where she knew the big trapdoor would be. She didn't know how she

knew it was there; she'd thought she was lost.
But there it was, still open, and she jumped
down into it before any of the pursuing
grown-ups could stop her.

She had to see him again. Nobody was making her. She just had to.

She went by herself down all those steps.
They kept moving around under her feet. All
of a sudden they'd curve and dip or get wider
or skinnier, for no reason. She wished somebody would be there to guide her, or at least to
warn her ahead of time how the steps went.
But nobody was. She had to figure it out for
herself.

She tripped a lot of times when the steps
rose up or sank. She kept running into walls,
because a minute ago they'd been somewhere
else. One time she fell and had to turn around
and crawl with her hands up the steps behind
her in order to get back on her feet. It occurred to her that if somebody had been there
to help her they'd have made things worse; in
this distorted and shifting darkness, she had to
find her own balance.

The steps kept going down and down. She'd
lost count of them. *Maybe I'll never get out of
here,* she thought, but that was just a habit,
self-indulgence. She knew she'd get out.

And she had to see him again.

Finally she seemed to be on more or less
level ground. She pushed her hands straight

out in front of her until they rested against the padded door. Trying not to think too much about it, she drew her hands back in, took a deep breath, and flung herself at the door. It swung open so easily that she almost fell, and she stumbled headlong into the underground room.

Teenagers were still sitting and lying around the room, but the circle was so broken now that if you didn't know there'd been one, you'd have thought there was no pattern at all. They weren't touching each other anymore, and of course they weren't touching Jerry. Some were slumped over in a sitting position, legs awkwardly crossed and hands limp in their laps. Some had tipped over sideways onto the mat among the scattered pillows. Their arms were bent and their legs were drawn up and their lips were pursed as if for sucking or kissing. They looked like pictures Lucy'd seen of fetuses in the womb.

Billy was still on the cot by the door. Lucy made herself crouch beside him and peer into his face, as if she wanted to kiss him. She didn't want to kiss him. But you had to know the truth. You had to understand as much about the truth as you could.

Billy was dead.

The truth was: Billy was dead. Jerry had killed him.

The truth was: Ethan was dead, too, but he wasn't here. She would never see Ethan again.

The truth was: Lucy was alive, and she wanted to be.

Stephanie and a few of the others had made their own smaller circle around the enormous body of Jerry Johnston. They were holding hands and swaying and trying to chant, but their voices broke. One by one they reached out and put their hands on him. Lucy dropped to her hands and knees, because she couldn't trust her legs to hold her upright, and crawled across the mat to join them.

The body was both bloated and collapsed. The eyes were craters filled with brown pus. The belly had imploded so that now it sank in as far as it used to swell out, like a pumpkin somebody'd hollowed out for Halloween. The rings glinted and hung loose on the fingers. The tongue, swollen and coated white, stuck out of the side of the mouth.

Lucy crawled to the top of the head, leaned way over, and put her mouth on Jerry's. It was cold and still, no sucking. It was so quiet, too; there wasn't any voice saying *darling*, saying *I need you*, saying *feel what I need you to feel and then give it to me*. There wasn't any breath.

Lucy sat back and put her hands on her own rib cage. Her breath went in and out.

She raised up on her knees again and leaned

forward and rested the heels of her hands on Jerry's chest. She lost her balance a little and her weight shifted, and her hands went through the shell of bone and flesh into the central body cavity. She cried out but didn't pull away.

There was nothing inside.

There was no blood. Her hands were dry and unstained. There was no tissue, not even dried-up pieces or little bits like sponge.

There was no heart. Lucy cupped her hands and scooped inside Jerry Johnston's corpse, and there were no organs at all. No lungs, which she'd always imagined as shaped like those seed airplanes that floated down from maple trees in the summertime and you'd find them all over the yard trying to start new trees. No purselike stomach.

No heart.

Slowly she withdrew her hands from inside the empty torso and slid them back up to lay them on either side of the head. With her fingertips she traced the eye sockets, the bridge of the nose, the jawline. There were indentations and cave-ins everywhere. Bones bent and moved. The point of the chin flattened under her palm; the nose punched in.

Then she pressed, not very hard, under and behind the ears, and the skull shattered. Jerry's head came apart in her hands, and she was holding pieces of his skull and clots of his hair. Once it broke, it wasn't a head anymore, and there was nothing inside. No thoughts. No power. No brain.

Jerry Johnston was empty. He'd eaten himself up.

Lucy heard the murmuring of Stephanie and the others around her. They were saying a lot of things. One of them was her name: "Lucy Lucy Lucy," a chant.

She heard voices and footsteps outside the door, and then it opened and light came in, just as she sat back from the emptied, heartless, brainless body of Jerry Johnston and put her hands in her lap. The police were here. Mom and Dad and Rae were here, calling her name, loving her.

Lucy thought her own thoughts. She felt her own feelings; many of them had no names, and needed none. She welcomed the blood in her own veins, the air in her own lungs, her heart beating, her brain working, and the rest of her life to live.

She stood up shakily and turned to meet her family. Just before they got to her to take her in their arms, she slipped one small sharp piece of Jerry Johnston's skull into the back pocket of her jeans—an amulet, a message, a secret code.

Then she said out loud, "I want to go home."

QUANTITY SALES

Most Dell books are available at special quantity discounts when purchased in bulk by corporations, organizations, and special-interest groups. Custom imprinting or excerpting can also be done to fit special needs. For details write: Dell Publishing, 666 Fifth Avenue, New York, NY 10103. Attn.: Special Sales Department.

INDIVIDUAL SALES

Are there any Dell books you want but cannot find in your local stores? If so, you can order them directly from us. You can get any Dell book in print. Simply include the book's title, author, and ISBN number if you have it, along with a check or money order (no cash can be accepted) for the full retail price plus $2.00 to cover shipping and handling. Mail to: Dell Readers Service, P.O. Box 5057, Des Plaines, IL 60017.